C000148557

A Tortured Soul

L.A. Detwiler

Published by L.A. Detwiler, 2020.

This is a work of fiction. Similarities to real people, places, or events are entirely coincidental.

A TORTURED SOUL

First edition. July 31, 2020.

Written by L.A. Detwiler.

To my husband

Author's Note

This book is extremely dark in its portrayal of domestic violence. It is uncensored, gory, disturbing, and upsetting in the way it approaches the subject. It was important to me that I didn't censor Crystal's suffering or sugarcoat what abuse can look like. I wanted to portray the true horrors of domestic violence in a way that will hopefully get readers talking. I hope that Crystal's story in the following pages upsets you. I hope it makes you frustrated that there are women and men who endure this kind of suffering. I hope that it stirs you to want change and to stop asking: Why didn't they just leave? I hope it helps you empathize a little bit more and to want justice for survivors.

I am not a survivor of domestic violence. The story you are about to read is completely fictional. However, there are monsters like Richard out there, both in male and female form. I hope this story makes you think about their victims and about what our world can do to stop monsters like Richard.

If you or a loved one is affected by abuse or needing support, be sure to call the National Domestic Violence Hotline at 1-800-799-7233. If you cannot speak safely, you can also log onto thehotline.org or text LOVEIS to 1-866-331-9474.

'Deep into that darkness peering, long I stood there, wondering, fearing, doubting, dreaming dreams no mortal ever dared to dream before.' ~*Edgar Allan Poe*

Prologue

I rock myself in the dusty room, the sunlight filtering through the blinds as dusk settles on the horizon. The splatters of blood on my T-shirt beg for me to change, but I'm too tired. How do you get this much blood out of fabric? How will I clean up this mess?

I sit in the bed where this swirling spiral of decay began. It was supposed to be a hopeful day, a day to rectify what remained of my life. Instead, it had been the day that incited the beginning of the maniacal end.

All good things come to an end—but what about the bad? The depraved? Do things of malice also come to a finale, or do they just continue on their merry way, torturing the downtrodden, the damned? I don't know anymore. I don't know anything at all. Maybe I never did.

My eyes are heavy with exhaustion, the turmoil of the past week plaguing me. Has it only been a week? Only seven days since the Crystal Connor I once knew transformed into a being I hardly recognize? Has it only been a week since the sins of my soul burned in anguish, filling me with a regret I can never reconcile for?

The Bible sits on the nightstand in its familiar spot, opened to the last page I read. The bookmark rests against the splayed pages, a visual reminder of all I've messed up. It may as well be a sign from God—I'm doomed. I hit my head

3

against the wall, terrified to fall asleep. I *can't* fall asleep. I know what's coming if I give in, and I'm not strong enough tonight to let that happen.

Tears fall. I rock back and forth like I have so many times. If I close my eyes, I can feel the weight of him in my arms, see those chubby cheeks, and remember what it was like to clutch him to my chest. I wish I could hold him once more.

And then, I hear it. My eyes bolt open, my heart surging with disbelief. It can't be. There's no way. But yes, as I silence my breathing and will my pounding heart to be quiet, I'm sure I hear it. Softly, in the distance, I hear the sounds of muffled cries, of screams, of him needing me.

I suck in a deep breath, maybe the first one in ages. The cries I've craved resonate through the house, a welcome melody in the midst of stunning sorrow. It isn't too late. He *is* crying. My heart leaps to hear the sound I'd so desperately wanted to hear all this time. I rest my head against the wall, feeling like maybe all will be okay. I sit, listening to the cries, the sound calming my soul instead of grating on my nerves. I'm so happy to hear his shrieks.

After a few moments, I'm not tired anymore. I stand from the bed, clutching at the locket around my neck, the familiar piece of soft hair inside. I don't have to open it to know it's there. I can feel him close to me. It soothes me to know he's near, even after all that's transpired. I cross the floor and peer out the window, studying the tree line I've seen so many times. At first, I couldn't look out there. The memories were too real, the scene too fresh. But things are different now. *I'm* different. I glance out into the fading light, perusing the edge of the forest. The darkness is macabre in a way that's familiar but eerily unsettling. I'm accepting of it, though. I've come to learn that life is sometimes meant to be uncomfortable.

But just as the cries are quieting and the silence of the house pervades again, I catch a glimpse of something that delivers icy, sheer terror to my heart. The peace that reverberated within is now shattered, a chill spreading like a virus in my veins.

'No. No. No,' I plead, shaking my head. My fingers clench into fists, trembling.

I put a hand on the window after unfurling my fingers with great effort. My trembling digits feel the grimy glass. I should be embarrassed about the thick layer of dirt. How long has it been since I've washed the window? Despite my fear, I can't help but wince at the crud, the scratchy filth irritating my fingertips. It's like I believe touching the cool, defiled glass will snap me back to reality. It will save me from what I saw. Certainly it wasn't . . . It couldn't be . . .

Like a sign, though, it appears again, right in the tree line, an angry, vicious sight that sends terror pulsing through every single one of my limbs. I bite my lip so hard, I taste blood. I devote my energy to steadying my breathing as I try to look away, but I can't. My gaze is cemented on the spectacularly petrifying sight before me.

I know what that means.

I know that he's almost here.

And I know that I am, in fact, condemned, body and soul.

Chapter One

Forkhill, Pennsylvania, USA

I first realize that something is horrifically wrong when the only screams filling the bedroom are my own. Shouldn't there be cries? Isn't that what happens? I'm too exhausted to move, fearing death might be upon me. Still, the question swirls, the terror slicing into my chest. I don't hear any cries. *Why aren't there cries?*

Weakened as I am, I manage to inch upward onto my elbows and peer at Sharon, the woman who lives near one of the bars in town. She once worked as a midwife, but you wouldn't know it to look at her. She is a far cry from the professional appearance and demeanor one would expect from the title. I glance over as she holds the baby in her arms. I wait for the cry, anticipate the joyous announcement of the sex of the baby I've been eagerly awaiting for nine months—really, for years. My miracle baby.

But the proclamation doesn't come. Sharon turns to me, her face wrinkled from too many cigarettes and too harsh a life. She is stoic as her eyes meet mine. She shakes her head gently, and I almost think for a moment I'm mistaken. All will be well. She'll saunter over, hand me my precious child, and congratulate me. She's just tired from the long day, I'm sure. She's just moving slowly.

It isn't the case, though. The congratulations never comes. Instead, I see the funeral dirge in her eyes. I hear it in the words unspoken between us. I splinter, right there.

'No,' I bellow into the murky, stale air that's tinged with blood and sweat. 'No.'

I've already cried out all of my tears in the past hours as I labored, unsure if I could survive such a draining event. I hadn't been prepared. I hadn't known how hard it would be. Still, I'd muscled through, knowing that all would work out. God would give me the strength. I would survive, give birth to my own miracle, and finally fulfill the purpose I'd been seeking. But there were other plans at work, I realize as Sharon silently shakes her head once more in confirmation, studying me over the bluish lump of flesh that isn't moving or crying.

'No,' I utter again, shaking my head violently, trying to sit up further. It's as if I believe the single word can combat reality. But words aren't magic wands. Denial of a fact doesn't make it any less real or true, and I certainly don't live in wonderland.

'I'm sorry, Crystal. Sometimes this happens,' she croaks, still holding my baby in her arms.

I want to scream at her, to yell that she's wrong in so many ways. I want to tell her that she must be mistaken, that God wouldn't do this to a woman like me. I haven't been perfect, it's true. But I've been good, overall. I've believed. I've prayed. I've sacrificed. *This can't be happening.* The thought relentlessly pounds into my head. It can't be. She must be wrong. I shake my head wildly as she cautiously ambles closer.

'Crystal, I'm sorry. It's no one's fault.' Her voice, weathered from cigarettes and age, cracks as she speaks. It isn't comforting, but I guess, in fairness, no voice would be at this moment. As she approaches, tears flood my eyes. I'd thought they were all gone, but they resurface to greet the morose occasion. She saunters closer, holding what was supposed to be my precious gift in her arms.

'No. You're wrong. I know you're wrong,' I plead, with whom, I don't know. With myself? With the baby? With the woman we hired as a midwife? With God?

'Do you want me to get Richard?' she asks as I clutch the worn quilt to my chest, pulling it close. I stare at the blood-soaked shirts at the edge of the bed, and then glance around the tiny room that is in a state of complete disarray. *I need to tidy it up. It won't do to have the room be such a mess,* I think, shoving aside the facts I simply can't face.

'Crystal, do you want me to get him?' Sharon prods again, and I turn my gaze from the shirts and the sheets that need washed back to the woman beside me. Richard. Where is he now? What will he say? He must be in the garage. He'd said this wasn't his scene, that this was all on me. Terror settles in as I realize it *was* all me—and it's all my fault. He's going to say it's all my fault again. And maybe it is. Suddenly, I just *can't* breathe. I begin to shake uncontrollably, a chill rattling through my body once more.

'Maybe we should get you to the hospital,' Sharon suggests, a warm hand touching my forehead. The same hand that was just touching my baby. I slink away from her blood-stained fingertips, her dry, cracked skin that scratches against me.

'No. No,' I say over and over. The word is stuck in my throat, and I cough it up like a loose piece of phlegm that just keeps catching on the way out.

I don't want a hospital. I don't want Richard. I want the baby, the one who was supposed to be mine. The one who was supposed to bring purpose to my life.

'Do you want to hold him? Sometimes that helps in these situations,' she says, coming closer, still cradling the newborn.

'He? It's a he?' I ask, a smile coming to my face. It's a he. Gideon. My sweet Gideon is here. Richard will be happy. He preferred a boy, a child he could teach to be a man. I knew all along it was a boy, had prayed for it even. A boy could make Richard happy. Our son would be something we could take pride in. He would make everything worthwhile.

Gideon Connor. He's here. My life is complete. Sharon has to be wrong. He's not crying, but that's okay, isn't it? My child is simply a sweet, sweet angel. He's a good baby already. He's calm and happy. That's all. He was so good these past nine months. Even in the last few weeks, when things were supposed to be difficult, I'd enjoyed the pregnancy. He never even kicked me or made me uncomfortable.

I look into the hazel eyes of the woman standing beside my bed once more. I take in her pale, craggy face and the dark circles that accentuate her deep, craterous crow's feet. My gaze dances over her face, following the lines and crevices with meticulous attention to detail. I follow a crease down her cheek, my eyes stopping on her wrinkled lips. Suddenly, I can't stand looking at her. I feel uncomfortable with her here, unhappy. I knew Sharon was a bad idea when we hired her, but Richard insisted that we couldn't afford a trip to the hospital, not without medical insurance. The garage has been doing okay, but he still thought it would be too expensive. And even if the garage had been doing well this past month, Richard insisted there were better things to pay for than a crooked doctor who would just steal all his hard-earned money for nothing.

So Sharon had seemed to be the best alternative. Richard knows her husband from the bar. One thing led to another, and suddenly Sharon, who had worked as a midwife a few decades ago, was the woman in the room with me with her too-bright hair and leathery skin, helping me to see the miracle through. I'd been a little nervous at first, but I assured myself it would be okay. We were in God's hands, and he would provide. He would endow me with strength. Like Mary in the stable, I'd give birth in the back bedroom, the stale scent of cigarette smoke and four-day-old trash in the kitchen reminding me of my humble roots. But it hadn't mattered. All that I cared about was that soon, I'd fulfill my ultimate purpose. I'd hold my baby, the true love of my life, for the first time. And here we were. Sweet Gideon had arrived. I'd done it.

'Let me have him,' I say, swiping the tears away, half-delirious from the trials of birth but half-exhilarated from the fact that I am a mother now. I've achieved my goal.

'Crystal,' Sharon says sweetly, and her eyes tell me exactly what she's thinking. She pities me. Stupid woman. What does she even know?

'Give me him,' I demand, the need to hold him against me trumping my typically polite nature.

'I really think you need to go to the hospital. I mean, I can clean you up, but with all things considered, you might need a professional,' she notes.

I'm done playing nice. Flinging the scratchy quilt aside, I reach up and snatch at my child, desperate to cling to him. She obliges, releasing her grip on his body and helping to place him on my chest. The weight of his body in my arms fills my heart, love surging for a child I've known for nine months. For those months, he was growing inside of me, consuming me, filling me. He was everything. I look down into his face, though, and feel the skin. Aren't babies supposed to be warm? He is supposed to be warm. He is silent, his face not the angelic, sweet, content smile of a newborn, but an apathetic, frozen look of a baby who never took a breath. His color is wrong. The coldness of his skin is wrong. Everything is wrong.

My breathing heightens. 'What did you do? What did you do to him?' I protest, staring at Sharon as I stick to the baby who has no life in him. His limp body flops against my chest, his limbs hanging at odd angles. I beg him to breathe, plead with him to come back to me. I can't lose him. Not him too. This can't happen, not now. *Oh, God, why? Why have you forsaken me yet again?*

'Please, no,' I shriek, as Sharon frantically tries to calm me down. She reaches for Gideon, but I won't let go. I snuggle him tighter against my chest and cradle him in the bed. Back and forth, back and forth. I rock him just like I'd pictured so many times. All those months in the rocking chair in the living room, I'd look out the window and picture our lives together. I'd give him the unconditional love he needed. We'd spend so many years together, growing and learning and loving and laughing. He'd be my sole reason for existence. He already was everything to me from the moment I realized I was pregnant. I'd give everything for him. But it wasn't just because it was my job. It would be because it's what I wanted more than anything else. I wanted to give my love to him. I wanted him to look to me for love.

I'd rock by that window, over and over, thinking about it all. Through all of the dark, boozy fights, the painful encounters, the thrusting inside of me, I'd stayed positive because I had the baby to think about. I could handle all of Richard's antics because it didn't matter. None of that mattered. All that was important was the baby. But now he was gone, ripped apart in a world too cruel and devious. He couldn't be gone. *No. No. No.*

I'd done everything I could. I'd been an obedient wife. I'd been a dutiful servant. Why was this happening? *How could this be happening to us?* I sob into my child, the smell of him nothing like I'd imagined. He doesn't smell of baby skin and milk. He doesn't smell of hopes and dreams. Instead, he reeks of death, pungent and decaying. He smells of loss and ache and disaster. He oozes with the bitter stench of a stale, fading life snuffed out.

I stare into the face of my child for a long while, tears clouding my vision and pain assaulting my heart. When I finally glance up, I realize I'm alone in the room, the peeling paint on the walls and the stagnant, rusty smell in the room emphasizing all that's been lost. Sharon is gone. I don't even remember hearing her leave. I don't know how long she's been gone. I don't know how long I rock my baby, his skin growing colder and stiffer to the touch. I don't know how long I sob and plead with a God who has abandoned me. But after some time, the door to the bedroom flies open, the familiar screech startling me as the brass doorknob slams against the notch in the wall, the house rattling in response. Things are about to get so much worse.

Richard hovers in the doorway, leaning on the frame. His shirt is covered in oil and grease. I study him through tears. I'm devastated for me but also for him. He'll never know Gideon. He'll never know his son. Perusing him, I think he's going to walk over to see the baby, to hold him. I consider the possibility that maybe things will be different, that we'll grieve this loss together. Maybe this will finally bring us together.

'Where's Sharon?' I ask weakly, feeling woozy from all of the sadness and trauma.

'I've sent her home. I don't need that bitch lurking around, telling me how to spend my money and what to do. We're fine here.' He struts across the creaky floor, and my breathing intensifies. The all-too-familiar dread sneaks in, a dark cloud over an already abysmal moment.

He stomps over to me, lurking above me in the bed as he stares down at us, the whiskey bottle in his left hand half-empty. Whiskey, not bourbon. Does it matter? Today, I don't think so. Alcohol weighs on his breath, surrounds him like an aura of gloom, but it's one I've come to know all too well. There's a quiet moment in which Richard seems to absorb the sight of Gideon's lifeless body. I detect a flicker of something in his eyes—a moment of sadness? Remorse?

Pain? I can't be sure. Maybe I'm only seeing what I desperately need to see.

Before I can get my hopes up, the glimmer becomes a conflagration I can certainly identify: rage.

'You stupid bitch. You stupid, good for nothing *bitch*. You fucking killed the baby. You're worthless, aren't you? Worthless. I should've gotten rid of you a long time ago. You're so lucky I kept you around. And for what? So you could kill the baby?'

The tears flow once more, and it's hard to breath.

'I'm sorry. I'm sorry. I tried. I'm sorry,' I beg, rocking Gideon again, squeezing his limp body tightly. *I did try,* I sob into Gideon's body, my face against his cheeks.

'It's dead. Why are you rocking it? You killed it. It's fucking dead.'

He throws the bottle against the wall and the crucifix I hung there crashes to the floor among the broken remnants of the whiskey. I shudder, and Henry's barks ring out loudly in the distance from outside the house. Richard grabs for the baby, but I squeeze Gideon closer. I can't let him go. I can't. I have to hold my baby. I need to hold him, to soothe him. I need to save him. I clutch to him like the lifeboat he is, my arms aching from the effort.

'Richard, please. I'm sorry. I'm sorry. I don't know what happened.'

And then, there is the familiar sound of his knuckles hitting my cheek. The pain stings, but this time, I don't flinch. I sink deeper into Gideon, into myself, steadfast and determined in my mission to hang on. My throbbing jaw doesn't deter me. There is a deeper agony I've come to know, a more extreme sense of hurt that goes well beyond the striking of his hand.

In the distance, Henry's barks echo louder, but barking can't fix this, even if the mastiff's intentions are in the right place. I imagine him yanking on the rope as he often does, the tree rooting him to the spot in the dirt he calls home most of the time. Richard says Henry's lucky he's allowed to live at all after all of the times he's come after him.

That's Richard's answer for everything. We're lucky. So lucky. I used to think that. I used to try to appreciate the good in life, to be thankful for what God gave us. But today, I don't feel lucky. I feel broken. I feel ruined. I feel scorned.

I sob now, tears and snot falling onto the baby I will never feed or coax to sleep. I press his tiny body to my face, inhaling a scent that just isn't right. I wish I could change everything. I ache for nothing more than to see him take a breath. He doesn't, though, and the next thing I know, Richard snatches the baby from me, my baby, despite my locked arms and violent grip. He is strong, after all. Always too strong.

'Richard, what are you doing? Give me him.' I'm hysterical now, screaming and crying as shock takes over my body. My words are grating squeals, barely decipherable. My arms stay frozen, as if Gideon's still in my arms. But he's not. Richard has my son, and I already feel the pain of his absence, my heart throbbing as it threatens to combust into a million pieces.

'It's dead, you stupid bitch. I won't have you sitting around crying over a dead fucking baby. You killed it. This is done.'

I wipe at my tears now and stare at Richard in disbelief. He carries the baby by his back leg, and I squeal at the sight of Gideon's sweet body swaying in the air, his head slapping against Richard's calf, clunking off the frame of the bed. There's no fatherly look in Richard's eyes as he dangles our baby, no sorrow or remorse. Only anger tinged with an even scarier hint of apathy.

'Richard, please, where are you taking him? We need to bury him. We need to get him baptized and then bury him . . .' I demand, struggling to get out of bed, still sore and weak from labor. I need to get up, though. The call of Gideon is stronger than any exhaustion.

Richard pauses halfway across the room.

'You really think I'm going to waste any amount of money getting some preacher over here for a dead body? You think I'm going to go through the trouble of burying a thing who didn't even take a breath? This thing isn't your baby. It's trash. And I'll show you what we do with trash around here.'

Horror clings to my chest, paints itself in my mind. Richard's never been a soft man, I've known that. But he certainly couldn't mean what he said, right? He's grieving too, isn't he? I claw my way toward him, woozy and unsteady. There is still blood all over my legs, and I'm terrified I'm going to pass out. I stumble onward, clutching at the sheets, at the wall to reinforce my stance.

'What are you doing?' I plead, my hands shaking and my head spinning. I lean on the bed, trying to steady my unreliable legs that shriek with pain. Everything hurts and throbs—my chest, most of all.

Richard doesn't answer, promenading out the bedroom door with Gideon. Tears dump from my eyes and blur my vision. I hear the screen door creak open and then slam shut. *What is he doing?* I want to chase after him, but my legs tremble and everything yelps in pain from just standing up. I trudge to the bedroom window, leaning heavily on the splintered sill as I look out toward Richard's garage, the lights still on.

Richard stomps across the yard, past Henry, who is tied to the tree by his decaying doghouse. Henry snarls at Richard, lunging on the end of the weathered rope, but Richard doesn't hesitate. He takes Gideon toward the tree line, and a hand covers my mouth. He can't be doing this. He wouldn't. But then, sure enough, he does the unthinkable, and I crumble to the wooden floor. I rock myself against the wall, banging my head against it. I slam my head over and over, the pain a welcome hint of what I'm feeling within.

I hope I bleed to death. I want to die. I need to join my baby. Mama always said unbaptized babies went to hell. I don't care, though. Heaven, hell, it doesn't matter. I want to be with Gideon. I hope I die. I hope I hemorrhage or get an infection or pass away from some complication from birth. I pray for the sweet, needed release of ceasing to exist. Of nothingness.

I just wonder if Richard finds me dead in here, will he do the same with me? Will he chuck me into the woods like a forgotten, rotting log? Will I land face down in the mud or the brush in the forest beside my baby? I've always known Richard was dangerous and cruel. I've always known he was something to fear. But what kind of monster does that? What kind of beast shows no remorse, no sadness for his own child? There is no forgiving this.

I cry myself to sleep that night on the floor of the bedroom, my cheek against the rough, splintered boards.

Gideon. My sweet Gideon.

Gone.

Chapter Two

I don't know how many days pass—Two? Four? —between the night Gideon dies and the night I decide to get out of bed and protect my sweet child. I spend countless hours whirling in a tormented state, the physical pain churning with the untamable grief into an unbearable concoction. I remember Sharon stopping by at some point to check on me, examining me and asking questions. I remember fading in and out of sleep, nightmares stirring me awake more often than not.

I remember Richard's stomping feet in the bedroom, a half-empty liquor bottle always close by. I vaguely recall him shoving a plate of toast at me, telling me to eat before I killed myself. He couldn't understand or didn't want to understand that death was the only possible reprieve.

But other than that, all I remember is slipping in and out of thoughts of Gideon, of dreams I had for him, and of the memories of his cold, rotting body in my arms. After days of crying myself to sleep, of lying in bed staring at the decrepit ceiling, I decide that there is something that must be done. Death isn't coming, and even though I want to, I won't take my own life. I can't do that. I know what God does to those souls. My mind begins to form the idea that drives me out of bed, an idea that although probably not wise, is necessary. I know what I should've done that first night, what I should've done all these nights that have passed. I can't sit around forever thinking about what needs done. Someone has to do it—and I'm the only one who can. It's all up to me now.

I peel myself out of bed, slipping my feet into the moccasins at the edge. My legs are unsteady and I'm still dizzy, but I don't care. It's not too late. I can do this. I've never been so sure of anything in my entire life.

My hands grab at the cracking walls of the bedroom, my steps slow and unsure as I make my way through the short hallway into the kitchen. Garbage litters the counter, and it smells of whiskey and rotting food. The house is a wreck. I need to clean. I'm surprised he's let me get away with this. I'm lucky he hasn't said anything about the state of the house. Why hasn't he said anything? One of life's mysteries. The dishes need washed. The counters need cleaned. The floor needs scoured. I have so much work to do. But right now, there is a more important task to complete.

I lean on the kitchen chair, catching my breath, as I close my eyes and steady myself. *I'm coming, Gideon. Mommy's coming. I'm sorry it took so long.* Why did I wait so long? I should've gone out that first night. I shouldn't have let him get away with this. I can endure a lot of things, but not this.

I gather enough strength to trek to the screen door and fling it open, the familiar shriek resonating through the darkness of the yard. Fireflies blink to one another, and the warm air envelops me as I make me way over the lifting plank on the front porch. A mosquito tickles my arm, dancing about trying to suck my life out of me. I ignore it, my mind set on the mission at hand.

I gingerly creep down the front porch stairs, one at a time, until my bare feet touch the dirt path that leads behind the house. I hug the rotting siding, not worrying about splinters today as I feel my way around to the back of the small one-story I've called my house but not home for all the years of our marriage. Henry stirs on his rope, tail wagging at the sight of me. I look at my dog, feeling bad for abandoning him these past few days as well. I need to get him food and water. Who knows if Richard has even bothered?

The light is on in the garage, and I hear some rock music blaring. I turn my gaze to the tree line, to the spot I'm after. I need to get to him. I trudge toward the forest, tears welling at the thought of what I must do. This isn't right. None of this is right. He should be here with me, in the rocking chair. He should be clinging to my breasts, feeding and living and breathing. He should be *breathing*. My breasts ache with the thought as I head forward. How different things could've been if he had only been breathing.

Henry's barking disconcerts me just as I'm reaching the edge of the yard. Fireflies continue to blink.

'What the *fuck* do you think you're doing?' a voice roars, startling me and pulling me out of my mission.

I suck in air, filling my lungs as fear usurps my body. I involuntarily shudder, and I hate that I do. I need to be strong for Gideon. I need to do this. I turn to see Richard, a greasy rag in one hand and a wrench in the other. Henry snarls on his rope, stretching toward us. Richard chucks the wrench at the dog and hits him in the side. Henry squeals, pulling back and sitting nearing his doghouse, licking the spot the wrench contacted.

'Richard, please. We need to bury him,' I reason, my voice soft as I automatically look at the ground.

Richard stalks over to me, and my stomach plummets. I sink into myself, shriveling up as small as I can. I bow my head piously, as Richard likes. *Please, God, let him understand.* He has to see. He has to know, somewhere deep down, that this isn't right. We need to make this right. He walks toward me slowly, wordlessly, and my pulse quickens. I close my eyes and flinch as I await his hand smacking against my cheek.

A tense moment passes, but there is no searing pain in my face. Richard gets close enough that his bourbon breath is hot on my cheeks. It scorches my lungs as I inhale. A formidable force that stirs fear in my already broken heart, he towers above me. I feel so small. I *am* so small.

'I told you that we aren't doing that. Did you hear me when I said that? Are you disobeying me, woman?' he asks, his voice unnaturally quiet and soft. He lingers on every word, his spacing and enunciation dramatic and languid. I hate it when his voice is so faint. I know it's a contradiction to the fueling fire burning inside of him. I know the anger is about to incinerate me. He's holding it back for maximum impact, storing it for the right moment to explode. I am forever being hurt in the aftermath of his detonation.

'Richard, I'm sorry. I am. But I can't leave him in the forest. He's our baby, Richard. Please. Don't do this to our baby.'

'How dare you think you can disobey me, you stupid *bitch*. I already told you. It's not your baby. It's *dead*. It's *trash*. Leave it right where I put it. You hear me? And get yourself cleaned up. The house is a goddamn trash heap. Get yourself together. I'm not going to have you laying around the bedroom forever. You have your duties to tend to, you lazy bitch.'

I take a deep breath, steadying myself. My head spins, and Richard's breath is still hot on my face. Terror threatens to seize me, but I shove it down. This isn't a time to back down. I can't stop now. I lift my chin, staring into Richard's eyes with an overt defiance, something I never dare to do. For a long moment, the two of us gaze at each other, his wicked eyes appraising mine. And then I do what I know I shouldn't. I turn from him and march toward the forest, my chin up and my eyes focused.

Before I can take three steps, though, Richard is upon me. He grabs my arm, his fingers digging into my flesh. I yelp in pain, desperate for relief but more desperate to get to my goal. I struggle and yank away from him, screaming out as Henry growls and pulls on the rope.

Richard is too strong.

I am too weak.

Before I can get away, before I can fight my way to my baby, I am on the ground, my back thudding on the hard earth. A jolt of pain stuns my body. My head cracks off the ground, and the next thing I know, Richard is on top of me, his hands around my neck. He squeezes, clutches at me, and I gasp. Tighter, tighter, tighter still his hands grip me. I can't breathe. *I can't breathe.* My neck's going to break. He's finally going to snap the whole way this time.

'Do I need to tie you out with the dog? Do I? Don't you even think about ignoring me again, you hear? Do you *hear*?' With each word, his grasp on my throat is tighter, and I start to slip away. My chest throbs and my head feels like it might just pop. The fireflies still blink in the background, and I think this might be where it ends. Richard on top of me, Henry growling, fireflies dancing around, and my baby rotting in the woods nearby. For a split second, I wonder if this would be such a bad way for my story to end. Maybe this would be merciful. Before the blackness takes complete hold, though, Richard lets go. He slaps me five or six times as I gasp and choke, my lungs aching as I suck in air.

'Don't even try that again,' he shrieks in my face, his nose against my cheek, his eyes lasering into me as I pant, everything sore.

He stands up, staring at Henry. 'You shut the fuck up, too. You're next,' he warns, kicking dirt at the dog before stumbling back to his garage, leaving me to stare up at the stars as I heave.

Tears fall down my cheek, but the balls of light above are a wonderous sight in the midst of the chaotic hell that is my life. How much pain can one woman endure? I don't know if I'm strong enough anymore, Lord. I don't know if I can carry this burden.

Henry quiets, and after a long moment, I sit up, my head aching. I drag my worn-out body toward the dog, who greets me with a tail wag. I lean against him and clutch his fur. I cry into him as I think about what's going to happen to me and wonder where it all went wrong. Then again, I consider as I rock my body gently in the dirt by the doghouse, I know exactly where this road to hardship started.

WHY DIDN'T DADDY COME for this job? Why did he send me alone? It wasn't like him to send me on errands, especially like this. He was always so careful with me. But that afternoon, he and Mama had been fighting more fiercely than normal.

'Crystal, take the truck and get that tire rim fixed,' he'd crowed at me as I sat on my bed, staring out the window when I was supposed to be reading. Monday evenings were reading time.

'But I still have reading to do,' I replied, looking at Daddy in the doorway. I could hear Mama in the kitchen, sobbing. I tried not to think about it. He took five even steps toward me, and my stomach clenched. Why did I say anything? At nineteen, you'd think I'd know better.

'What was that, Crys?' he asked me. I shuddered. I hated it when he called me Crys, but I couldn't say anything about it. Mama always said Daddy wanted a boy. It was his way of reminding me of that—I was a mistake, an unwanted mistake. He hadn't wanted a weak girl like me.

'Sorry, Daddy. Of course. Right away. Where am I taking it?' I asked. It was rare that Daddy let me take the truck. He'd taught me to drive at sixteen, but only as a precaution in case he needed a ride—or needed me to go out so he could do something more horrible to Mama than usual, something he didn't want me interfering with. But it was rare I was sent out. He worried I'd get into mischief, even though I barely knew anyone to get into mischief with. At nineteen, my life revolved *around playing secondary housekeeper to my Mama, church, and that was about it. I hadn't done well in school, but that was okay. Mama and Daddy always said education was wasted on girls, that we didn't need it anyway. I knew what my role would be someday. If I were lucky, I'd find a nice enough man who would provide for me. I would have a child, and that would be my purpose. Until then, I was trapped in this house following their rules—and their rules weren't always the easiest. But I knew I was lucky to be safe, to be taken care of. Daddy always reminded me that I was lucky. Mama too. Lucky Crystal. So lucky.*

'Down to the Connor garage. He's reasonable. Saw him at the bar yesterday, and he said he'd take care of it.'

I studied Daddy, his jaw clenching in the telltale sign. I wasn't a little girl anymore. I knew why he was sending me away. It had nothing to do with a truck he wanted fixed. It had everything to do with Mama and what he wanted to do her. I had lain awake plenty of nights, heard the yelps and the harsh words, heard the familiar sound of his fist hitting Mama's flesh. I'd seen the bruises, the blood, the devastating reminders of the cold, harsh truth. But sometimes, Daddy's whims were too dark for just a closed bedroom door between us. Even Daddy had principles, after all.

We were the weak ones. Daddy was the strong one. We were at his mercy.

I thought about saying no, like I wanted to do so many times. But what could I do? I knew all too well what price I'd pay if I spoke up. I wouldn't be able to change anything. Worst of all, I knew the penance I'd do, not only at Daddy's hand, but at Mama's. Women obeyed. That was the law of God. It was best to keep my mouth shut and do as I was told. I wandered out to the driveway to jump into the beat-up pickup truck, studying the dilapidated house as I did. What had brought me to this life? Was this really it for me? I hoped there was something more for me out there. I prayed for escape.

When I got to the garage and pulled up, I gingerly stepped from the truck and approached the garage.

'Excuse me?' I timidly said, standing in the doorway of the garage as the rock music blared at a ridiculous decibel. I leaned on the frame of the door, feeling nervous and out of my element.

'Hello?' I muttered again into the dark garage secluded on the windy path I'd driven down, away from town. Away from civilization, forgotten out in the middle of the woods. Beautiful in its own right. Peaceful and beautiful, the forest cocooning a tiny house like a magical getaway. Compared to the trailer court, it looked like heaven to me.

Richard Connor meandered out from behind a car parked in his garage. I'd seen him before around town. He wasn't exactly a secret, even though he lived out in an isolated section of town, trees and distance keeping him aloof from everyone else. In fact, he was quite the opposite of being a secret, his reputation marking him as infamous. Still, there was something about him that made my heart flutter as he walked toward me, oil and grease covering his shirt. Maybe it was his dark hair or his tan skin. Or maybe it was the way his muscles bulged beneath his shirt, a tight body that screamed power. Maybe it was that he was tall and walked with a sense of confidence, of purpose, I'd rarely seen and never experienced. Or, in truth, maybe it was just the fact that in Richard, I saw *something that I was so desperately craving at nineteen: an escape route I was frantic to claim.*

'Can I help you?' His voice was gruff but silky in its depth. Richard Connor was an enigma, even from the first moment he spoke to me. I liked the mystery that crept around his edges. I felt my chest tingle.

'My dad said you were going to help fix the truck? Denny Holt?'

Richard put down the wrench with a clink, walking closer to me, his eyes drinking me in. Suddenly, I felt underwhelming in my long skirt and turtleneck sweater. I felt like a stumbling fool.

'Ah, yes. Denny. Not a problem. I can fix it, but there are two conditions,' he said as he appraised me. He stopped in front of me, much closer than any man had ever stood. My breathing intensified.

'Yeah?' I said, trying to play it cool.

'One, you tell me your name. And two, you stay and keep me company. Gets pretty lonely around this here garage, you know?'

I smiled, his own grin warming me. The song changed on the radio, and I realized it was actually a song I knew. I felt at ease.

'I'm Crystal. And yes, I'd love to stay. Where else would I go?' I asked, shyly. I tried not to think about the questions Daddy would ask if it took too long. I would worry about that later.

'Good. Come on. I'll set you up a chair,' he replied, grabbing my hand and yanking me into the garage. The touch of his skin, ragged and rough, the hand of a true man, sent electric

warmth through me. It wasn't the hand of a boy like Timmy Grenshaw, the boy who had tried to kiss me last year in the hallway after school. No, this was different. Richard Connor had strong hands, ones that could save me. I was entranced. I was sold. I was taken by him before I could consider the danger of it.

I didn't care about his reputation or that he wasn't the kind of guy Mama or Daddy would approve of. Something told me Richard wasn't a God-fearing man, but I liked him all the more for it. Maybe, in truth, I liked him for what he represented—a true rebellion against the ideals of that house I was being held basically prisoner in and the repression of parents who made me feel weak. Following Richard into the garage, suddenly I didn't feel feeble at all. I felt alive. I felt vicariously strong through him. I felt like for once in my life, I could make my own choice; I ached to be autonomous, for better or for worse.

'So, I'm sure a gorgeous thing like you has a boyfriend, right?' Richard asked, and I stared into his eyes, the darkness of them speaking to me.

'No, not at all.'

'You a virgin?' he followed up, playing it off with a smile. I blushed, not expecting the question.

I nodded.

'Interesting. Very interesting,' he whispered, putting a hand on my waist and pulling me in. My heart raced as I thought he might kiss me, but then, before I knew it, he started singing loudly to the radio, pulling away as he jumped in the car parked in the garage and pulled it out, his driving reckless enough to startle me.

I sat on the metal chair he kindly set up for me, wondering what path that night would lead me down—and wondering if Richard Connor could be the man to rescue me from the house of horrors I was used to. Maybe he was the one I'd been praying for. Sometimes hope and rescue come in very unexpected forms, after all.

PATTING HENRY ON THE head one more time for confidence, I say goodbye to the stars, goodbye to the memories, and stand up on my two unsteady feet.

Sometimes hope and rescue do come in very unexpected forms, I remind myself as I breathe in and think for a fleeting moment about what I'm going to do.

Chapter Three
10 hours later: Tuesday Morning

I unfurl the corner of the rug, smoothing out the tasseled ends as I try to put every single string in place. My knees ache from the gritty, splintery texture of the living room's wooden floor. Richard refers to it as rustic, but I've always thought it was just plain ugly. Not that I would dare suggest that, of course. I straighten out the tassels into the rigid line like I've done so many times, each thread lined up with precision. Everything always has to be in its place.

I sigh, thinking about the mundaneness of the task. In light of everything, it seems so arbitrary to worry about the rug, but I can't help myself. Maybe it's a good thing that I'm thinking about something besides all that's transpired since last night. I feel maybe it's a sign. Maybe I'm going to be okay.

At the mere thought of him, though, my gut clenches and I feel as though I might be sick. I have to shove the fear aside. I have to be strong. I can't do this again. Richard said over and over I need to get on with things, that I can't keep crying. Maybe he's right about that, even if I don't want to admit it. It's time to get on with it all. What choice do I have?

I pluck the rag from the bucket and wring it out, the scent of bleach no longer assaulting my nose as I take the container to the bathroom to dump the grimy water down the drain. My hands sting, pruned from scrubbing all of the floors for the past hour, but I relish the feel of it. It's familiar, the notion of being productive, worthy even. There's nothing like the smell of fresh bleach, of laundry soap, of lemony freshness to make me feel valuable. The house might not be majestic or perfect or flashy, but it's spotless, as spotless as it can be at least. I always make sure of it. I might not be able to control much, but I've always regulated that. I learned early on that my survival depended on it. Setting the bucket aside, I stand at the threshold, taking inventory of the house.

Good as new—as new as 414 Peacoat Drive will ever be. Our humble abode, of course, had been a source of tension between my parents and Richard when we got married. Daddy didn't feel the tiny shack-like ranch and detached garage was good enough for me—ironic, since our one-bedroom trailer was hardly a castle, and Daddy was never the doting type. Still, maybe it's every dad's right to judge the next phase of his daughter's life and to emasculate the man she chose, even if she wasn't exactly a daddy's girl. And even if the man she married wouldn't dare let anyone emasculate him.

For all their differences, Daddy and Richard have their commonalities, some dark and some not so dark. They're both inarguably clean freaks, or rather, demanders of cleanliness. Neither liked a messy house, although arguably neither ever did much to contribute to an orderly living space. They instead rely on the women in their lives to pick up their messes, to clean up where they couldn't. Until the day Daddy died, Mama did everything for him. She was his caretaker, his servant, his worshipper in all ways. He wouldn't have it any other way. I wonder if this is my fate, too.

It's one of Richard's many ticks, his expecting everything perfectly clean. It's one of the things I've just learned to accept. In truth, Richard's obsession with cleanliness is one of the easiest to deal with. He likes things spotless and orderly. He *expects* things tidy and methodical and, with little else to occupy my days, I've obliged. Not that it's a bad thing. Cleanliness and godliness and all of that good business Mama had instilled in me over the years. It's hardly Richard's worst attribute, after all.

Truthfully, I'm fine with cleaning. It's what I'm good at. There are, I suppose, worse occupations of one's time, and there is something therapeutic about feeling the rag between my fingers, of washing away the filth in the house. Of wiping away everything I can, leaving nothing remaining like a great disappearing act.

Even if I wasn't a woman who liked cleaning, I would have learned quickly during our early months of marriage that it isn't always about me. Marriage is a sacrifice, and Richard always makes sure I understand that tenant fully.

Tears trickle now without warning, as they so often do ever since last night. Tears over everything that has gone wrong. Tears over everything that won't be. And tears over everything I can't quite set right. Then again, I think, as I wipe at my eyes, maybe I can.

As long as he doesn't show up, I can set things on a different, better path. I can make it all okay. I can serve my purpose and rise up. It's a thought pattern that dares to conjure up a foreign sentiment in my dented but still beating heart: Hope. Nevertheless, the cold, harsh truth rips through me like an icy, winter wind. The bitterness of it stops my breath, causing me to lean hard against the threshold, clutching at my shirt and clawing at my heart.

Hope never flies very far from Peacot Drive. I crash back to the muddied path, my heart denting a little bit more. True, Richard is missing, disappearing into the night like he's done time and time before. I squeeze my eyes shut, trying not to think about last night, about those fingers around my neck. I shove aside the aftermath of what happened, of the horrific feelings that overtook me. I wipe away the tears, knowing I need to be strong.

Richard's not here. I woke up from a restless sleep this morning to find the house still and quiet—and empty. His truck is gone, slipped away into the darkness of the night. Even though I should be worried, terrified even, a sense of peace takes over. Maybe this is exactly what I need to heal, to be okay again.

After all, I really shouldn't be worried. Richard's done this so many times. His truck is gone, off to another town with better booze and better women. I've grown used to it over the years, and so has everyone else. No one will blink an eye at the disappearance of Richard. It makes me feel a little bit sad for him—just a little. Out here on Peacot Drive, I've got nothing but silence. My only company is Henry. I've got all of this space, all of this empty space, to figure things out. For once, I'm thankful we live so far out from town.

Still, there's the sense of foreboding that this will end so differently than all those other times. Maybe it's because of the anger from Richard's reaction to me claiming Gideon, or maybe it's just that I'm feeling unbearably frail. Regardless, I'm rightfully on edge. Any second, he will end all of this. He will show up and destroy me for good. He will *certainly* be coming any second now. He has to be. I can't help but feel like this temporary reprieve from Richard, from my life, will be short-lived. How long could it realistically last? A few hours? A few days? Eventually, he'll come through that door, and it will all end there.

And what can be done about it, really? Hope hasn't clouded my vision after all. I never let it creep too far in. It is a tempting mistress so many lust for . . . until she shanks you in the gut. I protect myself against her, let reality guide my life. I know I'm nobody special, nobody strong. I'm a weak woman who depends on Richard for everything. For years, I've come to the conclusion that there's no escaping it.

I should at least enjoy the limited time I have to be free, though. I should be thankful for the reprieve, for the gift. I know it will be tough. I've never been good at doing things on my own. In truth, I've never had much practice. I've always been under the watchful eyes of Daddy or Richard, except for the benders Richard goes on. But there's always the knowledge that he'll come back. I think that's why he's okay with disappearing at random. Richard knows he still has control of me, even when he's not here—the knowledge that at any moment, he will return has always kept me honest. He keeps me on a tight leash even when he's out of town. And really, where could I go? I have no money of my own, no place to go, no life to build without him. I'm tethered as tightly to Richard as Henry is to the tree, but I lack both a foreboding bark and a set of puncturing teeth.

Nonetheless, things feel different this time, no matter how much I try to convince myself it's all fine, that this is just like the other times. Things don't feel exactly right. Who am I kidding? This isn't right. It will probably never be right again. I tremble, feeling like any second, that door will fling open and I'll be back on the ground, staring up at a starless sky this time, no fireflies in sight.

I'd thought about leaving the house for a while, of wandering into town, of maybe looking for a new dress or something of the like to take my mind of things. But I knew it was a terrible idea. I can't leave, not now. He could be here any second, and how would that look? How would he react? I would look guilty as sin, and I'd have to explain where I'd gone. I might not be the smartest woman in the world, but even I know that wouldn't be a good thing.

I tell myself to take a breath and then another. I remind myself it will be okay. This is nothing new. Richard's pulled this kind of thing before. In fact, a few hours missing for Richard is nothing, absolutely nothing in the scheme of things. How many weekends had he left for a bender, only to come home two or three nights tops, demanding dinner on the table and inspecting the house to see if it was clean? Or how about the time last year when he owed Blinky McMann four hundred bucks for a brake job gone bad, supposedly, and had left for four days? No one will be worried about

Richard Connor, that is for sure. And I shouldn't be either. He might be missed only because he is always causing such a scene in the town—and also because he is the cheapest garage in Forkhill. But no one will blink an eye. No one will worry.

He can take care of himself. He is a strong, able-bodied man. No one will be concerned that any harm has come to him. And after everything that's happened, after all these years, I really shouldn't worry, either. In fact, the emptiness of the house, the relative quietude is a relief to my weary soul. I walk with my head a little higher, with confidence that I can do this. I can make it through this. It's crazy that it's taken Richard being gone for me to understand that important reality—he is not the source of strength here. Not at all.

I shouldn't worry—but that doesn't mean I don't. It's just my anxieties are not really of the wifely type, something that makes me feel unabashedly guilty. Shouldn't I be feeling a bit intrepid for him? Shouldn't I wonder if he's okay after all that happened the night before he disappeared?

The icy terror shredding my chest isn't fear for Richard's wellbeing. It's perhaps the opposite. My unwavering, uncontrollable fear is that at any moment, he'll be here, standing right here, knowing exactly what I've done. I close my eyes and I can see him on top of me, choking me, Gideon so close yet so far away. I shudder at the horrific memory, and the fear surges again. I shake my head.

No. No. No. Stop it, Crystal, I tell myself. *That's enough. It doesn't do to dwell on the all the paths that brought things here, right here.*

I saunter into the living room, staring out the window. I lean against the cold glass, the bad memories flooding me no matter how hard I try to push them away. Looking out the dingy glass—I still need to wash the windows this week—I can't help but see the rage, the lack of understanding, the reckoning for sins. I feel it deep within, the same feeling I'd felt so many years under my parents' roof.

Just as they promised me, I know I'll pay for my sins, the ultimate price. But, until then, there's so much to do. So much to prepare. Because if he shows up at the wrong time, at the wrong moment, I'll pay with my life. That much I know. I need to get myself together, to think. I need to sort it all out and figure out what comes next.

Deep breath. Don't even think about it. Deep breath. Don't even think about it. I inwardly chant the words that have become my mantra, telling myself to stay calm. It wouldn't do to go crazy now. I have to keep it together. I'm, in truth, a terrible liar. I have plenty to fear. Still, I know this is no time to break.

Growing up in Forkhill, I know that everyone here has always seen me as the weak one. Maybe I am. Maybe I really am just Crystal Holt, the weak, and now Crystal Connor, the weaker. Maybe I'm just a fragile, flimsy housewife with no real direction or purpose. One moment of fortitude does not a strong woman make—does it?

But right now, I know I have to find some strength and some courage if I'm going to survive this. I know I have to be ready for when he is standing before me. Because he will come, I know it. Richard has ways of influencing, of impacting, and of seeing everything even when he isn't around. I know he'll make sure I pay for everything I've done. And with that awareness, my hands shaking, I finally allow myself to sink to the ground and sob, the reality of the desperate situation sinking in.

There is no getting out of this unscathed—in reality, I've already been marred over and over again these past days I've spent in hell. The best I can hope for now is to get out with some semblance of myself. That will be my mission, I promise myself, wiping away the countless tears after a long moment, the banging at the door startling me into action.

Chapter Four

I stumble to the door, leaning heavily on the walls. When am I going to be okay again? Will this pain ever go away? I'm exhausted, but even my tired mind knows this isn't just about physical pain. This is about the emotional wreckage that's been left in the aftermath of the hell I've been through.

Every step feels like a marathon as I drag myself to the screen door, wondering who it is. A piece of me fears it's Richard, that the door will open and reveal his ragged, angered face and this will all be over. I'll be worse off than before, and my single moment of freedom will be lost forever. He'll never let me live this down. But the thought is ridiculous. Richard would never knock. Who could it be?

I'm not feeling up to visitors, that's for sure. Not that Richard ever lets me have visitors, anyway. He says he is all I need in my life. He doesn't think I need distractions from my wifely duties. I was never very good at making friends. I was always the aloof one, the shunned one, the different one. Maybe that was why when Richard looked my way, I didn't hesitate to look back.

I make it to the door, wiping the hair from my eyes before pulling it open. Henry barks wildly outside as he yanks on his rope. *It'll be okay, Henry,* I think. *There, there.*

When I open the door, I'm surprised to see Michael Finnigan at the door, his baggy jeans and T-shirt wrinkled like he's slept in them. I haven't seen him in months, although he often brings cars to Richard to fix. I look at his receding hairline. That man really should wear a hat. I'm not sure why that comes to mind, but it does. He spits out some tobacco on the porch, and I shudder at the sight of the dark splatter on the tan, splintered boards. I'll have to mop that now. Richard would be mad.

'Where's Richard?' Michael asks, the lump of dip in his mouth skewing his words, watering them down.

'Not home,' I say, wiping my hands on my pants, looking at Michael as I do.

'What? Where the fuck is he? He's got a job to do. Told me last week he could fit me in. Shit.'

I shrug. 'Sorry,' I say. 'He's gone. Truck was missing this morning.'

'Asshole. Figures he'd take off. Did he say anything about when he'll be back?'

I shake my head. 'He never does.'

'Better not be like last time, when I had that 76' to work on. Asshole up and left for what, like four days? I can't wait that long. You tell Richard when you see him that Big Mike is looking for him and ain't too happy. You hear me?'

'I'll tell him. But I don't know when he'll be back.'

'Shouldn't be surprised, Missus. Should be used to Richard leaving. Always was a dick, even in high school.'

Michael kicks the porch, his worn-out boot stomping into the board. I lean on the door, breathing in and out, my side aching. Michael, apparently deciding I'm telling the truth, emits another expletive before turning on his heel and heading back to the truck, dented and rusty. He jumps in, slamming the door as Henry continues to bark on his rope. The truck starts with a clunking sound, and Michael peels out, down the secluded lane back into town.

I sigh. He's gone. But he won't be gone for long. He'll be back, and there's no telling what will happen if he returns and Richard's not here. Of course, he's not the return I fear the most.

It hits me then that Michael won't be the only one looking for Richard. True, it's not like Richard has that many friends. But he does have a sufficient number of customers. And when they come for their brakes or tire alignments or whatever else they need done, they won't be happy to find Richard gone. I squeeze my eyes shut, thinking about how bad this could be this time around.

I'm not strong enough for this. Too much has happened. Too much has broken. I can't do this again. The bills will be piling up, and the food stamps never go far. True, it's just me right now, and I don't have much of an appetite. But there's so much to take care of, and I just don't know if I have the strength. The day's business has already left me worn. Everything leaves me worn these days, though. I walk onto the porch, heading down the steps to go pet Henry, to sit with him a while. I think about letting him in the house, consider how nice it would be to cuddle up to him in the living room, sitting with a cup of tea and washing away all of the sorrow.

But I know I can't. He could be here any time. It wouldn't do to have Henry inside. It just won't do. Where would I hide him, after all? How would I stop him from doing what I know he'll do?

'Hi, buddy,' I say, walking to the dog, my only real companion these days. I sit in the dirt again beside him. My dress is covered in dust, but I'll take care of that tomorrow. It's laundry day tomorrow. No use in breaking the routine.

My eyes actually ache from a lack of sleep, and my hands hurt from the day's messy chores. The bedroom is still untidy, but I don't think my fatigued hand muscles can even hold a broom. I lean against the dog, who is happy for my company. He rests against me, unmoved by everything, untroubled by the demons that plague me. I rock back and forth, staring at the house that has in many ways become a prison. All of the worst moments of my life happened in and around that house. Who knows, however, how many more terrible moments are to come?

I think about how easy it would be to burn it down, to create an inferno out of the shack that's abandoned me in so many ways. It would be a relief to see it engulfed, a hellfire of truth and innocence going up in smoke. Instead, I clutch Henry tightly and ponder everything that's gone wrong. All those years of praying, of thinking faith could save me. Now, I don't know. I was good. I was. And where did that get me?

Guilt assaults me. I can't believe I'm even thinking like this. I need to pray. I need to atone. I need to be forgiven. I kiss the dog's head before standing and trekking back into the house. My feet follow the familiar path to the bedroom. I want to sleep, to tuck myself in like I have so many times and just fall into a senseless slumber. It's easier to ignore the world's realities.

I don't, though. I know what I need to do. I pull the Bible from the nightstand, flipping to the page I'm seeking. I find refuge in the pages, at least for a few moments. I read the words that I practically memorized in my teenage years. All those days spent worshipping in that little church. All those evenings kneeling before the Blessed Mother in the room in my parents' house. I know my way around the Bible. I just don't know if it knows its way around me, anymore. I focus for as long as I can, asking for forgiveness and strength. I don't know if I deserve it. God may be merciful, but he isn't blind. He knows what's happened. And so do I.

So will he.

I lean back against the headrest, thinking, remembering. I want so badly to forget, but I also don't want to forget. I want to remember what it felt like, that sweet body in my arms, that angelic face tainted by stillness. I rock back and forth, thinking about the baby and all of the hopes that died with him. I think about how, if only he had taken that first breath, things might have been different. It wouldn't have just been Gideon that was saved. It would've been me, too.

But it's too late for what ifs. Life is an unhampered train that just keeps chugging. It'll run you over if you don't get out of the way. I have no choice but to duck, take cover, and get ready for the next phase. I don't know how this story will end. I know where it started, though. And I know that it's not over yet. It's nowhere near being over just yet.

I ROCKED BACK AND FORTH in the chair, clinging to the soft yellow blanket I'd crocheted only three months earlier. It should've been pink. I should've made it pink. I held the blanket

to my face, wishing it smelled of newborn. Instead, it smelled of stale yarn. It smelled of death. It smelled of all the things I'd never hold, never have.

I rocked, tears falling and falling like they'd never cease. It'd been three days since my life had ended with the cramping, the blood, and the free clinic doctor's use of a single word I'd never thought I'd hear: miscarriage.

How could it happen? How? I'd prayed night after night for our baby, Richard and mine. From the moment I realized I'd been pregnant, I'd prayed it would be a girl. A healthy girl. I saw so much in that girl even though I didn't know her. I saw my purpose, my life, my escape.

Mama and Daddy, of course, had been livid when they'd learned the news. The one-night rendezvous with Richard had turned out to be a lifetime commitment. When I'd first realized that climbing into the back of the truck that night in his shop had led to my pregnancy, I was mortified, terrified, and sorry. I'd committed the greatest of sins. I'd gone against Mama and Daddy's wishes. I'd gone against the will of God.

Still, when I'd let Richard pull me into the back of that truck and peel my shirt off, I hadn't wanted to stop. The connection, the sensation of his rough hands moving over my smooth, untouched skin—it was what I craved. I felt needed and wanted. I felt special. I wasn't just Crystal Holt, the girl everyone looked over. With Richard, I was somebody.

My confession of my pregnancy to Richard hadn't gone quite as expected. He'd sworn instead of smiling. I'd naively thought maybe he'd be happy. His conversation turned quickly to money and how he was going to afford a mouth to feed. He'd tossed a wrench to the ground and grabbed a bottle of liquor from his toolbox. I'd sat in tears, staring at the ground.

Telling Mama and Daddy, though, that had been worse. I'd ended up sobbing, begging for atonement from God, from them, from the Blessed Mother. I'd spent the entire night on my knees, repenting for being a slut in Mama's words. I'd listened to Daddy slap Mama, blaming her for teaching me to be a whore. I'd cried so hard, I thought for sure I'd drown in my own tears.

Weeks passed. I hadn't heard from Richard. But eventually, Daddy dragged him into the house to tell me the news. He'd be marrying me that weekend.

'Won't have the town thinking my daughter's a slut,' Daddy had said as Richard stood in our living room, hands in his pockets. He refused to make eye contact with me.

I stared at my Daddy, at Richard. Nerves fluttered in my stomach. I hadn't expected to get married so young. I hadn't expected to get married to a man I barely knew other than having sex with in the back of a truck in a dirty garage. Still, this was my ticket out. Things had to be better, right? I'd be out from under my parents' roof. I'd be away from Daddy, from Mama. I'd be in my own family. And I'd have a baby to raise right. Richard would come to love me, wouldn't he? We'd be okay. We'd find our way. I'd make sure of it. I didn't know how Daddy convinced Richard to marry me, and I didn't want to know. I was just grateful he had.

Our wedding was official and nothing more. Richard said his vows with some enthusiasm thanks to whiskey courage. I'd worn a dingy white dress splotched with stains that Mama had found at the local thrift store. We'd said our vows at the courthouse in front of an audience of exactly two—Mama and Daddy. There was no fanfare. There was no loving first kiss. There was Richard roughly grabbing my face, kissing me sloppily, and then dragging me back to what was my new house.

And the first month had been—okay. I'd learned quickly that Richard had similarities to my father. I'd learned how to be a good wife, mostly from making so many mistakes. I'd learned that growing up and moving out wasn't as glorious as I'd thought. I learned that the secluded tranquility of Peacot Drive was as far from heaven as you could get, perhaps even further than the trailer park. I'd learned that my life would never be the thing of dreams, the life of independence my teachers at school had tried to get me to strive for. But I was okay with that. I had the baby growing inside of me. I had a chance to make things right.

But with that one word, 'miscarriage,' all that was gone. The soul-crushing word floated in the air.

I'd needed Richard to lean on. But he wasn't there. He'd spewed a few phrases to me about the goddamn expense of the crib I'd insisted on purchasing and how it had been my fault for eating unhealthy foods. He'd blamed me for the loss of his baby, but that had been it. There was no sorrow. There was no empathy. There was just Richard swearing about being tied to a goddamn deadweight. There was talk of how he'd have never married me if he'd have known child support wouldn't have ever been an issue. There was talk that he should just throw me back to my parents, make me their problem again.

The tears fell as all of the terrors that had become my life whirled about. I wasn't crying because Richard might leave me. True, it was unlikely my parents would take me back. They'd *refused to talk to me since I'd moved out, claiming I wasn't their problem anymore. Claiming I had my own life now to worry about. I hadn't even seen them in the three months since I'd gotten married, even though they lived a mere ten miles away.*

I wasn't terrified of Richard leaving me. I knew at that point he liked having me around, if nothing more than to feel in control. His relationship with me was about power, through and through. Without the baby in the picture, that didn't change.

My tears were for the baby I'd never know. They were for the life I'd wanted so badly that had slipped away. They were me mourning the baby I'd never got to meet. But they were also selfish tears for the girl I could no longer be and the woman I would never become. They were tears for the life I was trapped in and the hopelessness of a life without purpose.

That night, I swore to devote myself to my faith, to God, to anything that could make all of it better. I swore I'd be more pious, adhere to my wifely duties, and pray more often. If only he'd make it all right.

If only he'd bring me back my baby.

If only he'd help me find purpose.

If only I'd get pregnant again.

IT DOESN'T DO TO DWELL on the past. It doesn't. I know this. You don't need an expensive therapist to recognize this truth.

I peel myself out of bed, putting down the good book. I need to keep busy. Work is good for the soul and mind. I need to be occupied. Plus, when he comes, I want to look like it's a normal day. I don't want him being suspicious of me. I don't want him wondering what's going on. I head to the kitchen, staring out the window at the overcast day. I walk to the screen door, deciding to head out and clean the porch. As I do, the familiar screech comes back, and the handle jiggles. It's been broken for some time. It needs oil. Richard said he'd get to it. But Richard's not here. Maybe I could do it myself.

Richard would be furious if he knew I did a man's job. It makes him feel emasculated when I repair things around here. He does the fixing. He has very clearly defined jobs and roles in the household, as do I. I need to leave them be. I stare at the door, thinking. He's gone. I don't need to leave them be, do I? Maybe I can't fix the bigger things just yet, can't solve all the problems I have. But I can fix a flawed handle. Should I? Should I do it?

It seems so senseless to worry about something so trivial. Still, I let my mind crawl over the thought for some time, wavering back and forth over what to do. Finally, I decide to give in. I grab my keys and purse from the counter, in their familiar spot. I head out the screen door and let it slam shut. We never lock the door. There's no need. But I pause, turning to stare at the house. I think today I should lock it. Just to be safe. I should probably lock the door. Yes, yes. I need to.

I lock the door after struggling to turn the key. It's been so long since I've had to do this. Have I ever? I don't know how long it's been since I've gone into town by myself. Two years? Three? Even last year, when Richard disappeared for four days, I wasn't brave enough to go. I was too afraid. I must be a fool. I must be losing it. Maybe it's all the blood loss or the grief. I don't know, but there's no turning back now. My mind is set on it. I'm going to do it.

Maybe I should check the garage first. Maybe some of the tools I need are out there. Richard doesn't like it when I go in his garage. Maybe I shouldn't go in. I twiddle my fingers in anxiety. He wouldn't be happy at all. *But he's not here,* I remind myself. I could just take a quick peek around, see if there's anything in there that could be of use.

I head down to the garage, my hand freezing on the doorknob. I take a deep breath. It's all okay. It's not a big deal, I remind myself. It's going to be fine. Just a garage. That's all. I'm just getting some tools. It's not like it's a crime.

I walk into the garage, the smell of oil and gasoline overpowering me. I glance around the shop, dirty yet somehow orderly, too. Richard likes order. I saunter over to the toolbox in the corner. I have no clue where to even start. I've never searched through his things. Richard never lets me in here. I start pulling open some drawers, glancing at all sorts of tools. I don't know my way around the toolbox or even where to begin. Still, I can't stop myself from glancing through them. What am I even looking for? I don't know. My breathing is ragged.

Focus, Crystal. You can do this.

I open drawer after drawer, looking at all sorts of sockets and wrenches, screwdrivers and other parts. I come to the bottom drawer and peel it open. I freeze when I look down and see it. I stare, wondering if I should look in the envelope. Unmarked, stuffed in the bottom under some tools, it sits, begging to be opened. My hand gingerly reaches inside, touching the wrinkled paper envelope. I pull it out and peer inside.

Wads of green bills sit inside, crisp and untouched. My eyes widen. More money than I've seen flow through our house, sitting right here, piled away under tools. What is he doing with all this? And more importantly, where did it come from?

A moment of indecision. What to do with it? I think about shoving it in my pocket, taking it inside. It could help me. It could solve a lot of problems, couldn't it? It could open doors I thought could never open.

It might be a partial ticket out of here. Couldn't it? Couldn't it help me? For the first time, I see something creeping in, something I usually stomp down.

Hope, relentlessly resurrecting itself once more.

Money can't solve everything. But it could be a start.

I know it's a risky move. There are still so many other variables to consider. I have things to get ready, things to finish, before I even let myself dream of the possibility. And who knows how much time I have to work with? There's no way I could pull it off before he comes—could I?

And what would I do with the freedom? With the escape? Wouldn't he eventually find me? And then what would happen to me? It's all so mind-boggling. It feels like a bad crime novel, but one where the plans don't work out perfectly. This is more than just buying a train ticket and some hair dye. This would be forever, and I don't know if I'm brave enough.

Am I?

I stare at the money, the crisp paper feeling uncannily warm between my fingers as if it really is igniting something within. It quickly sizzles though, marred by reality and a lifetime of harshness.

Even if I did find a way to make the money work, to get out of here, it's dangerous. What is the money from? I don't know what Richard's been up to, but I don't want wrapped up in this. He'd never let me get away with this, whatever it is. After a long moment, the feeling of hope settles right back where it belongs, right where it always goes to hide when the reality of my situation sinks in. I sigh, tucking the envelope back as a new question surfaces.

Who is my husband? And what is he really doing in the garage? They're questions I should've been asking for years but am only now starting to.

I decide that whatever I need, I'll find at the hardware store. I have to get out of here. I can't be spotted in here. I'm walking out toward the front door when I stop again. My stomach plummets once more. There, in the inside corner of Richard's office, sits an unassuming yet familiar hammer. The handle is worn and dirty, decades of use wearing on the unsuspecting tool. It lays underneath a shoddy table, out of view.

But, by the head of the hammer, blood pools. Bright and oozing, the puddle spreads on the floor. This is bad. This is really bad. I stand for a moment, trying to calm myself. It's fine. Richard obviously just hit his hand. Maybe he just hurt himself. That would explain it. But that's a good bit of blood. A hit hand wouldn't explain that away. I stand for a long moment, wondering what I should do. Should I leave it be? Or should I clean it up? This doesn't feel right at all. He wouldn't be happy with that mess, though. Richard never liked a mess, after all. He wouldn't just leave a bloody puddle in his garage, his prized possession.

After a long moment, I decide that I must take care of it. He can't come here and find the garage like this. Things will be so much worse for me if he does. Thus, I trudge to the house, digging out the bleach and the bucket, taking a deep breath once more. I can do this. I can take care of this, I reassure myself. I utilize the next half hour to tenaciously scrub the floor, getting rid of the congealed puddle. I assure myself it's fine even though I know deep down it isn't.

After the blood is gone, I decide to stow the hammer in the toolbox. I put it in the bottom drawer, right on top of the envelope of cash. Would Richard be able to tell I was in there? I don't know. But there are bigger issues right now.

Maybe the true danger is just beginning.

I refocus, drawing my attention back to the screen door as I take the bucket and rag inside to rinse out. The screen door still needs fixed. I'm shaken from the discovery in the garage, both discoveries, but I settle myself down. It's okay. It's all okay. One thing at a time.

I decide that I do need to head to the hardware store to get some tools. They'll be able to help me, and I'd rather have new ones. I don't want to go back in the garage unless I absolutely have to, I think with a chill. I relock the door, head outside, and hop into the truck. Richard, of course, always takes the red truck out of town when he leaves. It's his favorite. The blue one is still here, though. I will myself to remember how to drive. Sometimes Richard has me drive him to the liquor store when he doesn't want to. But it's been a while. He typically only lets me drive at night when no one will see him being driven around. After all, he says, it doesn't do for a man to be driven around like some fairy by a woman.

I back down the lane, pointing the truck for town. I feel a little bit excited. I'm all by myself, and it feels good. Still, the farther I get from the house, the more my nerves creep in. Can I really leave? It feels unnatural to be this far away. I feel so out of control, which is ridiculous. I've never been in control, have I? Nonetheless, out here, I can't watch things. I can't keep an eye on how it's all playing out. I can't watch for him. I don't like the idea of returning home and being surprised. What would he do to me? Would I be able to play it cool? I don't know.

I follow the familiar route to town, looking at the trees surrounding the lane. It's been so long since I've been out. The last time I was out like this—my hand goes to my belly. Tears threaten to cascade down, but I stop them.

'Stop it,' I shout to myself, slamming a hand on the steering wheel. 'Breathe. Don't think about it. Just don't think about it. Breathe.'

I inhale and exhale slowly, feeling the weight of the air drifting out of my lungs. I bite my lip, trying to calm myself. As I come to a Stop sign at the end of the lane, I reach for the knob on the radio, turning it up. The familiar rock band comes on, the one Richard loves. I turn the music off. I'd rather listen to silence than that song. It takes me back to a dark place, bad memories assaulting me. I shake my head. That won't do either. What *will* do these days? I don't like who I'm becoming or what life is becoming. The eggshells I'm precariously trying to walk on now feel even more delicate than when Richard was home.

A few moments later, I'm mercifully saved from the inner monologue rattling me as I pull into Pete's Hardware. I put the truck in park, pulling the emergency brake on. I glance at my eyes in the rearview mirror. They are bloodshot, and the bags under my eyes really are noticeable. I haven't thought this part through. What if people ask questions? True, I haven't been in town for a while, but Pete knows me. Everyone knows me in this town. Everyone knows Richard. I'm not ready for the questions, the assumptions, the pitying eyes. I'm sure talk of the baby has swirled around. Sharon certainly couldn't have kept it to herself, could she? I don't want to deal with that. I just can't. And what if people ask about Richard?

Ridiculous, I remind myself. It hasn't even been that long since he went missing. Not like anyone will notice. Sure, the bartenders will wonder why his familiar stool is empty, but that's about it. No one will miss the town drunk, the town mischief maker, the town wreck. And even if they do, it's not like he hasn't done it before. Besides, it's not like I know anything anyway, I remind myself.

The pool of blood in the garage, though, comes floating back. I shudder at the thought, shirking it off. It's all okay. It was nothing. Nothing at all.

Still, it's the fear that they'll know about Gideon, that there will be pity in their eyes. I see it every time I walk into town. Their gazes fall upon me, and I know what they're thinking. *There she is. Crystal the weak. Crystal the abused. Crystal the powerless.* I used to see it as a kid, and then, after

I got married, I saw it even more. People like to stare and assume. But they don't like to step in.

I open the door to the truck, figuring I may as well go in before I lose my nerve. I just need to gather the needed items, pay for them, and get out. No one's going to say anything. People know better. They're afraid of Richard, after all, even if they won't admit it. Wouldn't do for it to get back to him that they've been talking. I lift my head with a little bit of confidence, but my eyes don't leave the ground. Old habits die hard. I tell myself to stay calm, but my damn hands are shaking. There's no stopping them. I hate this.

The bells tinkle on the door as I wander into the foreign territory. In truth, I really don't know what I'm looking for. The fluorescent lights reflect off the shiny linoleum in mesmerizing and disorienting patterns. It smells like rubber and oil simultaneously, and my nose turns. I'll just snatch up a bit of everything that grabs my fancy.

'Hi, Crystal. How are you?' Pete asks when he sees me. He stands behind the counter, the lights from above shining off his bald head. He's worked here for as long as I can remember, and I glance up to see the familiar smile. I don't see the pity I'd feared. I just see Pete. I remind myself it will all be okay. No one's going to ask anything.

'Fine. I just need some items. Broken screen door,' I mutter, grabbing a shopping basket as I march to the back of the store. My breathing increases. Why am I getting so stressed out? Why is it hard to breathe all of a sudden? I need to get it together. Going to the hardware store isn't a crime, even if Richard would have me believe so.

I nod in assurance at what, I don't even know. I plod to the back of the store, looking at the bolts and screws, assessing what size I might need for the screen door. I try my hardest to walk the aisles of the small store serenely, reminding myself I need to stay calm as to not draw attention. I don't want Pete telling him about this if he gets the chance. He won't be happy to know I was out and about, buying this stuff. It won't help my case, that's for sure. He'll be suspicious and question me about why I had come here.

It's innocent enough, though. What could Pete really tell? Of a housewife coming shopping for some tools and supplies to do some repairs? What's the harm in that?

Nothing to see here, thank you very much, I say internally, almost smiling at the words. I raise my head a bit more, taking in the sights of everything around me. Wire cutters and hammers and drills and all sorts of things I haven't ever had a need to buy. This is a man's world, but today, for just one moment, it is also mine. For a startling minute, I realize I like the feel of that.

Maybe it is just that the metal and vices and piping have nothing to do with my domestic side, the side tied to the baby, the thought of which sends radiating pain from my heart outward. Perhaps I like being here, my hands feeling the wrenches and pliers with a craving to hold them, because it is so foreign to my world—and right now, I am certainly playing a foreign role.

I'm not Crystal Connor, the subdued wife of Richard. Sure, it's temporary. He'll be showing up any day, any hour now. But for the moment, I can play the part. For now, I am free, my sweet innocence running wild into zones uncharted.

Even though I know it's wasteful, I make a rash decision. It's foolish, truly, because I must be careful with money. There isn't much left in the coffee can I robbed earlier, and I don't want to touch that money from the toolbox without knowing what it's from or if I might decide to use it later. I shove the thought of it aside. But I just can't leave all of this behind. I need that feeling of all of the items in my hands. I fill my basket with item after item, glee filling my heart in an unsettling way as I consider the possibilities.

What's wrong with me? Lord, I need to get home. I need to open the Bible. I need to pray. But right now, prayer won't soothe my soul. It's the set of items that Pete scans and places in the bags that makes me inexplicably happy.

'Fixing something?' Pete asks.

'Screen door. And a few other things that need taken apart around the house.' I answer too quickly. Pete studies me, and I feel for a moment like maybe he knows more than he should.

'Richard going to take care of it?' Pete asks warily. I notice his eyes fall to my stomach, assessing it. I pull my sweater around me, shuddering under his look. My eyes return to the floor, and the confidence that surged a few moments ago disappears.

I make a noncommittal noise that could be taken as a yes. I'll let him take that as a yes. Pete halts our nonsensical dance around personal topics and totals my items. I hand over the cash, and then I take the bag of miscellaneous tools and items I barely know how to use. I guess I'll have to learn. I need something to keep my mind off it all. Maybe I'll just do some practice, first. I can't screw this up. It would be such a disappointment to miss the mark on this.

I carry my bag to the truck, my hand absentmindedly drawn to my stomach, the place where sweet Gideon was not so long ago. Tears well. I hate that Pete reminded me. I hate that wordlessly, he can remind me of what I'll never, in truth, forget.

Gideon's gone. I'm empty. Things will never be right.

This bag of tools can't make it all okay. There's no fixing what's broken in the house. But I guess I have to try. That's all I can do is try to repair what I can. Loading the bags into the truck, my heart quickens. I feel the sudden need to get home. It's like I'm being pulled there, like something is telling me to get there fast.

He's coming. I know it. And I'm not there. There will be no stopping him now. I need to get there and face up to what he'll think I've done. I grit my teeth. I don't know if I'm strong enough. Not after Gideon. Not after all I've lost. Can I really keep this up?

I start the truck hurriedly. I don't know what will be there when I get home. I don't know if he'll be there, waiting in the kitchen, his judgmental gaze perusing me. He'll lean in close and tell me the news I've been terrified to hear for so long, the words that there's no recovering from.

I could end it all here, I consider. I could find the strength to hit the gas pedal, speed off into the distance, and never look back. But where would I go? How would I survive? And what would become of me?

I can't do it, I admit, as the truck points toward Peacot Drive. Maybe I'm not really that strong after all. My blood itches with a need to be there. I need to be there. Maybe it's Gideon calling me there, pulling me there. Or maybe it's the fact that I'm not finished with my to-do list. Before I hit that gas pedal and leave town—which I'm still not certain I'll do—I need to get so much in order. It makes my head spin. Am I smart enough to pull it off? Calm enough? Do I even have the resources? That's a topic I'll have to tackle later, if he doesn't show up first. It's probably a waste of time to dream about freedom, after all.

I'm coming, I assure my son as I stamp the pedal down harder, heading back to my now self-afflicted imprisonment. I'll do what I need to do. After all, maybe there's still some fire left deep down if I'm just brave enough to find it. And maybe I can set things right, set things into motion where they should be. I'll chase hope later, if I have time and the ability.

I go home to begin the tasks I need to complete, the tools heavy in my hands, but not as heavy as the heart within me. It takes me a long while to get it all done. I'm inexperienced, after all, and even though I try to shove them aside, the tears creep in as I'm completing the job. I hate that I cry. I hate that weakness. But it's to be expected, I suppose.

When I go to bed that night, I'm wearier than I've ever been, but it feels good. Oh, does it feel good to finally do something worthwhile. As I drift off, I think about the cleaning I need to do. I really have a lot to finish, but oh well. That's a chore for tomorrow. If he's not here by now, I think I have some time. I fall asleep in the empty bedroom, not worrying about Richard. Instead, I let sleep take me to a place where he can't touch me—or so I think.

Night One

My legs are heavy and leaden, like they're stuck in tar or molasses or maybe nothing. All I can think about is that my legs just won't move fast enough, they just won't work. I scream, begging my legs to move faster as the sheer terror and knowledge that I'm going to die if I don't hurry catches up to me. I need to get out of here.

As I attempt to run down the lane, familiar in some way, darkness descends on me. I run faster and faster, every step agonizing in the follow through. I'm wearing a white nightgown, the one that's worn and faded from my drawer, but as I look down, I realize there's blood splattered here and there. I don't have time to think about it, though. As I rush forward, the lane suddenly morphs into a forest, suffocating me with overgrown brush and vines. I'm ducking this way and that, trying to make my way through the claustrophobic scene, trying to feel my way in the oppressive blackness.

My heart races as I realize it's just so dark, and I'm so lost. Everything swirls around me and my stomach starts to hurt, vomit threatening to rise to the surface. I stop in the middle, the trees and vines whirling over and over like I'm on a demented tilt-a-whirl. I hear the beating of a drum in the distance, methodical and chilling. I try to scream. Nothing comes out but a stifled, soundless scratching.

I glance to my right and see it there. A grocery bag, spotlighted in the middle of it all. It's such an odd sight, contrasting with the darkness of the forest. What is it doing here? Did I drop it? The beating of the drum keeps pounding, the trees still whirring, but it's like time stops still around that bag. I walk over gingerly, and the forest creaks to a halt around me. My feet aren't heavy anymore. I feel noticeably freer. I stoop down, ready to reach in the bag.

'Are you sure you want to do that, Crystal?' a voice murmurs behind me. It's a voice I recognize in some depth of me, but I can't quite place it. The sugary femininity of it swirls around me, clunking into my psyche. Before I can reach in the bag, I turn to see her. Heather Granville, the girl who made my life hell in junior high. She's still the same Heather, but there are a few key differences.

Her hair is missing, patches strewn about the forest floor. Bloody gobs of skin hang from her head. I want to ask what's wrong, but I can't. I stare in confusion. What's she doing here?

'Be careful, Crystal. You don't always want to find the answers.'

Before I can open my mouth to ask the questions pounding into my head, she's gone, reduced to a malicious omen whispered in the forest. I turn back to the shopping bag. It's converted into a box, almost like a Christmas package. The shimmering gold wrapping paper glistens, a red bow on top. I reach down, scratching my leg on a spindly branch tossed on the ground. I crawl toward the present, the beating drum still pounding in rhythm with the movement of my limbs. Entranced, I untie the ribbon and slowly peel back the lid, anxious to see what's inside. But once it's open, I jump back. I shrivel away from the horrific sight that is truly the hallmark of the darkest nightmares.

I try to scream again, but it's no use. My voice catches in my throat. I scream and scream, but there isn't a sound. The drum keeps beating, louder and louder as I scurry backward, away from the box, the rotting corpse inside barely even human.

I scurry on the ground, crawling back like some sick and twisted crab crawling right into the boiling pot. I need to get away. I need to get home. Where am I? What's happened to me?

My hands feel the ground, leading the way backward, but suddenly I touch something warm and sticky. It's somehow familiar. As if I'm playing a twisted game, I try to identify what it is without peeking at it. It feels out of place among the dirt and branches. I finally turn to look at what my hand is touching. Red covers my fingers, splattering about. Suddenly, my hands are both dripping with ghastly amounts of blood. Have I hurt myself? Have I cut myself? I'm so confused. But when my eyes finally focus, I realize what I've touched.

A finger. A severed finger, the rough skin sagging around the ligaments, the bones. I scream again, and this time a sound comes out, but it's not the terrifying shriek I want to bellow through this hellfire forest. It's barely a muted whisper, a weak cry that goes unheard amidst the trees.

Where did it come from? What's it doing here? I wonder. But before I can investigate, I hear a thud nearby. I look to see another finger, dripping and jarring, land in the dirt to my left. The edge of the finger isn't a clean cut. It looks like it's been sawed, back and forth, back and forth, until the skin and *tendons and bone cracked into ragged pieces. It screams pain, my own digits aching at the mere sight of it.*

I stumble to my feet, needing to get out of this place. My eyes wildly search for the lane, but it's gone. Suddenly, I hear another thud. A finger, straight ahead. I think about running away from it but for some unknown reason, I'm drawn to it. I walk closer. Thud. Another finger, way up ahead. My feet creep along, the fingers pounding in distinct intervals on the ground, me following them.

Thud. Thud. Thud. Walk. Walk. Walk. It's a nonsensical game, an eerie investigation, but I can't stop myself even though my head tells me I should want to stop.

The sky darkens, darkens, darkens. I stand at the latest fallen finger, bloody and oozing. There's a chill in the air, my filthy and stained nightgown whipping around my legs. I look up. A house sets in front of me, shadows cast on it in an unsettling, unnatural way. There's a red mist of some sort, an inexplicable haze settling around the peeling white house.

I'm home, I think. I'm here. There's a familiarity to it, a magnetism almost that settles my flailing limbs, my racing pulse. But as I stare at the house, the screen door flapping back and forth even though there is no wind, I shudder. This isn't home. Not quite. Maybe not at all. It's not my home, yet it feels familiar.

Thud. Another finger lands on the front steps, and I consider stepping toward it. But just as my right foot is ready to stretch forward . . .

I BOLT UPRIGHT IN BED, sweat leaking from my forehead. My back is drenched, my white nightgown stuck to my clammy skin in uncomfortable ways. After a long moment, I catch my breath, squinting, telling myself it's okay. It's just a nightmare. Nothing more. Just the brain's way of processing the inexplicable and complicated elements of life in disjointed, fragmented ways. It doesn't mean anything. I'm okay.

I'm okay, I reassure myself, over and over, as I lie back down, pulling my knees to my chest, squeezing them tight, and telling myself it's fine.

Just breathe. Don't think about it. Just breathe. Over and over, I tell myself it's nothing as I glance down, checking for blood on my nightgown that surely isn't there.

I rock gently, tears cascading down my face as I stare over at the empty pillow beside me. I get up, find the bleach and the bucket, and I get to work. I clear away the grime that I can, making sure it's all spotless. It needs to be spotless.

I can make it all spotless, can't I?

Chapter Five

Henry's barking startles me as I sit up, the couch having enveloped my weary body. I stretch and try to place myself and remember last night. I must've fallen asleep after scrubbing the floor. What time was that? It's hard to tell, and I have no way of knowing.

I stretch my body, and my neck creaks. Panic roots itself in my brain. Is he here? Is Henry trying to warn me? Look at me. I'm an absolute mess. This won't do. But there might not be any time. I wonder if my short-lived freedom, at least the most I can hope to enjoy, is over.

Wandering to the kitchen, I look out the front window to see if the vehicle I've been dreading is out there. It isn't. Instead, another red rust bucket is parked in Richard's spot, and a guy I don't recognize emerges. Confusion rocks me. I haven't seen him here before. My heart beats crazily. I don't think Richard would like a stranger being here with me. I need to be careful.

Henry snarls on his rope. I'll feed him after I deal with this. Give him some meat. Richard never let the poor dog have any meat. I think today, I'll let him have meat. There is extra in the fridge, after all, thanks to Richard. Maybe I could even bring Henry inside for a while. But no, that's probably not a good idea. Just in case. I need to be careful. I can't let myself get too sloppy here. It could all be over soon. I shove the thoughts aside, reminding myself to stay calm.

The stranger staggers up the pathway, a stained, sleeveless shirt showing off saggy arms and poorly executed tattoos. He belches on his way up to the front porch. I study him, wondering what he wants.

'Richard here?' he asks when he gets close enough, his missing teeth causing a lisp.

'Not right now, no,' I reply from inside the screen door, not daring to open it. I don't want to let him in. Richard never wants me to let strange men in, but that's beside the point. I know I need to be exceptionally careful.

'Well, the asshole's supposed to fix my truck today. What the hell? Where is he?'

The way the man stares at me and keeps walking toward the screen door makes me more than a little uneasy. I avert my eyes like I have so many times.

'He's out. Sorry. You'll have to come back.'

But the stranger doesn't take no for an answer, creeping closer to the door. 'Well, I'll just have to wait for him then.' His hand rests threateningly on the screen door. I hold it closed, my trembling hands no match for his, I know. But I can't let him in. How will it look? A strange man in here with me, Richard missing. I know what he'll think if he happens to come in. The thought terrifies me. I can't have him thinking that. I *won't* have him thinking that. For one of the few times in my life, I find a strength somewhere within to stand my ground. Maybe it's the fact that Richard's gone, or maybe it's because I've already changed in the little time since everything has happened. But an unfamiliar surge of tenacity and persistence bubbles up. I raise my head and stare at him through the screen door. I muster up the courage I've only recently started to uncover.

'No.' It's a single word, but I say it with a vehemence that is both dangerous and demanding. It is accompanied by a deliberate glare, one that surfaces from a malevolent, hidden spot within. The man—I still don't even know his name—ogles me, a snarky grin on his face. I want to wipe it off. I want to make him know I'm serious. I unwaveringly maintain my death stare.

'Tough little lady, are we? What would your man think of that one?'

I just keep staring, an anger for all that's happened these past days bubbling under the surface. I can feel the surge of rage in my chest, a feeling unfamiliar.

'Go.' I slam against the screen door with my body, launching myself against the shoddy frame. The simple yet forceful act stuns the man, but I don't take my gaze off of him. After a long moment, he shakes his head.

'Fucking bitch. You're both going to pay for this, you hear? See how much business you get when I burn the place down.' He slams his fist into the porch post, spews a stream of expletives, and storms off.

Inhaling, I close my eyes, a smirk spreading on my face. Did that just happen? Did I really just tell him off?

Maybe Crystal Connor isn't as fragile as everyone in this town thought. Maybe she's not a broken-down excuse for a human being. And maybe it took Richard disappearing from my daily existence for me to see the truth—I'm stronger than he thinks. I'm more capable. And I'm smarter, too. I can handle things on my own, I really can.

It's been over a day since he's gone, but it feels like it isn't enough. Suddenly, the emptiness of the house doesn't feel terrifying. It feels like maybe it's exactly what it should be. I feel in control. I like it.

I head out and feed Henry some meat. It isn't cooked, but that's okay. He doesn't mind. He gobbles it up, practically snarling as I fill his bowl. I stroke his fur, and he slurps my arm. I shake off the slobber and blood from the raw meat before heading inside. I spend the morning doing some chores, tending to some things that need handled, and then sit in the rocking chair in the living room. I rock back and forth, staring out the window, my arms cradling the baby I know isn't there. I still miss him. God, I miss him. I wish he could've survived. I'd give up freedom for eternity if he could be here. I'd endure Richard and his harmful ways if it meant Gideon and I could be together. I'd do anything to feel him in my arms.

'Mama's here, Gideon,' I whisper into the now silent house. 'I'm right here. It'll be okay. We'll be okay.' Tears leak from my eyes as I wonder if it's true. Will we be okay? Will I be able to survive this? And how will I get through it? I have no concrete, pre-meditated plan. I haven't thought this through. How could I? He could be here any moment. What is there to plan?

I dare to let my mind dance over the possibilities. For a second, I see a glimmer of myself, dyed black hair flapping in a breeze by an ocean somewhere far, far away. Waitressing tables, smiling at a man who has manners and says 'please,' who doesn't look at me like a piece of meat. I see the nametag that says Carly or Scarlet or whatever name I want to be.

I see the possibilities of starting over, of leaving, of breathing in salty, fresh, free air.

Free.

But then the dream evaporates. Who am I kidding? He'd find me. It's too late to dream of that life. How would I even begin to start? And I can't possibly have much time. A few days, a week at most. And then he'll show up and it will all be done. That's not enough time to erase the past, to give myself a clean slate.

Nevertheless, the idea flirts with my mind a little while longer, makes me wonder what the first steps would be. Could I really pull it off, the unthinkable?

I'll think on it, I decide. I'll let myself at least dream about it. Because if I've learned anything these past couple of days, it's that you never know what you're capable of, not really, until the moment transpires.

For today, though, I have too much to do before I allow my mind to fly on fantastical flights of whimsy and dreams. Because before the dream life by the sea would take place, there are things that need finished here, things I need to do. The new Crystal can't become someone else without tying up loose ends, without creating a layer of protection. I touch the necklace that I haven't taken off, pressing my fingers against the cool, silver metal, thinking about what's inside. I can almost smell it if I close my eyes, that soft, soft scent.

I decide a hot shower is just what I need. I stomp into the bathroom, flipping on the light. It flickers a little in the familiar way. I undress, peeling off the filthy nightgown and tossing it on the floor as I turn the rusty knob in the shower. The putrid green tiles look even uglier than usual today. Then again, maybe I'm just seeing them for the first time like so many other things. Richard loves the color green. Suddenly, the color makes me want to vomit.

The pipes groan as water chugs through them. I step into the tepid water, never hot enough to really clean or relax. I rub my arms, staring down at the washrag that is molded to the spicket, maintaining its firm, drooping shape. My fingers smooth up and down over my shoulders, rubbing out the tension. There's no one to rush me, and I close my eyes, relishing in the fact there's no one to storm in. Sometimes, when Richard goes out and I'm allowed to be in the shower more than two minutes, I like to close my eyes and imagine I'm in some fancy hotel in New York City where the water runs hot and showers run long. I like to imagine there's someone waiting to wrap me in a warm, fluffy towel, to offer me champagne.

But my eyes always open and take in the cracked tiles of the shower, the aged marks on the tub, and the hardwater stains that taint the vision. There is never anyone waiting to wrap me up, only to break me down.

My eyes open, absorbing the sight of the hideous tile, the marks, the crunchy washrag that is now sopping up rogue droplets of water. I stretch my neck back, luxuriating in the feel of the water slapping my face. I breathe in the humid air, clearing out my lungs. I take a long time in the shower, long enough that I smile at how mad Richard would be. I savor the thought for a few moments more before I screech the knobs to off, the water droplets cascading down my body.

I saunter down the hallway, naked and damp. I stretch out on the bed, enjoying the freeing feeling. Richard always calls me a slut when I'm naked in the house. Or, if he's drunk, my nakedness always stirs a malicious carnal depravity in him, one that he fulfills without my consent. I shudder at the thought, reaching toward a pair of jeans and a shirt that is crumpled on the floor nearby.

The Bible sits on my nightstand, the familiar page open. I really should pray. I've been slacking, and Lord knows I have plenty to ask forgiveness for. But I just can't find the strength to right now. My mind wanders to practical considerations. I need to get some food. I need to get some real food. It's been how long since I've cooked? Richard wouldn't be happy. He would want dinner on the table whenever he got here.

But the truth is, I need to eat too. It's unhealthy, really, what I've been doing. I've been so preoccupied with everything else that I haven't taken the time to eat. I need to get to the grocery store. I think I'll do just that. I'll get the ingredients and make dinner and maybe I'll get a bottle of wine. I could use some wine. Not too much. I don't want to dull my senses. I make the plan, heading out, but then I look at the living room. My skin crawls. It needs to be cleaned. Just in case. If he comes in, I want it to be clean, right? No, I *need* it to be clean. Dammit, I wish I could just bask in this freedom. Why am I so hung up on this? Does it really matter?

Yes. Yes it does. My breathing speeds up as the reality sets in. I can't just escape this. Sure, I can wander into town and grocery shop today. Maybe even tomorrow or the next day.

But eventually, this charade will end, and it will all be even worse than before. I'm in danger, so much danger. My heart beats crazily and panic threatens to consume me. I raise a shaking hand to my chest, trying to assuage the fear.

I'll just clean the living room, I tell myself after a long moment. That will be enough. Then, I'll wander into town. I think about walking down the aisles of the market, alone, free to make the choices. I'm just going to clean first, and then I'll go.

But once the bucket is filled and the familiar bleach scent drifts through the house, I realize that maybe I shouldn't go. There's some cereal in the cupboard. I'll just eat that. There's so much to do here. I can't just leave. There's some laundry that needs done. And goodness, I really should store those tools I'm finished with somewhere. And should I head out and clean Henry's bowl? It's so filthy, and I feel bad about it now. Just a little. There are tons of things I could be doing. This place is a mess. I can't have it messy. I can't. It needs to be perfect. All picture-perfect.

I crumple onto the splintery living room floor, my hand rubbing over and over on the one particularly dirty plank. Tears start to fall. I can't just leave, I realize. I'll never be able to just leave, not yet. There's too much at stake. I'm stuck now, just as I've always been. I think about all the choices that led to this moment. Why am I being punished? Why?

Richard disappearing seemed like it could be such a good thing, but old habits die hard, and the freedom isn't really enjoyed knowing he could be here any second. My brain tries to wrap itself around the idea, but I can't. I just don't know what to think.

Focus, I tell myself. *Think. You can do this.*

Tomorrow, Richard will have been gone for two full days. It's not unnatural or unnormal. I still really shouldn't be worried, right? Not that I miss him anyway. But still, I have to admit, things without him won't be perfect. Our food stamps and assistance don't cover all that much. Richard's under-the-table money in the garage helps pay the bills. Without him, what will I do? What if he never shows up? The possibility of leaving is a wonderful thought, but I have to be smart about it. The fear of living in this prison is too much—but the fear of the unknown is sometimes more frightening. I've been out of work so long. There's no way I could find employment. I can't support myself, can I? I know I can't keep this all up.

There is the mystery wad of cash in the garage, but how will that look? And what if he shows up? Clearly, that cash is hidden for a reason. If I spend it, couldn't the police track it or something? I don't know. I wonder if it could bring a whole new level of complication down on me. Of course, does it get any more complicated? And what if I'm desperate? Then again, it's not a question of if I'm desperate. It's when.

I wish I could just hide in my bubble forever, but it's definitely wrong. Richard disappeared late Monday evening, the night he threw me on the ground when I tried to get Gideon. It's Wednesday and already, two people have come looking for Richard—and it's only going to get worse. Richard isn't one people will miss, but they will eventually notice his absence. And I know from today's visitor that they won't be happy if he doesn't show up for job after job. It doesn't look good, for sure.

Tomorrow, I might need to start looking for him. I'm worried, after all, of how it will seem when he shows up if I haven't even tried. What kind of a wife would I be if I didn't worry, didn't look for him? I need to make it look like I tried to find him, even if this is something that's typical behavior. I need to look like the dutiful wife Richard expects me to be, after all, no matter what path I choose to pursue. Whether I stay and he shows up, or I manage to get out before he does, I need to play the part, be smart about it all, and finish the important task.

But that's tomorrow. I still have some time. I lean against the wall, the floor drying. Bleach permeates the air, stings my nose, and makes me feel at ease. I inhale the pungent scent, breathing it in and out. I always thought if I were to take the coward's way out, I would do it with bleach. The smell is my refuge. It soothes my nerves, even now. Maybe it'll be okay. Maybe I could go into town for a little bit and get some food. If he shows up, what can he really say, huh? We do need to eat after all.

'Just don't think about it,' I say out loud, standing up from the floor to walk to the kitchen and retrieve my keys. I head out the screen door, lock the front door, and don't look back.

MY HANDS GRIP THE SHOPPING cart so tightly that my knuckles beam white. I don't dare make eye contact with the few shoppers, terrified they'll approach and ask questions. I don't want to deal with inquisitive, nosy neighbors. Word has certainly gotten out in this tiny town that Gideon has passed away. Stupid Sharon probably blabbed to the whole town. I squeeze the cart so hard, I think my hands might go numb. I just don't want to talk about it. I don't want people looking at my belly, making eye contact, and telling me without a word that they pity me. Poor Crystal. It's always been poor, poor Crystal.

They don't know. They don't know anything, I remind myself. The thought soothes me. The front wheel relentlessly squeaks as I shove the grocery cart down the produce aisle, wondering what I should get. What does one make for dinner when they're cooking for just themselves? What do I want?

I don't even know. I've never really got to pick my dinner, after all. Richard always decides. I ponder what the best choice would be, but I just can't settle on an answer. I don't even know what to make for dinner, and that frustrates me. How do I not know what I like? How is my life at this sad, piteous point?

'Stop it,' I mutter aloud. An elderly woman examining the skin of two pears, comparing them as if it's a life-or-death situation, looks over at me, startled. I smile weakly, apologetically at her. Wouldn't do for the town to think I've gone mad. Of course, under the circumstances, who could blame me? Still, I don't need any more rumors flying around about the Connors than there already are.

I wheel the cart to the deli, looking at some of the prepackaged foods. There's a roasted chicken, piping hot, in a tiny little shelving system. *It looks delicious,* I decide as my stomach loudly grumbles. Richard would never allow me to buy this. He'd call me a lazy cow if I refused to cook from scratch. This seals it. Precooked chicken it is.

I wander to the nearby cooler, eyeing the potato salad. I decide I'll get some of that, too. I add it to the pile, the contents of my grocery order looking sad. I veer my cart down a few more aisles, wondering if the freedom will prove to tempt my taste buds.

As I maneuver up and down the aisles, avoiding a young child here or there with tearful disdain, I find myself glancing at the familiar spots on the shelves. The kind of tuna Richard prefers. The crackers. The type of cheese he likes, right beside the one he hates. I can't get him out of my head, and I hate that. He's not even around to dictate what I do, yet he always is. He always determines exactly what I do. How in just a few years have I become so numb to who I am as a woman? As a person? As just Crystal and not Richard's wife? How have I forgotten so much? Will I ever find myself again?

In truth, I think, adding a few of Richard's items to the cart just in case or perhaps out of habit, maybe I haven't forgotten at all. Maybe the sadder reality is that there never was a just Crystal. Before Richard, I was my dad's Crystal. I've always been a pawn in this male game of domination and power. I've never known true freedom. Now, though, the more frightening question becomes: will I ever? Even when I have control, maybe I'm just fooling myself. Maybe I don't have what it takes to be in power. Perhaps I don't deserve it. I've failed, in truth. I've failed in so many ways.

My cart swerves down the frozen aisle, and I stop in front of the ice cream. So many choices, so many flavors and varieties. I smile to myself, taking a deep breath. I slide open the frosty door and let my hand reach for whatever container it wants. I let myself choose. Such a simple moment, but such a big one, too. I wheel away, staring down at the pint of chocolate chip cookie dough, a flavor I've never had. It'll be good to try something new.

The instant gratification of sticking the ice cream in my cart fades, though, as I wheel onward. Nothing good can last forever. My hands slide back and forth on the handle on the cart, and I stop to take a breath. My breathing is so rapid, yet I can hardly seem to fill my lungs quickly enough. My eyes well with tears, an all-too-familiar feeling. I need to get home. I can't do this. I need to get home, to take care of things. I need to pray and to study and to clean. I need to set things right. Things aren't right. I get into the checkout lane, unloading my items, trying not to make eye contact with the cashier. Luckily, the woman in charge is new or at least new to me. I'm thankful to not see someone I know. I can't answer any questions.

An Elton John song blasts over the supermarket speakers, and it calms me. Richard hates Elton John. I love him. My parents never let me listen to much music growing up, but when I'd take the truck to run errands for them now and again, I always turned on the radio, praying it would be one of his songs. The song soothes me. I like it.

Me, Crystal Connor. I like it. Not because someone told me to. It's all me. The thought softens my racked nerves.

The cashier apathetically spouts off the total, snapping me out of my wistful thoughts. My heart races again. I need to get back. I shouldn't have left everything as it was. What if he comes while I'm gone? This was a terrible idea. Everything could end right here. I can't have this happen. It isn't right. It isn't how I wanted it to happen. And I need to clean that floor. I really do. I think of the tasks at hand. So much to do today. So much to finish. But as I'm loading the groceries and getting ready to head home, a new idea comes to mind.

I smirk. Yes, yes. That will do just fine, I think, letting the cart roll away in the parking lot. It slams into a random truck, but I don't care. The fear, the nervous energy has morphed into something else.

Excitement. Energy.

It's going to be okay. Let him come. Let him come while I'm doing it. I don't care anymore. There are some things you just have to see through regardless of the consequence. God forgive me, but this is one of those things. How hard will it be, I wonder?

I suppose there are some things you just have to find out yourself.

I JOLTED AWAKE AS THE strong fingers yanked on my virgin hair, jerking my head back with such fire, I gasped. The Bible sat, splayed open in front of me on my tiny desk in my room.

'What's this?' Mother's voice beckoned as I grabbed my neck. 'You can't even take time for the Lord, our Savior? You selfish girl. You selfish, selfish girl.'

My heart thudded as she yanked me from my chair. The clock in the hallway chimed. Six o'clock. Had I really slept during Bible time? How had I been so stupid?

Mother dragged me out of my room, down the hallway to the living room. Father sat in his chair, staring ahead.

'She was sleeping again,' Mother confessed, my father removing the tobacco pipe from his mouth.

He shook his head. 'Should call you Peter instead of Crys. Get over here.'

I trembled, knowing what was coming. Father might not be a devout reader himself, but when it came to punishing me, he was always happy to oblige—and to follow Biblical rule on punishments. The hypocrisy of him was never something I dared to verbally question. It was just a paradoxical reality that was accepted, like Jesus dying to provide us with life. He stood, a familiar, fiendish gleam in his eyes. He liked this. Maybe he even lusted for it. It gave him power. My thirteen-year-old self trembled, trembled, trembled. Mother stood back, crossing her arms after crossing herself, as if I was the sacrificial lamb. Perhaps I was.

Father jerked me by the arm, dragging me to the hallway where the Blessed Mother statue stood watch, the Madonna standing vigil over a tiny but meticulously orderly shack. I tried to steady my breathing, to find a sense of buried courage, but it was impossible. I knew what was coming. In one fatal swoop, he ripped off my shirt, the buttons popping as he tossed it to the floor. I hurriedly tried to get off my skirt, my undergarments so

I didn't meet his force. So I didn't have to feel his gritty, leathery hands brushing up against my soft skin or lingering a bit too long. The nakedness was to instill humility in me, but I always shuddered at the way Daddy looked at me. Especially since I'd undergone big changes in my body.

'On your knees,' he barked, humiliation drifting through me. I plopped to the ground, the dirty hardwood floor beneath my knees digging into them. I didn't dare lean back. I folded my hands, rocking, praying for forgiveness I didn't think a statue could grant—not with the work of my father at play. A swift kick in the back almost sent me flying, but I pulled myself back up into position, not daring to waver. I knew what would come if I did.

For hours, I stayed, my knees throbbing. When I grew weary, a bucket of ice water woke me up. It was torture in its finest sense. But through it all, my thirteen-year-old self believed Mama was probably right. I knew what she'd told me since a little girl was correct. Women were sinful. We needed men to guide us to salvation. We needed my father to show us how to behave, how to live, how to serve God. I prayed hard that afternoon, guilt washing over me. I hadn't been vigilant. I hadn't been good. I hadn't been faithful. It was my fault. All my fault.

When my punishment had finally been deemed worthy and my penance served, my mother stomped into the room. Tears washed over me, praying that my mother would hold me in her arms, comfort me, would show me the love I craved.

'Get up. It's time to start dinner,' she spewed, handing me clothes to put on as she walked to the kitchen.

'I'm sorry,' I whispered, lip quivering as I tucked my freezing body into the refuge of the scratchy wool.

'God forgives the genuine and the hardworking,' she whispered, and then we spoke nothing more of it as she led me to the kitchen to continue my womanly duties.

I SIT AT THE KITCHEN table, plunking my spoon into the pint of cookie dough ice cream. It's delicious, I decide, savoring every bite. My hands ache from all of the work I've done, but I welcome the feeling.

Stuffing spoon after spoon into my mouth, I sigh with a realization that almost scares me.

I'm happy. For the first time in a long time, I'm actually content. This is what it feels like.

I glance at the door, my heart beating. I hope he doesn't come in. I hope he doesn't ruin this for me. He could always, always ruin it. I savor the next bite of ice cream a little bit more before putting the rest in the freezer and putting the spoon in the sink. Richard never lets me go to bed with dishes in the sink. I smile at the sight of the spoon defiantly sleeping in the middle of the stainless steel.

I grab the splotchy glass from the center of the table. It had been keeping me company while I devoured my snack, a nice centerpiece for the moment. It added to the mood.

I carry it up the steps, smiling as the contents jiggle in interesting patterns. Odd but magnificent. My smile widens, the fears of a few minutes ago fading. I get myself ready for bed, brushing out my matted hair and washing my filthy face. I climb under the quilt. It feels good to rest my overworked body, I realize as I settle onto the mattress.

I turn and look at the glass I've placed on the nightstand with fascination. I reach out to touch it, deciding to pick it up and roll it back and forth between my stained fingers. So worrisome. So different. So new. And dark. I always loved how dark it was.

I set the glass back down, sighing. I really shouldn't have dirtied a glass for that. How difficult it will be to clean. I think about getting up to scour it. I hate having dirty dishes sitting around. Richard hates dirty dishes. I smirk at the thought, thinking again about the spoon in the sink before setting the glass back on the nightstand. The Bible sits beside it. To think, the same words I read as a child, as a teenager under my parents' roof are right there within reach. How ironic. How odd. Who would have thought? I lie down on my side, facing the nightstand, the holy words sitting by the glass that threatens to usurp my calm. I drift off staring at them both, though, as a single question rotates in my head: how will I ever explain that glass away?

How will I ever explain what the glass holds? I laugh at the absurdity of it all as I fall asleep, thinking about all the possibilities but coming up with no rational explanation. In some ways, as I drift off, I feel anxious, like I'm being watched. But go ahead and let him watch, I think, as I chuckle at my own cleverness and fall right asleep.

Night Two

The waves blow my hair upward, upward. It's raining so hard that the drops belt my face. They're not just any raindrops, though. Red, purple, green, and blue raindrops splatter on the hot sand, plopping into the ocean, smattering on my skin. I look out as the waves roll on. They stop mid crash, a beautiful spectacle. I'm reminded of Moses standing in front of the sea. I wonder if I could part it. I start to try, but then, everything changes and suddenly I'm falling, falling, falling.

No scream comes out, as usual. Just a whimper, an almost inaudible whisper. What's wrong? I wonder. Why can't I scream? My stomach flips and flops as I fall down, down, a black hole, lime green geometric shapes floating by me. Where am I going? Why am I so alone? Where is everyone?

Just as I'm ready to land, I feel myself floating up, up, up. The sensation again throws me for a loop. I turn and see a black cat also floating by me. I wonder who he is. I reach out for the cat, but it hisses, screeching. I notice all of a sudden that it only has one eye. Where the other eye should be is a gnarly, gaping socket seeping with pus and blood. I feel like I've seen the cat before.

Before I can think too much about it or reach out for the creature, I'm standing in front of a floor-length mirror. I stare at myself, my hair a frizzy mess. My face is covered in lines. I look haggard. I don't recognize myself. In the mirror, behind me, I see a cross. It's as tall as I am. It is empty. I try to adjust amidst all of the disorienting sights, but my head just throbs with confusion.

I turn to look at the cross, but suddenly it's gone. In its place is a doll, one from my childhood. Familiar. Safe. I take a breath in the dream. It's all okay. All is as it should be. I sink to the floor, and suddenly, I'm in my childhood room, three or four. The dirty pink carpet beneath me welcomes me. I am home. All is well. I reach toward the doll, but I startle as I do. There's something missing.

An eye. Another eye missing. Where is it? I don't remember her eye getting hurt. So odd. So strange. There's a tapping on the window suddenly, and my heart chills. I look up and see a shadow. The tapping steadfastly continues. I stand from my spot, walking toward the window, leaving the doll behind. I scream, terror rippling through me in waves. Outside the window, staring back at me as it rolls about, is an eye. A bubbling eye, oozing and yellowed. Blood seeps from somewhere. It's a ragged, veiny eye, bobbling to and fro, looking so unnatural and staring directly at me. I want to take a step back, to run from the window, but I can't. I'm stuck, frozen in place gaping back at it. Tears well. I don't understand. I don't understand at all. And then, as I'm staring, an explosion. The eye bursts, fragments of goo floating in the atmosphere, splattering on the window. I shriek.

I turn around, but the doll is gone. She's gone, gone, gone. I feel the need to find her. I creep to the window, my feet now moving of their own accord. I crack open the window. It's easier than I remember. Ignoring the eye remnants on the window, I slip out, the chilly night air biting into my skin.

I walk through the grass, the night completely black. On my path to I don't know where, I notice there are glowing eyes peering at me from all about. Where are they coming from? Who is watching me? I don't like this feeling at all. Vomit bubbles within my aching stomach. I walk for a bit, the only light on my way the light from the glowing eyes. And then, I stop.

I'm here again. The house. The familiar yet unfamiliar house. The red mist settles around it. The peeling door screeches open and close, open and close. I take a breath. I want to turn around, but I don't. Something compels me forward. I know this place. It's okay.

I step forward, my bare feet now reaching the first step. The splintery texture stabs my feet. I pad up the steps, stopping at the porch. My hand reaches for the screen door, and I steady myself, a part of the red mist now, a part of this place.

I step forward again, my toes reaching for the familiar feel of the floor within. I don't turn around, looking forward as I plod over the threshold.

Chapter Six

When I stand in front of the mirror in the bathroom, cracked and weathered from years of abuse itself, I can't help but wonder how it got to this point. Growing up, I never really thought of myself as pretty. Modesty meant no makeup, and like every teenage girl, I was always centered on the imperfections I saw when I looked at my reflection. The dark circles under my eyes that begged to be covered. The tiny scar on my forehead from wrecking my bike. The nose that was too wide, the eyes too far apart. There was so much that needed fixed.

Still, looking back, I can see now what I couldn't then. I *was* pretty. I still had the bright eyes of a girl unsure of where life would go. And even though Mama and Daddy didn't sprinkle our house with kindness, there was a semblance of resilient softness there, a façade of love. They were harsh to me because they loved me—at least that's what Mama always used as a defense when Daddy got out of hand. *Love is pain sometimes, Crystal. Love is sacrifice, just like our Savior sacrificed for us.*

Standing here now, though, studying eyes that are anything but bright, I can't believe I'm looking at the same person. In many ways, I can't believe I'm looking at the same person from days ago. I peer into the eyes, the window to the soul, and I don't like what I see. Where once I saw a hint of purity, or at least an attempt at it, I now see a marred schism of darkness, a blackness spreading. I don't think I can stop the darkness's destructive path, either. It's far too late. I shake my head after squeezing my eyes shut, trying to obliterate the reality in front of me.

Don't think about it. Just breathe. Don't think about it.

My inhalations ragged, I draw them in and out, gaining some pretense of poise. I need to be lucid, to be cautious. Richard and the sheriff have never had a good relationship. This could go wrong in so many ways. But I know I have to do this.

I have to play the wifely part just in case. At least I can say that I tried. I'll tell him see, I was worried, terrified actually. I was loyal and cautious and did what any devoted wife would do. I need to be able to say that. It's my only chance at escaping the throngs of terror that will be unleashed upon me if I don't play my part correctly.

It's the only chance I have at survival.

I've learned the hard way over the years that we all have a role, we all have a duty to follow. My life has been a winding string of expectations to live up to, none of which were ever mine. Today, in many ways, is no different. Even without Richard here to bark orders, I know I am still shackled to him, still driven by his ways. I'm forever a prisoner in one way or another of the man I often wish I could forget.

'Stop it, stop it,' I shout, slamming my hands on the bathroom sink's counter, getting closer to the mirror as I rock back and forth. How can I think that? If I had never met Richard, I would've never had my sweet Gideon. His life wasn't in vain, was it? He was still here, even if only for a brief moment. I knew him and loved him—love him, I correct myself. I *love* him. I still can take care of him, make sure he is safe and his life matters. I need to do that for him. It's the only thing that really means anything now.

Guilt assaults me once more. How dare I think these things? What kind of a woman am I becoming? I always thought Richard held me back. What if the truth is that he held me up? I shudder at the possibility. It can't be true. I'm strong. I am. I will find my way. I'm on the right path, the righteous path. There have been too many signs to think otherwise.

Focus, I tell myself. I stare into my eyes in the mirror, behind the blackness, I see something else that's been hidden for a while.

Determination.

I won't let him break me. I won't. I need to dig deep, to find the strength and the wiliness to pull this off. I can do it. It just needs to be perfect.

'Hello, Sheriff Barkley. I need to talk to you. It's about Richard. I'm terribly worried that something has happened.' I practice saying it with the sweet softness the world is used to from Crystal Connor, but the smile that greets me in the mirror is unfamiliar, cunning, and manipulative. I relax it, just to sell the part. I dig deeper, thinking about the Crystal Connor from a few days ago. What would she say? How would she act?

A few days can change a lot. It's true. But right now, I need to pretend nothing's changed, that I'm just a scorned woman looking for a man who probably isn't worth her time.

Chapter Seven

I put on a floral dress and swipe a few dabs of powder on my nose—Richard doesn't allow me to wear any more makeup than that. I make myself look presentable, but not *too* tidy. Under the circumstances, it's understandable I'm not looking fresh and crisp.

After the long drive to the station, I wander into the building. I've been in a few times before, mostly to defend Richard or to pick him up when things went wrong. Things always go so, so wrong with Richard.

My stomach flops at the prospect of talking to Sheriff Barkley, but this is nothing new. I've always been nervous around the man. I think it's because when I look at him, I know without a doubt that he recognizes the truth about my marriage. It's not like it's a huge secret. Richard is never subversive about his need for power, for control, and for domination. Everyone in town looks at me with pity, mostly stirred by the knowledge that Richard is the abusive man of most women's nightmare. I am the object of their sympathy, flirting with danger because I'm too stupid to leave, at least in their eyes. If only they knew the whole truth.

At the front desk, Pamela Weaver sits, typing away, chewing her gum too loudly. A shoulder pad in her sweater is slipping out, and an annoying song is playing on the radio beside her. Her whole demeanor seems out of place for a sheriff's office.

'Can I help you?' she asks, blatantly perturbed by my presence. She snaps her gum, and I shudder. Richard hates when women chew gum.

'I need to see Sheriff Barkley,' I murmur, fiddling with the thin gold band on my left hand.

'Don't we all. He's pretty busy at the moment with a big case. I could have one of the deputies talk to you.'

'No, I'd rather see Sheriff Barkley, please,' I reply, adamant but calm. I want to see him, to ease my mind. It would be better to see him.

'Have a seat, then. It might be a while.'

I do as I'm told, hunkering down on the stiff chair, tucking my purse on my lap. I fiddle with the zipper of it, back and forth, trying to settle my mind. I haven't done anything wrong. I need to remain visibly calm but concerned. I remind myself that I'm doing the right thing by being here, playing the correct role. Minutes tick by until they feel like days. It's a long, long while before Sheriff Barkley makes it out to greet me.

'Mrs. Connor. What brings you by?' he asks, extending a hand to me. His skin is rough and weathered, but his handshake is gentle. I like that he shakes my hand. I stand to look at him.

'I need to file a missing person's report. Richard's been gone for over forty-eight hours.' I utter as he leads me to his office. He gestures for me to have a seat before shutting the door.

'Were the circumstances suspicious? Any reason to believe he's in trouble?' Sheriff Barkley asks. His demeanor is calm, unassuming. I know what he's thinking—this is just one of Richard's typical scenarios.

'No. Not really. I mean, he just up and left Monday evening. But it's Thursday, and I haven't heard from him, and I don't know, Sheriff. I just have a bad feeling, you know? I have a feeling in my gut.'

He studies me from across his desk for a long moment. 'Crystal, I heard about the baby. I'm sorry.'

I freeze, panicking. I wasn't expecting this. Why is he bringing up Gideon? How does he know? Of course, though. The curse of the small town. Everyone knows everything about everything. I try not to cry, averting my eyes.

'Thank you,' I murmur, the falsity of the words transparent and cracking.

'I'm not trying to sound insensitive, but, well, does the baby perhaps have something to do with Richard disappearing?'

My eyes snap to attention and I stare at Sheriff Barkley. 'What do you mean?'

'Was the baby what drove him to leave? I know loss can incite all sorts of feelings and behaviors in people.'

I take a deep breath. 'I don't know. I honestly don't know. Look, I recognize it isn't uncommon for Richard to disappear. He's done it before, it's true. But this time just, well, it feels different this time. I'm worried. I just, I don't know. I worry something happened to him.'

Sheriff Barkley sighs, leaning back in his chair. 'Well, thank you for stopping in. Let's get the paperwork started. We can fill out the report and go from there. I'll do some snooping around, see if I can find him. But between you and me, Crystal, I've lived in this town a long time. I've known Richard practically his whole life. I wouldn't worry too much. He'll be back before you know it, I'm sure. He'll be back here, being Richard, driving us both crazy. I don't think there's anything to worry about.'

I look at the sheriff, wanting to tell him there's oh-so-much to worry about now. That things will never be worry-free. That I can't see a way out of this. But I don't.

Instead, I nod my head like the sweet woman I'm supposed to be. I let him be in charge. I listen as he walks me through the paperwork, and I meticulously, painstakingly fill out the document. When I leave, Pamela cracking her gum as I head through the door, I exhale, not even realizing I'd been holding my breath. Step one done. Richard's reported. This should help me, should hold up my story when he shows up. I have proof that I tried to find him, like a perfect wife would do.

I slide into the truck, holding the steering wheel. I glance in the rearview mirror, steadying my gaze. That was hard, but I did it. Getting the sheriff involved is always risky—that's what Richard would say. The law usually brings more harm than good. It's a risk I had to take. In the long run, I think it will prove useful.

Regardless, I know what I need to do now.

Chapter Eight

I dash up the stairs, winded from all of the chores. It was exhausting today, draining. Maybe I'm just tired because of where I've been and what I did. Still, there's a sense of exuberance persisting, even with all the weariness I feel. I smile, thinking about how good it felt today. I rush to the sink to wash my hands, scrubbing and scrubbing as the pounding at the door continues. I shudder, wondering who it could be. Henry barks maniacally outside, reminding me that it's time for his meat. First thing's first, though.

Sheriff Barkley promised to swing by with updates, to be in touch soon. Certainly he hasn't found something already, has he? I thought it would be days until I heard from him. In truth, I'd hoped it would be days. I'm getting quite used to my new routine. As awful as it sounds, I'm okay with Richard not being around. Happy, in fact. So happy with my life I've found in the days since he's left.

And the more time that goes by, the more I convince myself I can do this.

I convince myself that good can come from such loss and pain.

I assure myself that this is my chance to get away, to start over, to become a new version of myself. But first thing's first, I realize as the pounding continues. One step at a time. One day at a time. One moment at a time.

My heart pounds now. This could all be over, though. I could be getting the news I've been dreading. Or, perhaps, it's just another one of Richard's jilted customers. That case isn't as bad, but it's certainly not ideal, either. My head rings, all of the thoughts crashing into each other. It's hard to think. I don't want to answer the door. It's time for my studies, after all. I need to go and study. I have so much to pray about, so many answers to seek.

'Richard, it's me. Cody. Open up.'

My head spins at the familiar voice. No, no, no. This won't do. Not at all. *Not at all.* Henry continues woofing vehemently as I dry my hands, examining them, avoiding the inevitable. I glance around. The place is tidy enough. I need to make sure, though. Cody and Richard are close. I've learned that the hard way. He's Richard's eyes and ears. I need to be wary.

'Coming,' I assure, trying to keep my voice from wavering. I glance at the basement door, noticing it's ajar. I wander over and shut it, straightening the dish towel on the way back. I dry off a spot on the counter, the knocking continuing.

I take a breath, knowing I can't put it off any longer. I walk to the door, fling it open, and offer a weak smile, the screen door between us.

Cody's face is stern, and he glares at me through the door. My twentysomething brother-in-law whose face has always reminded me of a weasel scowls, as always. Thinking it over, I've never seen the man happy. He's much scrawnier than Richard and, I suspect, a great deal less intelligent. I've always imagined that his feelings of inadequacy around

Richard drive his badger-like demeanor. He is, in fact, just as bad as Richard. Maybe worse in his own right.

'Where's Richard?' he barks. 'I need to see him, now.'

It's a demand, his hand yanking on the screen door. I stand in the doorway, but I know it's no use. This wild animal is on the prowl, and he won't stop until he gets what he wants.

'He's not here,' I reply, my eyes darting around the house as Cody storms into the kitchen, blowing past me. My blood pressure surges, my chest squeezing. I don't want him here. Not like this. I can't have him here. I know what he could do.

'What do you mean he's not here? I need him. He's supposed to be helping me.'

'With what?' I ask, trying to distract him as he leans on the counter.

Wrong question. He's in front of me like a frothing pit bull before I can retract the words.

'Don't worry about it, you dumb bitch. Jesus Christ, you're all the same. You, Kimberly. You get too much freedom. Richard and I need to talk. We both give you too much freedom. You think you have the right to go around asking questions.'

I shudder at the words. Kimberly is Cody's wife. I've only seen her a few times. Richard and Cody don't really let us get together. I think they're afraid we'll compare notes, realize what we're dealing with. There's strength in numbers and power in awareness.

'He's not here. He's been missing. I reported him this morning.' My words are choppy and frank.

'You *what*? Are you stupid? Why would you do *that*?' he bellows, furious.

I take a step back. 'I don't know, Cody. I just, I think something's wrong. He disappeared without a word.'

'Probably a reason for that, you idiot. Now you sent the sheriff on his trail. Nice going. Nice fucking going. Oh, he's going to kill you when he gets back. You're done for. Wait until I tell him what you've done.'

Tears well in my eyes. This is getting messier and messier. Cody paces in the kitchen. I eye the living room warily.

'Fuck,' he shouts to no one in particular, and I begin to wonder what he and Richard are up to. All those late nights out, those arguments in the garage. I have no doubt he and Richard are up to something unsavory. How does Richard's disappearance throw a kink in their plans, though? This complicates things. Why would Richard up and leave if he and Cody actually had some sort of plot?

'He'll come back. And when he does, I'll be here. I'll be here to tell him what a bitch you were when he was gone. Your hours of freedom are numbered, Crystal. And then you'll be on your knees, begging. For your life. I'm telling you, you'll regret this.'

I shake as he walks toward me, a silent prayer on repeat in my head. It's a serenity prayer I used to say over and over when Daddy was in one of his darker moods, when he would come at me with the same crazy eyes I've seen in Richard and, right now, in his brother. Still, I waver, my knees wobbling and my stomach muscles clenching.

Cody touches my chin, his thumb caressing me before he painfully turns my head. His fingers apply ample pressure to my jawline. He leans in and whispers in my ear. All of the hairs on my arm stand at attention.

'You better be afraid. Because when he gets back, you'll pay. And I know this—he'll be back, Crystal. He always comes back. Remember that when you're out gallivanting and having a good time. There will be hell to pay eventually. You'll have to pay for your mistakes.'

Panic swirls. What does he think I've done? Does he know where Richard is? Is this all a manipulative plan—but for what? I thought I was running the show here, but now I don't know. Maybe I'm just a pawn in some demented game.

No, no, no. It can't be. I rock back and forth after he lets my face go.

He stomps toward the door, pausing to turn and look at me. 'Oh, and Crystal?'

I whimper, afraid of what's next. I can't even manage to string words together in response.

'It smells like shit in here. You better get cleaning. Richard won't be happy that you've been slacking on your womanly duties.'

He flashes me a malignant grin. I shudder. He turns, flings open the screen door so hard it crashes against the siding, and heads to his truck, swearing at Henry as he does. I sink to the floor, shaken and shattered. I curl up on the linoleum, rocking back and forth. Back and forth.

Forgive me, Father. Forgive me.

THE SUN POUNDED DOWN, a few wispy clouds floating in the bright blue sky above. There was a soft breeze blowing through my hair and the trees, but I didn't mind. I closed my eyes, leaned my head back, and stretched out my legs.

It's going to be okay, *I told myself.* I'm better now. Things are better.

The months had passed slowly, insidiously, as I wept myself to sleep during all hours of the day. Richard hadn't been there like I thought he would, and it was harder than I expected. I'd gone through the cycles of grief over and over and over. I'd cried alone, rocking in my chair, wondering why my baby girl had to disappear.

I hated that word. Disappear. I hated that there was no real, true symbol that the baby had ever been here. Like one of the wispy clouds, she had just floated away, the only memory of her the feeling of yearning in my heart, in my soul for her. The miscarriage rocked me to the core for months, for years. I was never quite the same.

Richard blamed me. I knew it. I could see from the look in his eye, from the harsh words he spat at me, from the demands to get over it. Sometimes, it seemed like he was happy the baby was gone. One less mouth to feed. One less worry. Still, even if he hadn't wanted the baby, a harsh reality I'd only come to face in the past few weeks, he felt rage at the fact I'd failed him.

I'd failed. He was right. I hadn't lived up to my potential. I had been lacking somehow. Maybe Mama was right. Maybe I hadn't prayed enough, or maybe I needed to repent, to atone for past wrongdoings. Maybe this was God's way of making me serve penance for my sins. I hated the thought that our Savior would be so cruel. Still, cruelty wasn't a foreign entity to me, not by a longshot. Life was sacrifice. Love was sacrifice. That's what I had to understand.

I heard Richard cursing in the garage, throwing a wrench or other tool aside. I flinched, my eyes opening. I'd reveled in the peaceful moment in the sun for too long. I was jolted back to reality.

But this reality was better than the devious reality of the bedroom, wrapped away in a cocoon of myself, praying for death. I needed to reconnect with the world. I needed to repent. I needed to atone. There was always so much to atone for. I stood from the porch, ambling to the garage.

'Richard?' I murmured when I got to the threshold. 'Richard, can I make you lunch?' I was meek, afraid to enter his territory. I learned last week what would happen if I did.

Richard emerged from the back of the garage, his T-shirt smeared with grease. He appraised me, his eyes shifting up and down over my body. I held back a shudder, averting my eyes. I hoped he liked the dress. I was trying my best. I just needed him to see that.

'About time you fucking clean yourself up. What, you think you're going to lay around that bedroom for the rest of your life? I didn't marry you so you could be a fat ass mooch.'

I wanted to tell Richard I'd been out of the bedroom for weeks. The latest bout of depression over our lost baby girl had lifted, and I'd been scrubbing the place up and down, hurting my fingers so much from the cleaning. I wanted to remind him how I'd been the perfect wife these weeks, making up for lost time and pouring myself into something to help numb me to the pain. Most of all, I itched to reiterate to him that we lost her, the sweet baby, and that I was still grieving, just as he should still be grieving. It didn't matter how much time went by. This month, that date, would always be so hard. I wanted him to understand. God, I so desperately wanted someone to understand.

But it wasn't my place. I needed to be a good wife. I needed to obey. Isn't that what Mama always said? She prepared me for this role. I had to stay in my place.

'Yes, Richard. Okay. I'm sorry to bother you. I just wanted to see if you wanted lunch.'

He smirked as I trembled under his glare. He crept toward me, and I fiddled with my fingers. My ribs ached from the memory of what power he held over me, what pain he could inflict. I prayed I hadn't angered him. I'd learned the hard way what happened when his temper roared.

Richard, after all, wasn't the man I thought he was. Then again, maybe he always was. Maybe he was exactly who I thought he was and that's why I chose to walk into the garage that fateful day. Maybe I chose him because he was familiar. He was exactly the kind of man I understood—and no matter how bleak that understanding was, isn't the familiar always welcome? Don't we crave what we know? Then again, that was assuming I did the choosing. In reality, I'd always known Richard was the one in charge. He's always been in charge.

He walked closer and closer until his hot, tobacco-laden breath puffed against my cheek. He swiped at my cheek, and I squeezed my eyes shut, telling myself not to cry. This was my husband. I loved him. Why was I so nervous? But it was a dumb question. I knew why I was so nervous.

'So you want to know if I want lunch, is that right?' he asked, whispering.

'Yes, Richard.'

I smelled the booze on his breath. He'd been drinking again. I should've known better. Why hadn't I learned? Maybe I was as stupid as he said I was. I was always too stupid.

He snatched my jaw, squeezing tightly. 'Don't you think that's something that's understood? What, you think I'm going to let you off the hook? That I'll just starve while you lay around that house, eating my food I'm working to earn? Is that what you thought?' His voice surged with intensity, and he gritted his teeth.

'No, of course not. I'm sorry.'

I trembled, my constricting chest making it so hard to breathe. I hoped it all would be swift. I wasn't strong enough to handle anything but something quick.

There was a long pause, and I waited for the assault. I started silently praying, chanting the familiar words in my head. I needed to put myself into enough of a trance that the pain lessened. But before I could get through one Hail Mary, Richard let go, flinging my jaw out of his hand like I was a defiled object to be chucked aside.

'Pathetic. Truly. You're lucky I married you. No other moron would want you. Especially now. Just remember that if you think you can do better. Remember that if you think you can wander off and slut around with other men. You can't do better, Crystal. You can't. And if you try, I'll kill you.'

Tears pooled as I studied the ground. 'I love you, Richard,' I said, hating myself as the words spewed. How weak could I be? How could I love the man who hurt me so much? How could it be love? But I did. I did love him. He was familiar. He provided for me. I was his. It was my duty to love him, no matter what. I said those vows. I was a woman of my word. Mama always said to be a woman of your word.

He stomped away, ignoring my final words.

'I love you,' I whispered to the ground, tears falling freely as I trudged back to the kitchen, not even bothering to wipe at my eyes as I made lunch for my husband.

Chapter Nine

Scrub, scrub scrub. Swish the brush in the bucket. Scrub, scrub, scrub.

The rhythm of my scrub brush mixed with the scent of bleach swirls around me, lulling me into a trance-like state. The sun is setting, and Sheriff Barkley hasn't shown up. I haven't heard from him since going to the station to check for updates. Should I go back down to the station? Should I go to him and try to find answers? How long until he figures this all out? I don't know anymore. I don't know what to do.

I scrub, back and forth, back and forth, my brush following the lines of the familiar floorboards. It seems like I have to scrub more often. My knees ache from being on the hard floor, but I don't stop. I need to keep it clean. The house smells bad. So, so bad. Tears well. I'm failing at even this.

I keep scrubbing, rinsing the brush every now and then as I clean, clean, clean. My knees are creaking as I fling my body back and forth wildly, overexaggerating every movement. At least I have something to do. But the mindlessness of the job isn't helping. My thoughts keep wandering, pondering over whether Sheriff Barkley is actually searching for Richard, wondering if he'll actually turn anything up.

Why do I care? It's stupid, really. Richard isn't here. That's all that matters. No one goes looking for the wild lion when it isn't bothering the flock, after all. It's silly to worry. I'm losing it. Maybe I've been in the house alone too long. Maybe not having Richard to talk to or to yell at me is making me a little crazy. I don't like that thought and snuff it out hurriedly.

After a long while, I stand and study my work. The wet spots on the floor soothe me. All better, at least for now. I take the bucket, ready to dump it. And then my eyes land on something else in the hallway.

The Blessed Mother.

I've walked past her so many times these past few days, but I haven't seen her, not really. Eyes averted, I shudder as I walk by her, thinking about what she must be thinking. Would she pity me? I don't know. Maybe. I hate the thought of her seeing me like this.

I set the bucket down now, entranced by the familiar face ahead of me. I take the time to look, to really look, at the worn statue sitting on the shelf in the hallway. Richard always hated that statue, swore that it cluttered up the house and that it was hideous. It had been a housewarming gift from Mama. At the time, it felt like a haunted relic, an insidious reminder of the agony I'd suffer in atonement.

I walk closer, the chipping robin's egg paint of the statue's headdress eerie. Her face is worn, ragged, and dirty from years of penance. I kneel before her, staring at her, tears welling. I think of all the times as a child I knelt before her, forced by Mama to beg for forgiveness. I think about all of the times I stared into those unsettling eyes, the pupils too large, thinking about how odd it was to put so much weight on a statue. I remember all of the hours kneeling before her, Daddy whipping me with the belt, my screams echoing off her ceramic feet. I remember all of the holy water ablutions, the sacrifices at her feet, the rituals of a family who put too much faith in a religious idol and not enough faith in each other. Still, she is like a familiar photograph that becomes so ordinary, you walk by it without really seeing it. She's blended into the background of our humble house and become a thread in the needlepoint that is Peacot Drive.

Tears fall as I rock back and forth, staring up at the statue that was both my refuge in my parents' house and my own personal hell. I don't know what the statue is anymore. I don't know. But right now, I'm clinging to anything familiar, and so I find myself crawling toward her, touching her, tears flowing. I scooch back from my knees, plopping onto my bottom, wrapping my knees into my chest. I stare up at her, those eyes peering down on me with judgement like so many have before.

'I'm sorry. I'm sorry. I've messed up. I'm so sorry,' I cry, truly acknowledging the statue for the first time in years. I beg for things to be okay although I know that even the Blessed Virgin can't make any of this okay. It's too far gone, even for her.

My head pounds, and my pulse quickens. The Blessed Mother. Why didn't she help me? Why didn't she save Gideon? At the thought, I look up at her putrid face, and I shudder. Am I losing it? I must be losing it. Because for a second, I could've sworn—

No, there it is again! I leap to my feet. I'm positive. I walk closer.

The face. It's smirking. A barely noticeable smirk, but upon closer inspection, I'm sure of it. The line of her lips, it curves just enough. She's definitely smirking. I shriek at the statue. How could she do this? How could she? After all of those years I sat at her feet, basking in the shadow of her judgement, how could she let this happen? Tears fall. Gideon. Sweet Gideon.

Evil monster.

I snatch the statue from its stand, the weight and bulk of it feeling unruly. I know what I have to do. I charge to the basement door. I can't avert my eyes any longer. I can't avoid her. I need to be rid of her. I need to have the statue gone. Too many bad memories rest in her robes, and too many fears are tucked in her eyes. Too much anger lurks in her sneer.

I don't bother with pulling on the light cord, hurrying my way down the steps in the darkness. I can't have her up there, studying me, judging me anymore. I can't. She's not who I thought she was. Through the blackness, I saunter through the murky, dirty basement, the dirt floor underneath my feet gritty and chill-inducing. I need to scrub my feet now, I think. But there's no time for that. I wander to a back corner and chuck the statue there for safekeeping. A pang of guilt assuages me, but I ignore it. Some things have to be done, and some things change.

I'm heading to the stairs, and I pause for a moment as my feet contact the first splintery board. I listen, hearing the faint, muffled screams. I look back to the dark corner where the statue is. Dammit. She's screaming. She's definitely screaming. Tears well again.

Don't think about it. Just breathe. Don't think about it.

I march up the steps, slamming the basement door. I head straight to the shower, turn on the water, and get in with my clothes on, desperate to drown out the basement screams and to wash away the memory of that mocking smirk.

Night Three

I pour the cereal into my bowl and retrieve the milk from the fridge. The house is empty, silent, save for a single mouse sitting in the corner of the room. I wonder if the trap will get it. I'm sitting now, the bowl in front of me. I'm spooning the cereal into my mouth, but something doesn't feel right. The cereal tastes odd. The texture is off. Confused, I pause, reaching into my mouth. I pull the chunk of cereal from my tongue and look down into my hand.

I shudder, dropping a bloody toenail onto the wooden table. My stomach flops, and fear takes hold. How did that get in there? I look down to my milk, pink now. I stir the spoon, confusion still setting in. I sift through the milk, lifting my spoon over and over, horror flooding my entire being.

There are no pieces of cereal in here. Instead, my spoon lifts up toenail after bloody toenail. I shove the bowl back, covering my mouth as I shake my head. What's happened? I'm going to be sick. Oh, I'm going to be sick.

I run to the bathroom, but when I get there, a murky red haze fills the room. It's an oddly ethereal fog with a reddish tint. I freeze at the threshold. Do I go in? I don't know. I take a step, but then, on the floor, it rolls. Back and forth, it rolls. I lean closer. What is that? And then my scream catches in my chest, rattling in my lungs. I cough and sputter, needing to get away from it. I pant, exhausted, the sight of the baby's severed head *rolling around and around, around and around. I think I hear it scream. What the hell is happening? What's happening to me?*

'Crys,' a voice chokes, coughing and sputtering. I turn my head to the screen door.

I stand, daring to walk closer even though I want to run the other way.

'Crys, I know what's going on here,' the voice rasps. I look, the tucked in shirt, the perfectly pressed pants familiar. The voice, although throaty and guttural, is recognizable, too. But it can't be. It can't be him.

He's . . .

I look at the figure standing in the doorway.

'Crys, come on,' he says again, rattling the door. I shriek. It is him. *He's the only one who regularly called me that. Richard would use that name once in a while to get a rise out of me, but there was only one man who called me Crys.*

Daddy.

'No,' I whisper. What's happening? It can't be him. I walk closer to the screen door, terrified. I need to be sure. But before I can get a closer look, he's dashing through, chasing after me. I make a run for it, heading to the back of the house. Once I'm in the middle, though, things shift. This isn't my house. I'm so confused. Nothing's the same.

Photographs on the wall aren't of anyone I know, and the furniture is all different. The floor is murky, muddy even. I'm falling now, tripping in the middle of some great room.

I scurry backward, trying to get my footing, trying to get out of here. But I can't. I keep falling, falling, a reddish mud gripping my bare feet. He's coming closer now. My breathing intensifies. There's no escaping him. What does he want? What will he do?

Please don't, Daddy. Please don't do it.

But it's too late. I look up, deciding to look into his face this time.

There's no face. Where Daddy's face should be is a gaping, seeping hole, blackened flesh rotten and crumbling. His features are gone, and it's like I'm staring into a darkened tent, his skin flapping in the breeze.

The scream I emit now is one from the depths of somewhere outside of me, somewhere I can't even begin to understand.

Chapter Ten

It isn't even dawn yet, but I need to get out of here. I need to think, to stretch my legs, and to escape the house. The place is doing something to me, truly. The dreams I keep having aren't healthy, especially with everything else. It wouldn't do to lose it now. I can't lose it, not yet. I have to keep my wits about me.

A walk. Yes, a walk will help clear things up. I'll feel better, getting out of that house, getting some air. Some fresh air is all I need now. That's all.

I amble into the blackness, the morning chill biting through my thin, threadbare sweater. But I keep walking. Down the lane, past Henry who stares at me. I trudge past Richard's garage, shuddering at the spookiness of it. I power onward, to where, I don't know. There's a winding, overgrown path in the forest. I follow it, not worrying about the fact it's not light enough out yet to venture into the brush. What's the worst that could happen? I'm not that worried anymore.

Trees above me and vines and bushes darting out at my feet, I keep walking. The sun is getting ready to peek over the horizon as evidenced by the fact that the blackness isn't completely inky black. It's fading into a hazy, grayish black, the kind right before dawn or right after sunset. The best kind of darkness. I breathe in and out, the chilly air hurting my lungs, but I savor the pain. It means I'm still here. I've still got another day.

It's going to be a particularly draining day, I know. I have things to do today. I can't stay cocooned forever. Reality will come knocking, and I have to be prepared. So today, I will take care of things, be pro-active. A tingle jolts through my body as I realize I'm not home right now. Oh, this could be bad. I hate the chains I feel to that place, though. I shrug the thought aside. I need to break them a bit. I need to step out. There's nothing wrong with stepping out, after all. What could anyone say? Who could blame me? Hands in my pockets, I walk on and on until my calves ache. My body has been through hell and back, but the human body, well, it's resilient I suppose. It can handle amazing things. It can endure exceptional circumstances. I should know, after all.

My feet plod on, for how long, I don't even know. It feels good to not have to think, to not be surrounded by the fears and memories within those walls. It feels good to break away. For a moment, I think maybe I'll just keep on walking forever. But I know I can't do that, not yet. There's still more I have to do. But if the next few days go as planned, maybe . . . just maybe . . .

I have a number for the women's shelter a few counties over. I'm going to call it today, see if I can find a shelter in another state. Maybe in one of the Carolinas, near the beach. It would be a start. I feel like maybe they could help me with the new life. Maybe they wouldn't ask too many questions. I need to be far away from him. I need to make sure he can't track me down once I'm gone.

But I couldn't stay there forever, not for long. I'd have to figure things out quickly—a job, a new identity. Otherwise, it will all be pointless. Otherwise, he'll find me.

Still, I know I can't stay here forever, either. What's left here for me? Nothing but darkness and torture, worse than the nightmares I've been having. There is danger and fear lurking around every moment. My freedom is sucked away by the knowledge he'll eventually reclaim it. If I can get things sorted through, get some things organized, maybe that secret stash of money in the garage will come in handy.

Unless Cody gets to it first. Or unless he comes back and ruins it all.

Maybe I should leave today, I think. What's stopping me?

But I know the answer to that. I know there are things that my soul needs to finish here. For Gideon. I owe him that much. I can't leave yet. Soon, but not yet.

Still, I should be getting ready. I'll call that shelter today. I'll get a plan in place. I'll get the supplies I'll need, and then, when the job is done, when all is right, I'll disappear. At just the right moment.

I wonder what Richard would say if he could see me now, marching into the darkness without a single care. Marching forward with hope and an escape plan. It would make him possessively mad. That makes me smile.

Richard. Over three full days gone. I sigh. I can't avoid it forever. Something's clearly not right at all. What will people say if he never shows back up? What if this town never figures out what happened to him? Or to me? I picture the black-haired woman standing by the ocean, but I know it's not so simple.

I'm tainted. I'm ruined. I'm lost in so many ways.

Even if I do make it out, I can't just wipe everything away. Some sins can't be cleansed, and some lives can't be saved. There is no starting over for me completely, and as sad as that is, it's something I've come to accept. The best I can hope for is a few weeks, a few months of freedom, of feeling the sun on my face, of choosing which way to walk. Life isn't fair, even if God is. Life isn't merciful, either. We deal with the hurdles we're given, we make our choices, and then we're left to reap what we've sown.

And reap, oh reap will I.

I shake my head. Too deep of thoughts for too early. I yawn. I barely slept a wink last night between the dreams and the screams. That statue really needs to stop it. I'm going to have to bury her soon if she doesn't stop. I need sleep, especially for today. Today is going to be trying. I need to dig deep, to find that Crystal smile. I can't have people pitying me or worrying. It won't do to have them worry.

The sun is peeking over the horizon now, the light from it brightening the path. How long have I been walking? I really should be getting back now, shouldn't I? I've been gone long enough. There's no sense in trying to escape now. I know how that will end. It doesn't take one of the devil's fortune tellers to know that.

Mama always hated fortune tellers. Once, when I was in high school, some of the girls I talked to were going into town to see one. Chrissy Harris wanted to know if her Mom was going to survive her bout with cancer. I wanted to go and see what it was all about. But Mama found out, and I spent that night kneeling in front of the statue, seven hours and seventeen lashes.

What would Mama think now? What would she say if she were here? I'm pretty sure I know what she would say, and I don't think I'd like it. After Daddy died, Mama went down to Georgia to live with her sister. Said there was nothing here for her. I wasn't surprised, but the hurt did cut deep. It still does. I've come to learn that's life.

It's too bad I can't turn to Mama now. Georgia would be a good place to get away—but Mama would never understand. *Stand by your man, Crystal.* It's the lifeblood of her ways, the mantra of her heart. She would never be okay with my need to escape.

Loneliness. It's the evading emotion that marks my life, even now. Being alone in every way. We are all alone, just in different ways.

As I stomp back to the house, my bones weary and my head pounding, I freeze. Because suddenly, I'm not alone at all. I shake my head, tears welling. No. No. No. I take a step forward, blinking. It can't be real. It must be a waking nightmare, a delusion. I'm losing it. I am. But as I step forward, he bleats, the noise startling me. He stares at me, defiant, stomping, right in the middle of the road.

Where did it come from? There are no neighbors for miles and miles. I'm all alone out here. Where did the goat come from? I stare at it insolently at first but then apologetically. This can't be good. No, it can't be a positive omen at all.

'I'm sorry. I'm so sorry,' I say to the goat, to the universe, to myself, to the baby. To him. To everyone I've ever known. I crumple to the road, the dirt greeting my knees as I sink down, hands folded in a familiar position.

'Please forgive me.'

I rock back and forth, and the goat eventually wanders off, but it's left its mark. It's made its point. I know what's happening now, and I know there's no stopping it. I sob in the dirt for a long time, trying to sort it all out. But I know now that it's irrelevant. No matter what choices I make, no matter what I do from here on out, it's sealed. My fate is settled. There's no escaping the truth.

When I finally pull myself up to my feet, I run, not walk. I dash home, through the screen door. It might be irrelevant, and it might not matter, but I need to clean. I need to feel that rag between my hands, the floorboards under my knees. I need to waft in the smell of the bleach. Maybe I just need to cover up the cold, hard truth I've been trying so hard to hide. And maybe, just maybe, today will be the day it all comes crashing down. I scrub and scrub until my hands ache. Then, I carefully pull the tassels on the rug taut and straight. There, there. All better now.

All better indeed.

Chapter Eleven

Pamela's hair is in braids today. I study her, the way the perfect blonde hair is woven into the intricate design. Her face is still pretty, tight, but the braids look ridiculous. I think they make her look childish. Then again, Richard always loved braids. Maybe that's why I'm being so harsh. I hate the reminder of the not-so-distant past.

'Mrs. Connor, what can I do for you?' she asks through crackling gum. The phone rings, but she ignores it. There's a lot of hustle and bustle, even though the town is so small. It seems like a hectic day. I wonder what could be going on. Have they found something? Have they found something about Richard? My stomach plummets.

'I just came to check on the report I filed. Is Sheriff Barkley around?' I ask, twiddling my hands, looking at the ground now.

Her gum snaps as she wheels backward in her chair, peeking at the office nearby.

'Hmm . . .' she mutters, leaning back so far I think she might fall. 'I think he's busy. On the phone right now or something. But have a seat. I'm sure he'd like to see you.'

At her words, I glance up and stare at her. He'd like to see me? What does that mean? Have they found something? Have they found evidence already? Oh God, this could be bad. My mind flashes back to the hammer, to the blood.

Could Sheriff Barkley have found something already? Is that possible? And if he did, this can't be good. Not at all.

Just breathe. Don't think about it, I tell myself as I sink into the uncomfortable metal chair, trying not to think about the similar metal chair that used to be in Richard's garage. I cling to my purse as I set it on top of my floral-patterned dress. Suddenly, my eyes follow the pattern, the swirls and vines running into rose after rose. This is too much. Why did I wear this? This dress is way too over-the-top. It screams that I'm trying too hard. I don't want him to think I'm trying too hard. It's just sad.

How should I act in this situation? It's tricky. Then again, I've lived my life within the confines of Richard's expectations. I've lived the past years meticulously weighing every word, every action, every sentiment. It's not easy dancing on eggshells day in and day out. One gets tired. More than that, though, one gets unaccustomed to how to walk on regular ground. This, of course, is not regular ground, not at all. How would I know how to act in this situation? How many times must a woman report her husband missing?

Not very often, if she's lucky.

This gets my wheels turning again, though, and I fiddle with the handle on my purse, worn and faded. Why this time? Why is this different? Richard's disappeared time and time again. Why is this time different? Why am I here? Why am I so worried? Sheriff Barkley must be wondering what's going on, for sure. Why did I feel the need to report him as missing? Why did I feel like this had to be different? And only two days in? I don't have a good answer. I don't. It was a gut feeling. That's all. Would that be good enough? Did that make sense?

I ask myself if it makes sense to me. It doesn't. But I guess sometimes a woman just has a feeling, and sometimes a woman has to go by that. Life can't be lived only on the margins of science. Sometimes life has to be lived by the heart. God, do I know how true that is.

I sit for what feels like forever, my back against the chilling metal chair, my head resting against the mint green walls in the waiting area. Phones ring. Papers shuffle. A few deputies float in and out. Every time one comes through, I shudder, wondering if they'll have turned up something.

What could they possibly find?

Then again, what couldn't they find? My mind travels back to the wad of cash, the mystery of its origins something I've tried to shove aside. There's too much to think about, after all. Still, it's something I probably should be concerned about. What was Richard into? What did he get wrapped up in? And whatever it is, how long until the sheriff's asking questions I can't explain? How long until he comes rapping on the door wanting me to explain the inexplicable? I shudder at the thought. Richard, oh Richard. You've sure left a mess behind, haven't you? I think about how that wad of cash represents so much now—the hope of salvation, of escape, of possibility, of potential danger. It makes me realize how delicate my life is right now, how one discovery could lead to my dreams crumbling down. It's all risky. It's all complicated. It's a delicate dance, and I don't know which way to step.

Then again, life with Richard is always a mess. A beautifully disgusting mess, oozing with pain and torture. There's not a prayer out there to absolve the pain he's caused. I breathe in again. It won't do to think about all that now. It won't do at all. Focus. Focus. Focus.

'Mrs. Connor?' a voice asks, and I look up to see Sheriff Barkley. His stoic face offers a hint of a smile, and I find myself weakly grinning back. He's a nice man. A good man. When you're married to one of the bad ones, I guess you have a knack for seeing the good ones. If only I could've used that methodology years ago. For some things, though, it's too late. Way too late.

I rise from my seat, sliding the metal chair as I do.

'Sheriff Barkley. I just wanted to stop by and see if there are any updates,' I offer meekly.

'Come on back,' he says, adjusting his belt, standing tall with his chest puffed as he studies me. For a moment, my heart flutters. Why do I need to come back? Is it that bad? What has he found? But then I calm myself. Procedure. It's all procedure.

I saunter back to the office, which is tidy yet also disheveled somehow. Everything seems to have a spot in the organized chaos. A stapler sits perfectly perpendicular with the edge of the desk, and a dish of paperclips rests right beside it. The desk, however, is covered in folders, stacks and stacks sitting on the edge. Paperwork clutters the top of the desk, and I fight the itch to organize it. I fold my hands in my lap once I sit down to resist the urge.

'Mrs. Connor. How are you holding up?' he asks me, his fingers intertwined as he leans on his desk, as if ready to hear every word.

For a moment, I feel like I'm in a therapy session. I open my mouth, and then close it again, taking a breath. *Don't say anything foolish. Don't say anything that will give away how you're feeling. He doesn't really want to know how you are. He doesn't really need to know all of your complications.*

'I'm okay. I'm doing okay. Thank you,' I say noncommittally, eyes averted.

'Well, since yesterday, I've done a bit of digging. I've put out a dispatch to other stations with Richard's license plate number and the make and model of his truck. If he's spotted or pulled over, I'll hear about it. I also swung by a few of Richard's haunts you told me about. Asked around. No one's seen him since the night he disappeared. He was in at Fifth Street Pub earlier in the afternoon he went missing. Apparently, he got into somewhat of a fight with Joe Johnson over a game of pool but nothing out of the ordinary. Typical Richard behavior. No one's seen him since.'

I sigh, nodding. 'Okay.'

Sheriff Barkley gets out a notebook, flipping to a new page. 'Have you thought of anything else, Mrs. Connor, anything at all that might be helpful to the case?'

Flashes of the money blaze through my head. I feel myself getting sweaty, but try to rein it in. I hope I'm not looking gray or burning red in the cheeks. I don't want to give anything away. I'm not ready to answer that question.

'No, I haven't. I've been racking my brain. I don't know, Sheriff Barkley. I know this is going to sound silly, but, well,

I'm just worried. I know this isn't out of character or anything, and who knows, he'll probably show up in a day or two, having been on some bender or out of town or God knows where else. I know my husband isn't the most reliable man. He isn't the must trustworthy. I know that. But something feels . . . different this time. It's nothing concrete. It just feels so different. I'm wondering if Richard will ever come back.' I weigh the power of my final statement. Maybe I'm trying to judge the situation from Sheriff Barkley's eyes. Maybe I'm looking for reassurance that my freedom might be sealed, that escaping might be a possibility. Or maybe I'm just hoping to lay the groundwork for when I don't come back, either.

Sheriff Barkley sets down the pen he's been holding. He looks across the desk at me.

'Hey,' he says, and then he pauses. I look up, staring into his face. 'Listen,' he continues. 'It's going to be okay. I really don't think you need to worry yet. Richard is a rough one, and yes, he's not trustworthy. But the man always comes back. You know that, and so do I. For better or worse, he always shows up and raises hell. This will be no different. But if you're worried, well, who am I to judge? You're his wife, after all. You know him better than me.'

'Thank you. Thank you for all of your support. I do feel bad. I'm sure you're a busy man, and to be bothering you with this. Maybe I'm crazy. It's been a tough few weeks. Maybe I'm just overly sensitive, you know?' I offer, tears welling.

Sheriff Barkley reaches across, patting my hand. 'Don't feel bad. It's my job to help take care of those worries, even if I'm not really wanting to find the missing. Listen, I know things have been rough. I know Richard has made things really hard for you. But I'll find the man and bring him home. I will. Don't you worry about it. Men like Richard never get far before they come back. Now, I'm going to go later today and check in with his brother. See if maybe he has any information. I'll get a hold of you as soon as I hear anything. I'll keep you posted. And if we don't hear anything in a day or two, I might swing by the house, see if there's anything we're overlooking. See if maybe there's any more cause for concern or clues Richard left about where he was headed. If you happen to come across anything, don't hesitate to call me, okay?'

I take a breath in and out. I hadn't expected this. Cody will not like this. And if Sheriff Barkley shows up at the house, this could get a whole lot more complicated. He'll definitely be searching the garage and everything else. I think about the wad of cash and Cody's erratic behavior.

I can't leave just yet then. This seals it. I need to keep a handle on the sheriff, on the situation, before I abandon it all. I need to buy myself a safety net of time.

I need to finish arranging things here before I even think of starting over. I've been patient. I've endured Richard's abuse. And like Sheriff Barkley said, Richard will show up eventually. But there's no reason to believe it will be today or tomorrow. And even if he does, well, maybe things are different. Maybe I'm different. Maybe even if he did show up, I'd still keep hope alive. I'd still find the courage, the strength, to escape this torturous life, to clean it all up and head off into the sunset.

Besides, Sheriff Barkley still doesn't seem too worried. Richard's fine. That's what he believes, and that's what I need to believe too. It's all fine. I can't let on how worried I am. Maybe it's a good thing that the town is so small and that Richard's made such a bad name for himself.

'Thank you, Sheriff. Thanks so much.'

'Oh, and Mrs. Connor?' he asks as I stand from the chair.

'You can call me Crystal, please,' I say, smiling sweetly as I clutch the chair for support.

'Crystal. You don't have to drive the whole way out here for information you know. I'd be happy to come to you.'

'That's so sweet, Sheriff Barkley. But it really wasn't any trouble. It does me some good to get out of the house, all things considered. Keeps me busy. I'm keeping the house going so that when Richard comes home, it's all ready for him, you know?'

'Well, you take care. And let me know if you need anything, all right? It'll all be okay. He'll be back before you know it. Enjoy the peace and quiet while you can.'

I smile and nod, heading out the door and to the truck.

'Bye, now,' Pam shouts, her gum cracking again. I jump at the sound, and then put a hand to my chest.

I breathe out. Everything's okay for now. They haven't found anything of concern. But then again, it's not okay. Not at all. Because as I get into the truck, ready to drive home, itching to get back to home base, I shudder. My knuckles grip the wheel, and the cold sweat is back, dampening my forehead and the small of my back. I shake my head as I drive down the road, toward the unknown.

After all, like Sheriff Barkley said. There's really nothing to worry about. Richard should be back in a few days. Everyone's expecting as much. I should enjoy the peace and quiet for now. But how can I do that when I know he *could* show up at any moment? How can I relax knowing then when he gets to the house, when that vehicle pulls up, all is going to change, and getting out of this mess will be so much harder? How can I breathe knowing that my life will be over, and that Sheriff Barkley will no longer believe I'm a good woman looking out for her husband—because there just might not be a Crystal Connor left standing?

I better be ready. I need to be ready. I've been slacking. Things aren't perfect. They need to be perfect. I need to clean. I'm out of bleach, though. Richard always prefers bleach. He says it smells like clean. He says the chlorine smell is a powerful reminder that the house is sanitary. Richard's all about being sanitary.

I decide to swing by the market. I hate that I'm not going straight home. I really should be there in case he shows up. I need to be ready just in case. But I also need the bleach. I can't clean the house properly without it, and it's so important to keep it all just right. Richard wouldn't like it if I wasn't cleaning properly. I need to get the job done. I need to play that familiar role, the dutiful wife. I need to play it better than I ever had in case he realizes what I've done. Because what I've done, well, it's unforgivable. It's destruction in the purest sense.

In the parking lot of the market, I sit for a moment, my head on the steering wheel. I murmur the familiar prayer, begging for forgiveness. Why did I do it? How can my soul ever be all right?

I sit with my tortured soul for a little while, the silence of the truck's cab enveloping me in a glassy horror of my mind's own doing. I squeeze my eyes shut, the tears falling. There's no turning back. There's no undoing it all. I have to be strong and hope that I'll be ready when he comes—or long gone. One or the other. I tell myself I can do this. And until he shows up, I'm just going to have to keep going. I'm going to have to make the most of this time, just like Sheriff Barkley said. I'm going to have to try to find some peace for my weary soul, some solace of a simple kind, or at least some apathy. I'm going to have to sort through it all, make my peace, and then carry out my plan to freedom. I can't break now. I can't.

Crystal Connor is weak but she's also unbreakable when she needs to be. I think Richard needs to know that. I think he will know that before it's all said and done. Or at least that's what I tell myself as I chant my mantra in my head, sauntering into the mart to fill my cart with bleach, some of Richard's favorite foods, and a few boxes of hair dye just in case I get the chance to be the new woman Richard will never, ever get to meet.

Chapter Twelve

I scrubbed the dishes, my hands stinging from the hot water and soap. Staring out the window into the abysmally gray day, I'd let my mind wander, thinking about how differently life turned out than I hoped.

Empty. That's the word I'd use to describe it. I stared into the empty yard, cleaning the dish, my mind and heart and soul equivocally empty. I felt beyond lost and alone. Shattered. I thought the agony was never going to stop.

It had been two years since I said goodbye to that sweet baby girl, and I thought with time, it would eventually be okay. I imagined that Richard and I would march into a future not as bright but still glistening with possibility. We'd find a new way to function, a new dream of forever. I thought he'd find a way to love me despite my shortcomings. I believed I could find a way to bring that love to his heart, to connect with him, to turn his callous heart warm again. I could fix him. I could help him. He needed me.

I'd learned over the years we'd been married that Richard didn't have the best upbringing. Mine was certainly no picnic, but Richard, well, I'd argue his was even worse. The constant drunken rages from his father, the abuse at his mother's hands. The fake illnesses and the doctors and the plain lack of love. Starvation, neglect, and terror were hallmarks of his childhood.

True, my life had been no breeze. But at least my family got one thing right. At least they gave me a sense of faith, a religion to cling to in the moments of darkness. Richard had been given only superficial, false gods to cling to—his pride, his masculinity, and the idea that he needed to protect them both at all costs.

Those hopes for Richard to become something more should've been dashed. Still, somewhere deep inside, I'd clung to the theory that Richard just needed to be shown love to know love. I'd seen glimmers of who he could be—I just needed to help him polish those traits.

I'd seen the way he helped the old lady from the market jumpstart her car on a cold day the previous winter. I'd seen a tenderness in the way he smoothed a strand back from my face, the way his kisses could sometimes be charming and the thing of dreams. With every dozen dark moments, there came a sliver of hope, just enough to reel me into Richard's grasp and make me believe I could help him be the man I wanted to love me. I felt like maybe it was my purpose to bring Richard to a better version of himself, to help him see a different life than the one his family had shown him.

Nevertheless every time I got close to thinking I was making progress, we'd take at least ten steps back. There would be the sweet kiss followed by the whacks across the face for a simple mistake—a wrong type of salad dressing at the store, an overcooked piece of meat, a misplaced glass. Anything could send his fists flying at me. It seemed like everything did.

Still, I wasn't a quitting woman. I'd said my vows. I'd sworn to God that for better or worse I'd love him. And so I would. But lately, I was beginning to wonder if this marriage had been part of God's plan at all. I'd wondered if, like Mama said, I'd been a disgrace to everyone, that my one sin would lead to a lifetime of penance. Because Richard certainly made me repent, like it or not.

I kept scrubbing the dishes, staring into the void and wondering if that was it. Would that really be all my life entailed? Guilt lurked in the corners of my thoughts. How could I be so selfish? Richard did provide so much for me. Many people weren't as lucky as me. I had a roof over my head, food to eat, and a warm place to sleep. I had a man who provided the basics for me. I didn't have to lift a finger outside of the home. I had a man who was tough and stoic, who could fix just about anything

Except for his own warped mind. Except for his own power-hungry nature. He couldn't fix those things. And maybe I couldn't either. I sighed. When did life get so messy? When would I ever get a break?

The screen door screeched open. I turned to see Richard staggering through the door. My heart palpitated as I let the dish I'd been aimlessly scrubbing plunge underneath the water. I stared at it for a moment under the suds, wishing it could be so easy for me to disappear. Richard's unsteady gait told me all I needed to know. I shuddered, realizing it would be the kind of day I dreaded, the ones that were wicked enough to cast a lengthy shadow over me for days and days to come.

'I can get dinner started,' I meekly offered, rushing to the refrigerator. Maybe it would be okay. Maybe he'd be distracted.

He stumbled toward me, and I froze in place. God, please tell me he wasn't in the bourbon. Because I knew what kind of days bourbon days turn into. I steadied my breathing, telling myself it would be fine. He wandered up behind me, wrapping his hands around my waist. I dried my hands on my apron and swallowed as his hot breath harangued my shoulder. I inhaled slowly. Bourbon. The spicy hotness of the liquor on Richard's breath told me all I needed to know. I tried to assuage my wild fears, my leaking eyes.

'Shut up about dinner. There's plenty of time for that. I have some needs that need met.' He spun me in his arms, pinning me against the counter. His movements were jerky but purposeful.

Tears welled as I looked into the familiar haze of his eyes. It was more than just alcohol peeking out from his pupils. In his gaze, I saw the recognizable sadism lurking within them, a redness of intention that alarmed me. I squeezed my eyes tightly shut, thinking about what had happened last time he'd drank bourbon. I'd tried so hard to shove the thought aside. We were married. He was my husband. There was nothing wrong with being forced to please your man. It was all fine.

But I knew that it wasn't. It wasn't fine at all.

'Richard, I'm not feeling well. Please, let me make you dinner,' I whispered.

'Shut the fuck up, you slut. You're mine. I can do with you as I please.' He grabbed the nape of my neck, pinching hard. I squealed in fear, which I knew was a mistake. My fear only enlivened him even more. With his other hand, Richard grabbed at my shirt and shredded it off, the tear making me jump. It sent me back to those days in the hallway, Daddy's gruff hands ripping at my shirt in the same way.

'Richard, please,' I said, still hoping I could get out of this. I knew what was coming all too well.

'Get on your knees. Now,' he demanded, shoving me to the floor. I landed on my knees hard, and I whimpered as he unzipped his pants and let himself out in the middle of the kitchen.

I knew what I needed to do. I knew what I should want to do. He was my husband. There was nothing wrong with intimacy. I tried to balance perfectly still, knowing that to struggle would be to encourage him more. Tears welled as my body tensed.

Richard touched himself and walked behind me. I stayed on my knees, shaking. With a swift kick in the middle of my back, Richard threw me to the floor, my hands splaying out from under me. My chin cracked off the linoleum. I whimpered, and Richard let out a chuckle. He liked it when I whimpered. He liked the feeling it gave him.

Pain radiating from my chin, Richard mounted me, shoving himself deep inside of me until my body ached, until I cried out in pain. Thrust, thrust, thrust, each one accompanied by mind-bending pain. Each thrust making me pray for it to be over, making me squeal animalistically in agony until my cheeks flamed red. Over and over inside of me as he crushed me onto the floor. When I stayed silent, holding the shrieks in, he grabbed my hair with a hand, bashing my skull onto the floor until I whimpered again. I screamed in pain as he grunted in pleasure. The whole time, I stared through tears and through my aching mind, studying the floor.

It's so dirty. I should've cleaned it better. Why didn't I do better?

When he came, he dismounted, kicked me in the ribs, and zipped up. He strutted to the fridge and reached for a beer before heading outside. I jumped when he slammed the screen door. Tears pooled on the floor. At least he was gone. Still, I didn't dare move, knowing the pain would intensify if I did. I lay for a long while, my cheek on the floor, the stench of Richard and rape oozing through the kitchen.

Mama wouldn't like that I used that word, I thought. Women are meant to please their husbands. Rape doesn't exist between husbands and wives, she would say.

But maybe she would change her mind if she knew Richard. I pushed myself off the floor, gasping in pain as my whole body ached. I headed for the bleach and the bucket to clean my own blood off the once clean floor.

Chapter Thirteen

Tires on the gravel road send a jolt to my heart. My breathing intensifies as I turn from Henry's bowl, the food plopped into the dirty container. I spin to face the truth at the road. My hands shake as I wait to see what vehicle will be coming around the slight bend in the road. Under the cover of trees, the engine revs.

Is it time for the reckoning? Is it him? I cross myself, feeling blasphemous as I do. I consider dropping to my knees, begging for God's mercy. But I can't. I can't let him see me like that. I have to hang onto some sense of pride, even if it means hanging on until the very end. I will not make myself a martyr, not yet.

A tan truck gasses it up the road, screeching to a stop behind the red truck. I squint, trying to figure out who it is. I haven't seen the truck before, but then again, Richard's garage is always full of vehicles I don't recognize. I take a breath, realizing this isn't the worst-case scenario. It's probably just a customer I'll have to get rid of.

But then a bald-headed man emerges, biceps rippling. And in his hands is something that sends a shiver right through me again. Henry emits a growl as the muscular man stomps toward me, the crowbar swung over his shoulder like a baseball bat. I steady myself for the fight that's surely coming, wondering what the hell Richard's done now.

Chapter Fourteen

My fingers grip the handle on the knife that's in my pocket, tracing the dried specks of blood on it. I never used to carry a knife, but things have clearly changed. I squeeze the knife, Richard's prize possession, wondering if it'll be time to put it to use again. I steady my breathing, my eyes lasering in on their target.

Just breathe, I remind myself. I'm capable of this. I'm capable of so much more than I ever thought.

'Little lady, where's your man?' the gritty voice barks as he marches toward me. Henry yanks on his rope, and I consider letting him loose. I think about scaring him away, letting the huge dog do his guarding job. I think about ending this right now. But curiosity gets the best of me. I need to know what he's here for. I need to know what Richard's done. I need to figure out what scheme he has going and if it will hinder or help me in the long run. I need to know what I'll be running from, what secrets I need to keep at the women's shelter in South Carolina, the one I settled on to get me started when I'm finally done here.

'Not home,' I reply confidently, my palms sweating as I grip the knife tighter. His hands are loose around the crowbar, his grin defiant. There's a scar above his eyebrow. I've never seen him before.

'Is that so?' he asks, swagger in his walk as he finally comes to a halt in front of me. There are a few feet between us, but I start calculating how quickly I could close the gap if I needed to.

'Yeah, that's so. Who are you?'

He smirks, shaking his head. 'None of your fucking business. Let's just agree I'm about to be your louse of a husband's worst nightmare. The fucker has it coming after what he's done.'

'Well, sorry to disappoint you. But he's not here, and I don't know when he'll be back,' I reply calmly, coolly. Henry still yanks on his rope, barking and snarling as if he's thirsty for blood. I think he is.

'You know, it isn't smart to tell people you're all alone when you're a frail woman like yourself. A bad man might take advantage. A man looking for vengeance might just settle for taking it out on you. It would be a shame if your pretty little face got damaged.'

I pull the knife out of my pocket, holding it in front of me. My hand trembles, but my eyes are steady. It feels good to wield power, to be able to stave him off.

He shakes his head. 'Ballsy, aren't we? Should've known Richard's slut would be a bitch.'

'Get out of here,' I demand through gritted teeth. I don't blink, don't breathe, just in case I'm forced to thrust the knife into his flesh. I imagine the feel of the blade plummeting into the skin between his ribs, hearing his yelp. I imagine the feeling of slicing and hacking away the pieces of his abdomen, of his arms, of his face. I picture the skin flaps splattered in the dirt, like an abstract art display to be pondered. I like the image. I've always thought about being an artist.

'I don't know what scam you two have going. But I'm not done here. Someone's going to pay for what Richard's done. I'm getting my money, whether it's from Richard or from you. If I have to ransack this place and club you both to death in the process, I will. You understand?'

'And if I have to slit your throat right here, I will,' I reply, taking a step forward. He stares at me defiantly, challenging me as if we're participants in a duel. I notice his fingers grip the crowbar tighter, sending a shiver of fear through me, but I stand my ground. I can stomach this. What do I have to lose, after all?

Through gritted teeth, he bellows, 'You tell that motherfucker that I'm not playing anymore. He better get his ass back here. And Cody too. You tell Cody that I'm coming for him. We had a deal. And I'm not going down for this. You hear me?'

'Get out,' I bark, stepping forward, brazen and stoic.

After what feels like an eternity, the man curses and turns, storming to his truck. He stomps on the gas, peeling out and driving off, almost hitting a section of fence on the way.

I breathe a sigh of relief, my hand shaking violently. Who the hell was he? And what dealings does he have with Richard? I think about the money in the envelope, wondering what could have possibly transpired between Cody, Richard, and the mystery man to get him so angry. What has he been doing in that garage? And will the asshole come back?

I steady my shaking hands. I'm no weak flower. I'm no fragile pansy. I'm no longer the Crystal Connor who would cower in the corner, waiting for some strange man to come back for vengeance. I've changed. I'm different. I can handle this, I realize, smiling as I look down at the knife, the specks of blood instilling a sense of confidence. Maybe I can handle myself after all. Maybe that man should be afraid. Maybe they all should.

I make a decision then, stirred by the recent events and the confidence that has grown. I meander into Richard's garage and beeline for the drawer. I shudder at the sight of the familiar hammer but shove it aside. I claim the envelope of mystery cash, counting it to make sure it's all still there. It is. I smile as I squeeze the envelope tightly, feeling all sorts of feelings of hope and promise in that wad of paper.

I pat Henry on the head before wandering back into the house. I head upstairs, lifting the floorboard I loosened in the corner of my closet last night. The floorboards seemed like the perfect spot. When he shows up, he won't look here. I insert the envelope of money into its spot, gingerly lowering it beside the hair dye I bought. A few more things to add to my collection, a few more debts to collect. And then, once the final debt is paid, I'll be out of here. I'll be on my way.

When I head downstairs, I pull the knife back out of my pocket. My fingers run across the handle, and I know what I need to do.

I can still put the knife to good use.

Chapter Fifteen

T he screen door slammed as Henry's barking resonated through the forest. I startled awake in the rocking chair where I'd been perched after a full day of cleaning. My heart pounded wildly. How could I have fallen asleep? How could I have stopped keeping watch?

I jumped to my feet, struggling to steady my breathing and get it together. I smoothed out the yellow dress I was wearing. Richard hated that dress. How could I have been so stupid as to wear it? I knew he'd be back any moment.

In the time since we'd lost our baby girl, Richard had started disappearing more frequently. Sometimes, I'd wake up in the middle of the night to an empty driveway, his truck missing. Sometimes, he'd disappear for hours, a day, or even three or four days. But this time was different. This time, it had been five whole days without Richard.

Five nerve-racking days. Where was he? When would he back? He always, always came back, typically more volatile than usual.

I walked to the kitchen, questions swirling. When I reached the area, I saw Richard heading straight for the refrigerator. His eyes were both blackened, his gait shaky at best.

'What happened? Are you okay?' The questions flew out at the sight of my husband, clearly hurt. Everything else took a backseat to making sure he was physically okay.

Richard slowly turned staring at me, a sneer on his face. 'What do you care? Doesn't look like you missed me too much.'

I stepped closer as Richard grabbed a bottle of beer from the fridge. 'Richard, I've been worried sick. Where have you been?'

Richard turned slowly, slamming the bottle on the counter. Before I could even think, he was stalking across the small room, slamming me backward into the wall.

'Don't worry about where I've been, you hear? I don't answer to you. I had things to take care of. Important things.' His fingers tightened around my jaw as he flung my head backward. The searing pain radiating from the base of my skull blurred my vision for a moment, but I could still see his wild eyes close to mine. I couldn't move, couldn't breathe. The fear rising up in me was so much worse after being away from it for days.

I hadn't realized how peaceful, how quiet it had been without him. Perhaps because there was always the lingering fear that at any moment, he would come back. I'd lived my life for five days as if he were still there.

'I'm sorry,' I murmur.

'Sorry? Sorry for what, you fucking bitch? What did you do while I was gone, huh? The place is a wreck. What, were you cheating on me? Do you think you can run around doing what you want while I'm gone?' His fingers tightened as he pressed up against me. I could feel him harden against me and worried what was coming next. I squeezed my eyes shut.

'No,' I choked. 'Richard, I've been here.'

'And you didn't think to check and see where I was? Huh? You didn't get worried and try to find me? What kind of a wife are you?'

Confusion at the contradiction whirled, making me realize the truth I'd known all along. There was no winning with him. I was damned no matter what I did. He was in control.

He was strong.

I was weak.

I was his plaything at his mercy.

With one final shove he tossed me aside, stomping back over to his beer to take a swig. I didn't dare move, crumpled against the wall, staring at the floor and wishing I could disappear. I stood like that for a long moment, my neck and head aching, my heart hurting. Fear surged. I prayed it would be over, that Richard would stalk off to bed and leave me to pick up the pieces. But a few moments later, he was back in my face, taunting me with slaps and sneers.

'You listen to me, woman. You listen here. What I do away from here is my business. Who supports you? Who provides for you? Do you fucking think I provide this life for you doing a couple of brake jobs? No. It takes resourcefulness. I'm smart, and I handle it. But that means you don't ask questions. And you don't stray from me. Because I promise you this, I'll always be back. No matter how long I'm gone, I always come back. And so help me, if I find this house not in the condition I would expect or if I find you so much as doing one thing I don't approve of, I'll kill you. You hear me? I'll fucking murder you.' He pressed against my trembling body as sobs racked me.

'I'll take that axe from out back,' he whispered in my ear, his fingers twisting around my wrist so hard, I knew I'd have a bruise. 'And I'll chop your head off. I'll split you into pieces, and no one will be the wiser. You think anyone would find your body out here? And you think anyone would care? Just remember *that. I've got the power. I provide for you. I can change that at any time you become a liability. And don't even think you can get away from me. I'm resourceful. I'm wrapped up in all sorts of things you have no clue about. So don't even think for a second you can get away with anything, Crystal. I'm in control here. You got it? You're never leaving me. Fucking never.'*

I nodded wildly, just needing to appease him, to get away. He flung me to the ground and gave me a hearty kick. I considered myself fortunate that he wasn't interested in anything else. For a long while, I stayed crumpled on the floor, sobbing into the linoleum that smelled of bleach from my cleaning earlier in the day.

I cried for the life I'd lost when that baby girl died. I cried for the hopes of a normal life that died with her. I cried for the pain in my head and my heart that Richard inflicted. Most of all, I cried because I knew Richard wasn't bluffing. He would kill me. And he wouldn't need a good excuse to do it. I was trapped in every sense of the word. And he was right about another thing, too. I was too weak to do anything about it.

Crystal the weak would never be able to rise up.

Would she?

Chapter Sixteen

I pace back and forth in the house, wearing a trail in the floor. I really shouldn't. I can't. This isn't a good idea. There are so many reasons why I should just stay here, stay put. It's safer here. It will be safer if I'm here. He'll be safer.

I exhale, my hot breath falling on my own chest, the tank top I'm wearing showing more skin than I'm used to. When Richard is here, I tend to stay covered. I've always ascribed to modesty standards, but it goes beyond that. It just feels smarter to hide my skin, to keep my shoulders, my neck hidden away. But today, it's hot, and I'm sweating up a storm. My emotional health is more important than modesty. Besides, there's no one here to see me, after all. There are perks to being alone, I'm realizing. I keep pacing, my fingers linking my hands behind my back. *Think, Crystal. Think.*

Staying right here is the wise thing to do. I can keep an eye on things, can watch out for his vehicle to come rattling up the driveway. I can be prepared—although I don't think preparation will help at this point. Sometimes it isn't a good thing to see the devil coming, especially if you've already been damned to hell.

Still, it could be a good move to wander into town. Swing by a few of Richard's old haunts, do some digging. Gather a few of the supplies I'll need once I secure my chance to get away. When it's the right time, I'll be ready to dye my hair, slip into the night, and drive off for South Carolina. To start over.

Plus, going to town might give me some information that could be of use. Maybe they could help me dictate the trail that he'll follow. And maybe, just maybe, they'll give me the information I need to stay safe, to buy some time.

It could work. The good thing about being perceived as weak and piteous is that no one suspects you are capable of much. They trust you with things they normally wouldn't because they just don't have faith that you'll be able to do anything with it all. Yes. Yes, this could be a good thing.

Then again, there are also the questions. If someone asks me about that sweet baby—*no, stop, don't go there. Don't even go there. You've been doing so well. Don't let your mind unravel now into that dark abyss that is your sense of loss. Don't be enveloped by the choking, sobbing sorrow that racks your hardened heart. There's no use. You've done your best. You've done what you can do to keep him safe. It's all gone now. It's all over. That can't matter right now. There will be time enough to think of sweet Gideon, to ponder what it all meant. For now, you must keep your eye on the prize.*

I touch the locket around my neck and caress the smooth silver.

'Yes,' I announce to no one. 'This will do.'

I will go into town and track down some of Richard's old stops. I'll ask questions. It will keep my mind off of everything here and, more importantly, I'll look like the dutiful wife. I'll be the good wife Richard expects. Then maybe things won't be so bad for me if he shows up. I'll still secure some safety for myself, a chance to get away. The South Carolina dreams won't be dead. Yes, indeed. Great idea. I smile and chuckle a little at my own ingenuity. Sometimes I do surprise myself. I hurry to the bedroom, ruffling through drawers. I need the right outfit. I need to look pious but also sorrowful. I need to dress the part. It's all about looking right for the role I'm playing now.

I settle on some plain jeans and a simple baby blue sweater. It's innocent enough, even though it is quite loose. I try not to think about why the sweater is so baggy. I look like the sweet, innocent Crystal from a couple of weeks ago, the one who was anxiously waiting to welcome her baby into the world. Other than the missing belly and my aching bones, I do look the same. I look like the same Crystal from a week ago who spent her days cleaning the floors and doing dishes and picking up after Richard's messes.

Not much has changed, I appreciate as I smooth down my hair, grab the keys, and head out to the truck to wander into town. My hands shake as I peel out of the driveway. I won't be gone too long, though. I need to do this. I need to make my appearance. Because sometimes inaction simply isn't a choice.

ALTHOUGH THE SUN ISN'T even in the middle of the sky yet, the morning dew barely gone, there are cars in Blinky's Tavern's parking lot. Of course there are. All of the regulars will be here, burying their faces in steins of beer instead of facing the real world. If Richard were around as usual, he'd be here already, too. I hate to think about how much money he racks up in tabs each month between here and his other favorite bars.

I walk through the creaky door, the blinking neon sign out front beckoning me in. I waft away the puffs of smoke, choking as I enter the dingy bar, the haze disorienting me. Some rock songs fill the radio, and the stools are already lined up with customers.

A redhead stands behind the bar, her white T-shirt accentuating the fact that she isn't wearing a bra. The low neckline leaves little to the imagination. I cross my arms across my own chest, feeling paranoid and self-conscious even though I'm clearly dressed in an appropriate way. I feel all of the men at the bar and the redhead turn to see who has wandered in, automatically suspicious of a new face. I offer a weak smile, take a breath, and walk toward the bar.

'Can I help you, Miss?' the barmaid asks, mindlessly wiping down the black, glassy countertop in front of her.

I amble closer, trying to look poised and not terrified like I am. This isn't my scene. I probably shouldn't be here. Still, I ask myself: why not? I have nowhere I have to be. Why *can't* this be my scene? For a moment, I think about taking off the baby blue sweater and sporting only the tank top underneath. I think about straddling one of the stools, ordering a bourbon, and settling into an afternoon of drowning my own worries in the bottle. But I know that won't do. I have to stay focused.

'Hi, I'm Crystal Connor. I'm just wondering if you've seen my husband, Richard, if you know where he might be.' I decide to just get to the point.

A man nearby whistles, slapping his hand on the bar. 'You poor thing. Married to Richard Connor, huh? Damn. I didn't even know he had a missus.'

I avert my eyes to the ground. This was a mistake. I'm just asking for trouble. What did I really think I'd accomplish here? These guys are so drunk, they'll probably forget this conversation in thirteen seconds.

'Come to think of it, I haven't seen the bastard in a while. Carl, have you heard from him since last Friday?'

I look up to figure out who Carl is. A man with a moustache who is sitting on the corner stool rubs his chin.

'No, haven't seen the fucker—excuse my language—since he took me for my last twenty in that poker game. Bastard was card counting from what I've heard. Shouldn't be surprised though, with all that shady shit the guy was up to.'

I squeeze my eyebrows together. 'What do you mean?' I ask, staring at Carl. The other men quiet, looking at me with the familiar pity. What do they know that I don't? This isn't what I expected. I came here for one particular reason, and this isn't it. What am I missing that everyone else knows? Richard, what secrets were you keeping? And could I use them to my advantage? Am I brazen enough to use them?

'Oh, nothing for you to worry about, darling. I'm sure Richard's fine. The thieving bastard's probably just out on a joyride somewhere. I'm sure he'll be back irritating us all soon.'

I think about pushing it further, especially when I see some other guys whispering to Carl. I turn my attention to the barmaid.

'Honey, I haven't seen him either. Who knows where he could be? When you run with a tough crowd and deal in some shady things, you never know what'll happen. Listen, if I were you, I'd just lie low. Keep your hands clean and enjoy the peace. I've seen the temper on that one. I can only imagine what it's like to live with him. If something happened, well, maybe he got what he deserved, you know? Might be a blessing in disguise. I, for one, wouldn't miss him.' She winks at me, and I nod. Looking into her eyes that are accented with way too much purple eyeshadow, I feel an odd sense of comradery like she gets it. Like she knows more about Richard than the others. I feel like she can see through his thinly veiled façade and recognize him for the monster he actually is. I don't know why, but it makes me happy to know that. It makes me feel relieved and a whole hell of a lot less guilty for my own façade.

'Well, thank you. If you hear anything or see him, just let Sheriff Barkley know. He's on the case now.'

'Yeah, we saw him yesterday. He came by and asked a lot of questions. Never did trust him,' the first man I talked to offers. 'You need someone to walk you out? Never know who might be lurking around these parts.'

'Thank you, but I'm fine,' I reply, meaning it. I turn on my heel and head out the door into the sunshine, taking a deep breath.

No one knows where Richard is. No one has any clue what's happened to him. But they suspect it has something to do with Richard's shady dealings, whatever that means. Richard, Richard. What were you up to before you left? Drugs? Something shadier? I think of the wad of cash in the floorboards, my salvation money. I definitely need to be careful. Sheriff Barkley's bound to dig up some dark truths any moment now, and I need to be ready to keep my hands clean, just like the bartender advised. I look up at the bright sky, thinking about it all, and wondering where to head to next.

Ultimately, I decide I've done enough investigating for one day and made enough public appearances. Right now, I need to get home. I need to be there just in case. I have some cleaning up to do. And I also need to do some searching—if Sheriff Barkley's going to dredge up some shady secret about Richard, I need to know what I'm going to be dealing with. I need to see if I can uncover some truths. Then again, how am I going to make that happen? It's not like Richard's talking. It's not like Richard's doing anything to help at all.

I might just have to get creative and find my own ways to make the missing reveal the truth.

Chapter Seventeen

I pluck the tiny purple flower from the grass, twirling it between my thumbs as I plop down. I've wandered out into the warm sunshine, the tall grasses enveloping me. I always loved these purple flowers as a child. Of course, they're technically a weed. Mama always made sure to point that out when I picked them for her.

I wonder what Mama is up to now. I wonder what she'd think of me if she were here. I wonder if she'd still be quick to judge—the flower, of course. Sometimes I miss her, just a little bit. Sometimes, I wish she'd been able to see Gideon. I wish things were different. So different.

I spin the purple flower between my fingers. So delicate. So tiny. So insignificant in the scheme of things. I sit now, hugging my knees to my chest, staring at the sky, wishing I could make everything behind me disappear—the house, the garage, the threat of Richard. I wish I could just be absorbed by the ground, right here, swallowed whole. I wish I could pick my own gravesite, overgrown or not. But there's still so much work to be done. I can't give in yet. I can't finish up. I have to accomplish my goals. I have so much to do before he gets here. I owe it to myself, to Gideon. I need to finish what I started.

A few weeks ago, I had no idea what was coming my way. I had no idea that I'd deal with the greatest sorrow of my life—and follow it up with a newfound freedom, a change that was unexpected. How long will it last? This is the biggest question now. I don't know if I'm strong enough to face the ending, after all. I don't know much of anything anymore. I pick at the flower, plucking each petal off from the tiny flower.

He loves me. He loves me not. He loves me.

The old game comes flooding back from my childhood, the old wishes and hopes for my life. I'd sit in the grass, praying to God for a man to save me. I wanted nothing more than that Prince Charming of my fairy tales to come riding in and rescue me from everything in my life.

I had no idea that my Prince Charming would turn out to be even darker, even scarier than the villains of the fairy tales. For at least the villains had a cause, a purpose, and a predictable nature. There's no foreseeing what the man I'm married to is capable of, and that still terrifies me. Even when he's not in that house bossing me around, the cold, hard truth is this: I can't underestimate him. I can't get complacent. I have to be cautious, even now. Danger is always, always lurking. He still has the power to destroy me. Always. It's a fact I'll have to live with forever, no matter how many miles I manage to put between us. I shudder at the thought, glancing over my shoulder to examine the house. The porch is still empty, and the driveway only houses the red truck. I'm safe for now. I'm okay.

Gideon's okay.

I wonder what he would have looked like when he got older. Would he have my plain-Jane qualities, my soft jawline and mushy face? Would he have inherited my dull, dirty blonde hair? More importantly, would he have housed his father's sinister, manipulative eyes? Would he have housed even more qualities of his father's?

I picture Gideon with sandy blond hair, dashing through the surf as the waves crash inward. I've only ever seen the beach on television, the little that I've watched. The women lounging, reading magazines and eating chips while the kids play in the surf. I picture Gideon building a sandcastle, his laughter mixing with the gulls' cries while I lie on the blanket, watching him. Smiling, happy. A normal family filled with love and sunshine moments.

But then the imagined moment turns ominous, Gideon stomping on the sandcastle. His boyish laughter turns darker, louder, more familiar. Suddenly, his adorable smile is the vicious sneer of his father, of Richard, and his eyes are burning with a rage I know too well.

I startle, shaking my head, sobs choking me. Ice runs through my veins at the thought. I don't know which is worse—losing Gideon or thinking that he could have lived to become another Richard. I don't know indeed.

He loves me not. Or he loves me? Which one is it? I forget which one I was on. I stare at the delicate flower, the last petal sitting, waiting to be plucked. I toss the stem, my vision blurred from the water draining from my eyes. I guess we'll never know which one it is, although I have my suspicions. In a harsh world, I guess it's sometimes impossible to tell the difference anyway. What's the use?

I run my sleeve across my eyes, swiping away the tears that fall for a future that will never be anyway. I wipe my palms on the grass, biting my lip as I stare out into the vast horizon. There's no breeze to lift my hair, no movement of air to soften the sweltering temperature. I let the sun's rays burn into my skin, searing right into me. I like the feel of it. It reminds me that I'm still here, that I'm still alive. It reminds me that I'm still human.

I lean back, stretching my neck to the sky like a cat, my legs flat in the tall grasses. I stay like this for a moment, soaking in the sun, swaying a bit to a soundless tune playing in my head. I wish I could sit here forever, all of the complications a thing of the past. I wish I could just bask in the sunlight, in the nothingness of the day. I wish I could just be Crystal, staring into the vast unknown with optimism instead of fear. But we don't choose the hands we're dealt. We don't get to pick what scorches us or how long we can stay put. Some things are out of our hands. Even Richard lost control now and again, although he wouldn't admit it. Control is relative. Power is relative. We're all at someone or something's mercy.

I open my eyes, taking a deep breath. There's work to be done. I can't afford to luxuriate like some rich housewife any longer. I promptly drag myself up from the ground, wipe off the grass from the back of my legs, and bite my lip to stop it from quivering. I know what I have to do now. It can't be put off any longer. There's work, hard work to be done. I've been dreading this one for days. But as I saunter toward the house, my mission in mind, something even more terrifying than fear creeps in.

My lips widen into a grin as my heart feels at ease. I guess one really can get used to just about anything, after all. And

I guess you never know what you might actually enjoy until you try it.

He loves me not. That was the last petal. I'm suddenly sure of it.

I SHOULD BE TIRED AFTER the day's ventures, but I'm not. I'm energized, in truth, as I hop out of the shower, the steam filling the bathroom. I towel dry my hair, peering into the fogged over mirror. I swipe at it with my still-wet fingertips, smearing and smudging it. Usually, I wouldn't do this. What can I say? Without Richard hovering over me, I guess I can afford to take some risks. I look at the woman in the mirror. I hardly recognizing her. The faint hint of a smile that's on her face, the big eyes, the confidence in her stance. It's fabulously foreign, but fabulous all the same. I lean on the sink, thinking about all that's transpired. I can't believe what I've done. Yet, I also can. Is it ridiculous that when I say goodbye to this place soon, I'll actually miss this? I'll miss that feeling, that almost arousal-like joy I got from the job well done.

I head to the bedroom to pick out an outfit. What does one wear on a day like this? I browse the dresser, my limited options making me feel sad. I look at the dowdy housedresses that Richard prefers, the plain, simple clothes. I should really be wearing my normal garb in case he shows up. It wouldn't do to call attention to myself, after all. Not after what I've done, especially after what I've just done today.

But I don't know. There's something sad about putting on that wardrobe again. I don't want to. I just don't think I even can. I'm not that woman anymore, I realize with a startle. Have I really broken that mold? Time will tell. Regardless, Richard's not here to tell me I have to be that woman, that I have to wear that outfit. Maybe Sheriff Barkley's right without even realizing it. Maybe I should enjoy the freedom a bit. After all, it's been a hard day. I've done my duties, all of them. I pause for a moment, feeling like I'm on the precipice of either disaster or triumph. What to do? What to do indeed.

He loves me. He loves me not. Don't even think about it. Just Breathe. He loves me.

My head starts spinning, and I lean on the dresser, steadying myself. It's going to be okay. He's not going to show up today. He would've already if he was going to. Besides, I'm not a prisoner, not anymore. I can go run errands, after all. And that's when the resolve kicks in. I need to take care of this errand. I have to. I toss on some jeans and a T-shirt, scrunch my hair, and head to the kitchen. I grab the keys, hop in the truck, and am off again for the second time in one day.

A woman could get used to this freedom.

'CRYSTAL CONNOR? IS that you?' a voice beckons from the other side of the clothing rack. I pause, my hands holding out a flowered dress I've been debating on buying. My heartbeat quickens. A face peeks out from around the rack, and I see the familiar brunette who lives by Sharon. Shit. This isn't what I needed.

'Hi,' I offer, my tone non-committal, returning my attention to my shopping. It's been so long since I've bought a new dress. I don't think I've bought one since I married Richard. But today, well, I just want to get something new. Even if it's impractical—once he shows up, I'll never be able to wear something like this. It's a waste of money, and I need to save my resources if I'm really going to start over. But today, I just don't care. I need this. I'm desperate for a moment of normalcy. I need something new to walk into the new life that's hovering out in front of me.

Kara Johnson walks closer and grabs my hand in hers. I can't help but notice how wrinkled her skin is, far too wrinkled for her age. She must share in Sharon's pack-a-day habit.

'I'm so sorry. Sharon told me all about what's happened to you.'

I withdraw my hand from hers, yanking back my wrist like a serpent's just twisted around me. I stare into her eyes boldly, glowering as something in me snaps. How dare this woman presume to know my struggles?

'Sorry, I didn't mean to pry,' she adds, seeming to sense my discomfort.

'I'm fine,' I note, staring into her blue irises.

'It's just, well, I'm sure it can't be easy, with Richard gone and all.'

And maybe I'm imagining it, but I swear the women smirks. I swear that her eyelids flutter just a bit. What is this? Does she know something? I'm so uncomfortable. And something else. Something unfamiliar.

I'm angry. Rage-filled. Possessed by a disturbing sense of hatred that is sudden and biting. My fingers snap at her wrist, clutching onto it, and she gasps. Another woman across the store eyes us with wariness, but I ignore her.

'What do you know about Richard?' I demand, and my fingers tighten around the bones. I tell myself to get ahold of this flareup of anger, that I can't draw attention. But that's the thing. I can't stop it, even if I want to. Once more I am powerless—but this time, I am powerless against the toxic anger boiling inside of me, to a primal urge I didn't think existed.

'Nothing, nothing. I just heard that you were at the station, filed a report is all. I don't know anything about it other than that.' There's a terror in her eyes, and I'm surprised. Is she afraid of me? It's almost laughable. I've never incited this kind of reaction in anyone. But seeing the nosy woman squirm at my command, it's—I don't know. It's something. Emboldened, I press on.

'Does anyone in this town mind their own business? Huh?'

'I'm sorry, Crystal. I was just worried is all.'

'Well worry a little less about me and more about you. I'm fine. Really.'

I fling her wrist out of my hand, and she immediately backs up, studying me. I stare at her, shock painted onto her face. For a moment, I panic. What have I done? This can't be good. If she goes to Sheriff Barkley and tells him . . .

What? What am I so afraid of? Who can blame me after all I've been through? It's about time Crystal Connor shows this town she's not some mouse to stomp on. She's something else entirely.

Kara slinks away, back into some rack across the store. I notice she eyes me apprehensively as I scamper about the store, looking for a dress. Things aren't as exciting now, the interruption ruining my good mood. I try to shove the thoughts aside. I can't let that woman ruin a good thing, not now.

I finally settle on a bright blue dress with a white collar. It's expensive, but it's okay. I've swiped a few twenties from Richard's secret money. It's not like anyone's counted it, and I deserve this. Richard owes me this much. Even if Sheriff Barkley finds out about the rest, he won't notice this money gone missing. At least I hope not. It's a chance worth taking.

I don't know why I'm so adamant about this dress. Who is there to see it? If Richard were home, it's not like he'd appreciate it. And I'm pretty sure a nice dress will be the least of my concerns when I hit the road, when I leave this mess behind. Still, I walk to the counter to pay for the item. The teenager working at the register talks with a monotone voice, but I don't care. I smile at the rush of making the purchase. Oh, this is grand. Grand indeed. I walk out of the store, smiling at Kara just for fun on the way out.

Who am I?

Crystal Connor, that's who. It's about time this town starts to get to know her before it's too late. I walk to the car, the bag in my hand, and start up the truck. I consider going for a cup of coffee, but no, I better not push it. If he shows up, I should probably be there. After all, he needs to get to know Crystal Connor, too. No sense in hiding it from him, I think.

Life is still complicated, and there's an enduring, icy terror that threatens to usurp me periodically. But today went so unexpectedly well. It showed me that perhaps this could all be okay after all. Maybe there still is something to salvage of my life, something to strive for. Maybe I don't have to be the Crystal Connor Richard molded me into. I just need to keep at it and believe. I pull into the driveway, and I notice Henry is barking up a storm. And I also notice there's another vehicle, a black Camaro, parked in front of Richard's garage. My heart pangs. Now what?

I exit the truck and see her standing there, leaning on the back of the truck. And even though her arms are crossed, I notice one significant detail.

There's a pistol in her hand. Apparently, she's figured out a little bit of who Crystal Connor is as well. This can't be good at all, I realize as I slam the truck door, leaving the brand-new dress on the passenger seat where it belongs.

Chapter Eighteen

I walk up to Kimberly, my sister-in-law, with growing trepidation. I don't avert my eyes, keeping them on her, and especially on the pistol. What does she know?

She stands up straight, pushing off from the car. The pistol is steadied and pointing straight at me.

'Kimberly?' I ask meekly, not sure what else to say.

Her face is a straight line, her dark purple lipstick accenting the gruff facial expression.

'Where the hell is he? Have you seen him?' she asks, stomping closer, the gun trained on me.

'Who? Richard?' Why does she care about Richard? What's in this for her? Has Cody sent her? I start to unravel inside, feeling like I'm going to heave up my intestines. My knees are wobbly, but I tell myself to be strong. This was always coming. I just didn't think in this way.

'No, you bitch. Cody. What happened to him? What do you know?' Her voice echoes off the garage now, and I jump.

I put my hands out in front of me. 'Kimberly, I don't know anything. What are you talking about?'

'The son-of-a-bitch didn't come home. He's been gone for two days, Crystal. Two days. Now don't go telling me Richard didn't have something to do with this. Good for nothing asshole. Where is he? Where is he hiding?'

Confusion racks my brain. Cody's gone too? Did Sheriff Barkley get a chance to talk to him? Could this be related to Richard? I don't understand. I'm losing control here. I've already lost control, in truth. I've got a gun pointed at me.

'Kimberly, listen. I don't know. I've been to the station to report Richard missing because I don't know where he is, either. I really don't know what's going on.'

She studies me for a long moment, as if trying to assess whether or not I'm telling the truth. The woman barely knows me. I don't know why she assumes she could detect my tell. Still, something in my words must convince her. She drops the gun to her side.

'Dammit, I'm just so frustrated. Where the hell is he? What is this? Cody doesn't do this sort of thing, not usually. Not like Richard. He's so worried about me and keeping an eye on things at home that he doesn't just take off without telling me. What the hell is going on, Crystal?'

'I don't know. I really don't know.' I feel like a broken record, replying with the same statement.

We stand for a long time, two sister-in-laws who are more strangers than family, thinking about what a messed-up situation we're in. Wondering how this is all going to turn out. Wondering how Cody fits into the puzzle.

'When's the last time you saw him?' I ask now that the tension has calmed.

She sighs. 'Two nights ago. I came home from my shift at the diner, and the sheriff's car was here. He was just leaving when I showed up. Cody was agitated, so agitated. I asked him what was wrong, but he blew me off. That was two nights ago, and he hasn't come home. Where could he be?'

My blood runs cold. Sheriff Barkley talked to him. This can't be good. What did they talk about? And why would Cody leave? My mind flashes back to the money in the garage.

I want to ask Kimberly, but realizing she still has the gun in her hand, I don't want to stir her again. I doubt she knows anything anyway. I'm guessing, though, that the talk with Sheriff Barkley incited some fear in Cody. Maybe he had to get things in order, whatever things they may be. Or maybe with Richard missing, their illicit plans are falling apart. Because I'm certain that whatever Richard was up to, Cody was involved too. I wonder if it's just a matter of time until Cody reappears here, angry and on a war path, determined to find Richard's secrets.

I sigh. Richard's not going to do any talking, that's for sure. This just gets messier and messier. What have you done? *What have you done?*

'Look, if Richard shows up, I'll see if I can find anything out, okay?' I say to Kimberly, who glares back at me, frustrated and hesitant.

'Yeah. I'm sure Cody will come home. Who the hell knows anymore, though, you know?'

'Hang in there,' I say to her, meaning it. I look at the woman with long, black hair and think about how in another life, in another family, maybe we could've been friends. The sister-in-laws who go for manicures together or help prepare Thanksgiving dinner together for a big, jolly extended family. But life didn't deal us that hand, not even close. I wonder if Kimberly is as lonely as I am most days. I wonder if she lives with the fear I do. I'm sure in some fashion, she does. She must. Then again, I really don't know her at all.

Kimberly nods at me before climbing into the Camaro, backing up, and driving off. I sink to the ground by the garage once she's gone, thinking about how messy this all is. Where is Cody? What does he know about Richard? And what are the two of them caught up in? Secrets are never a good thing. I should know. But there's no use in dwelling on it all now. I have to hope that wherever Cody is, he just stays far away and takes care of whatever problem he and Richard have created.

The glass house I'm building is about to come crashing down anyway. I don't need anyone giving it a kick, after all.

Night Four

T error begs to escape from my body in shrill cries, but no sounds happen. I struggle and struggle, but my lips won't part. My stomach drops as reality sets in. My mouth is sewn shut. The truth slams into me with the force of a train, but I can't move. Someone must've sewn my mouth shut, I realize, as I try to wriggle my lips open. That's got to be what's happening.

I squirm and squeal, but it's no use. I can't escape, my mouth feeling like it's permanently glued shut. I need to scream. I need to get out of here.

I wiggle free, the ropes that were holding me down weak and pointless. They're no match for me. I jump off of the cold, metal table, terrified. I need to run out of here. Where am I? Am I in the hospital? I think I'm in the hospital.

I run, the gown I'm wearing wrapping around my legs, threatening to trip me. Off I go, out the door, some faceless beings shouting at me on my way out. How are they shouting? Where are their mouths? It's an eerie question I don't have time to ponder as my legs carry me forward, into the darkness of the night. The moon shines down, lighting the way. I run through mud and muck, running, running, inhaling through my nose deeply. I worry that my nose will be plugged and then I will die. I try to free my mouth, jiggling my jaw, but it's no use. I can't get it open.

I run and run for what seems like forever. On my way through the forest, raven's caws resonate through the deadened trees, an unsettling symphony that stirs me even more. I trip on a rock on the lane, my face smashing against the ground. Dammit. Dammit all to hell.

I do a weak push-up, still unable to move my lips, to scream, to cry. My arms shake as I lift my body up, ready to keep running to a destination unknown. I just feel the need to keep moving. The ravens keep screaming. Are there more of them now? I think there are more of them.

I run and run and run until finally, the trees clear and a pasture sits before me. I walk through it, slowing down, uncertain about my footing. It wouldn't do to trip again. My breathing is labored as I march through the pasture. Suddenly, it appears.

The house. The familiar house with its unfamiliar vibe, the red fog swirling around it. I know I should be afraid, the haunting aura around it repelling and demented in its own right. But I'm not fearful. I know this place. I do. I saunter up gingerly, my breath steadying. I hope I can find answers within. I need to figure this out. I need to speak up. I can't be silenced anymore. Through the squeaking screen door I go, into the kitchen. The pictures on the walls are different this time, but they're still not mine. The décor is off, and the floor plan is slightly skewed. Nothing is quite right yet. I take a deep breath in and out. Even though it's unfamiliar, I feel comforted somehow. I feel at home, more and more each time.

This time, I saunter to the white door in the back of the kitchen, the one that leads down those basement steps. The handle is glowing, and I'm mesmerized by it. Why is it glowing? I ache to touch it, even though I know it will burn. My fingers unfurl, stretching toward it. But before they can touch the steamy, hot brass, there's a thud behind me, a stomp on the ground. Footsteps. I turn to see a sight I can't even fathom, can't begin to interpret.

What is it? Who is this?

The creature—for this does not seem human—is tall, faceless, and foreboding. He wears jeans and a T-shirt, but these familiar elements seem a ruse to distract me from its hovering nature. It walks toward me, methodically, menacingly. Step. Step. Step. I shake, backing up, careful not to lean against the hot doorknob. I can't lean against the doorknob.

'Please,' I want to say, but my mouth is still sewn shut. I can only murmur. I can only make muffled noises, my lips unable to pull apart. This only seems to excite the creature even more. It tosses two huge, gangly limbs on either side of me, pinning me against the door. The hot doorknob sizzles against my robe. I might catch on fire. The thought terrifies me, this place going up in flames as I stand here, unable to scream.

I squeeze my eyes shut, trembling, as the faceless creature leans in. I open them in time to see it's shapeless face contort. A mouth opens in the middle, its milky face literally parting down the center. Tears fall crazily, my whole body quaking violently. From the center of its face, a long, slender tongue emerges, creeping toward me, darting toward my eye. I shake. I slink back. I squeeze my eyes shut and pray.

But no wet, sloppy sensation touches my face. I peek out from behind my eyelids when a sizzling, scalding noise beside me startles me. The creature's tongue is wrapped around the doorknob, the hot metal scorching it. I shake, shimmying out from under its limbs, backing up slowly as to not draw attention. The creature doesn't make a sound, standing there as its tongue burns, burns, burns.

I sink to the floor, unable to move or scream or think.

I am home now. This is home now.

Chapter Nineteen

My eyes throb, my heart thudding, as my hand rubs the cover of the good book. I trace patterns on it as my eyes leak, as the early morning light streams into the room.

Have I been awake all night?

No. I must've slept some because that was when the nightmare came. It jostled me awake, my chest throbbing as my lungs heaved for air. It was all just a bad dream, I reassure myself. Nothing to worry about. Still, I know there's more to it. Sometimes, nightmares aren't as distant, as fantastical, as we'd like to believe.

I should be praying, I know that. I should be on my knees by the bed, rocking gently as I read the verses that outlined my childhood, my whole persona. I should be begging for a forgiveness that I know I don't deserve. How have I abandoned it all? I pick at the skin around my fingernails, the guilt finally racking me. I've forsaken the one thing I can cling to, my God. How could I have abandoned him?

It's been a trying few days, for certain. But that's no excuse. Now, more than ever, I need to pray for my soul, for his soul. For all of us, really. Still, as my fingers trace the cover in methodical patterns, my fingertips dancing over the crusty leather cover, I can't bring myself to crack it open. My mind dances and darts through the memories of the nightmare, the faceless creature and the burning tongue creeping into every fiber of my being.

How did I let it all go so wrong? How did I let it go this far? What's happened to me?

I should've got in the truck, taken the money, and left. I should've used this as an opportunity to do something different. But a nagging thought inserts itself into my brain, twirling around and dancing with the truth.

I had needs within that I had to take care of. It wasn't just Richard keeping me hostage here. No, it was something more menacing at play. Years of torment, after all, change a person. Or maybe, just maybe, they help the truth of the person finally emerge, a truth that would have been repressed in other circumstances.

I don't know how much time passes, or how long I stare from the bed at the window, thinking about it all as a fatigue pounds against my skull. But eventually, tires on the gravel road and Henry's incessant barking stir me. My heart thuds once more. I hear the car door.

It's too late. I'm too late. There will be no penance, no forgiveness now.

He has come at last.

I squeeze my eyes shut through the salty tears. This is where it ends. I've ended it all, and my own version of darkness will now consume every dream, every hope, every prayer for redemption left.

Chapter Twenty

'Mrs. Connor, I'm sorry to bother you at this early hour. But I need to talk to you,' Sheriff Barkley says when I finally parade to the door, steadying my breath. My fingers shake, but I tell myself to breath. Just breathe. Don't think about it.

'What is it, Sheriff?' I ask, rubbing faux sleep from my eyes to mask my trembling fingers.

He stands outside the screen door, as if waiting to be invited in. Richard would've never let him in. He didn't trust anyone with the law. I step outside, closing the door behind me as I wrap my arms to cover my chest.

'Cody Connor. Have you heard from him?'

'A while ago. A few days ago. Not anytime lately. Why?' I ask, taking a deep breath.

'Kimberly reported him missing yesterday. Said she wondered if Richard had something to do with the whole situation.'

'Oh,' I reply calmly as I focus on Henry's barking in the background.

'Crystal?' he asks, readjusting his hat as I focus my eyes back on him. 'Anything at all you can offer? When did you see him last?'

'Before he went missing, I'm sure. He stopped to see Richard. But he's still missing, too, as you know.'

'Hm,' Sheriff Barkley murmurs, nodding. 'Was he acting strange?'

'He was acting like a Connor,' I reply, and I feel the sheriff soften at the familiarity of the phrase.

'Well, it's alarming, in truth. Two brothers now missing. It complicates the investigation a bit.'

'I hope they aren't wrapped up in something,' I reply, saying what he certainly must be thinking.

'You don't mind if I have a look around, do you? See if maybe there are some hints as to where Richard might've gone? It's been a few days, and I don't know, with Cody missing, things just don't quite seem right.'

'Is this official?' I ask, my heart pounding. Richard wouldn't like him looking around. He doesn't trust the law.

'No, no. No search warrant or anything. Mrs. Connor, you know I'm still skeptical about all this. I'm sure those two are just up to no good. Got themselves into some crazy dealings or something. But if that's the case, well, my priority is looking out for you. Would hate for an innocent to get wrapped up in something messy.'

I smile sweetly, leaning on the screen door. 'Thank you, Sheriff. I appreciate that. But I'm sure Kimberly's just overreacting. Those two have been known to take off together. I'm sure they'll turn up.'

I do my best to stay calm. I need to convince him all is okay, which isn't going to be easy now that I've been to the station twice. What was I thinking reporting him missing? I should've left it all alone. Dammit. Dammit. Dammit. The last thing I need is the sheriff lurking about, creeping around Richard's things. That won't do. I need to turn this around.

Sheriff Barkley eyes me suspiciously.

'Everything okay, Mrs. Connor? You look mighty tired. Something keeping you up?'

I bite my lip on the inside, the salty taste of blood seeping through. I see a growing hint of something—suspicion, maybe? —growing. I can't have that.

'I'm okay. Just a lot going on. Trying to figure out how to pay the bills and everything. Wondering when Richard will come home, and what he's been doing. But I'm fine. I'll manage.'

He nods, crossing his arms. 'Well, listen, I haven't given up. I'll get to the bottom of this. I'm going to go do some digging, see where Cody was last seen. If you hear anything from either of them, be sure to give me a call. And if it's okay, I'm just going to peek in the garage since that's where you put on the missing report as the last place you saw him.'

'Of course, Sheriff. Take a look. Take your time. Can I bring you some coffee while you work? Something cold?' I relax into the side of the house as Sheriff Barkley says no thanks to the drink. He tucks his hands into his pockets, glances at me for a long moment as if deciding whether or not to believe me, and then finally ambles away toward the garage. I think about accompanying him, but I don't know if I can play this part anymore. It's too nerve-racking. I think about the money I swiped from the garage that's tucked safely away. There will be no trace of it, though. What am I worried about? There's nothing for Sheriff Barkley to find in the garage, after all. I've cleaned up the hammer. The money is stowed away, just waiting for me to use it.

But what if there's something else? What if Richard has other unknown surprises hidden? I should've taken the time to investigate. I ball my hands into fists, squeezing them tightly. I'm not cut out for this, not smart enough. I should have thought to look. I should've been faster, should've been gone by now.

Focus, Crystal. Focus. You're going to be fine. Sheriff Barkley's on your side, I remind myself as I watch him walk to the garage, take a look around. I hold my breath, wiping my palms on my dress. After what seems to be an eternity, Sheriff Barkley emerges. He walks calmly, stoically toward me. I wonder what he's found.

But when he gets closer, he just nods. 'Nothing out of the ordinary, but I only had a quick look around. I'm going to look into some other potential leads, but I might be back to have a closer look,' he says. I paint on a sweet smile, turning the corners of my lips up too far. He'll be back. And what will he find when he returns? Will it be too late?

Will I already be gone, in one way or another? I squeeze my fingers back into balls again, nodding at Sheriff Barkley.

'Okay, then, Sheriff. Thank you. I'm sorry to be such a bother over what's probably nothing.'

He tips his hat at me. 'It's no bother. And I don't mean to concern you, but I have an odd feeling about this, with Cody missing too. Could be foul play.'

My heart thuds at the words as Henry's barking and snarling continue to echo in the background. Mixed with my fears, the noise from him shreds my nerves. Sheriff Barkley stares at me, his dark eyes shimmering. He stares a little longer than feels comfortable, but I keep my forced smile on.

He tips his hat again and turns, slinking down the front lawn to the driveway. Just as I'm ready to breathe a sigh of relief, though, he stops and turns. Panic rises.

'Mrs. Connor?'

'Yes?' I ask as steadily as possible.

He eyes me for a moment before nodding toward Henry. 'Be careful. That dog looks a little vicious. Wouldn't want to hear about something happening to you.' And something in the way he looks at me sends a shiver through my spine. My head whirls so fast I think I might pass out.

What does he think he knows? What did that all mean? Why did he say that? And is he really on my side?

I nod meekly and stay, frozen, until Sheriff Barkley gets in his car and peels out. Even after I can't see his car anymore, I stand, staring into the vast wilderness that has been forced to bear witness to the unraveling scene around it.

Chapter Twenty-One

I drag the scrub brush back and forth, over and over. So much dirt to get rid of. It needs to be clean for when he comes. Dammit, it just has to be clean. At least I have some more time now. My knees ache as the hard, gritty texture of the floor grinds into them. I keep scrubbing, the smell of bleach intoxicating and hypnotizing. It settles my fraying thoughts and steadies my shaking hands.

It's all okay, I remind myself. Whatever Richard is wrapped up in isn't my problem. It isn't like I knew about it. It isn't like I can get involved in that. And Cody missing, well, that's no issue either. I have bigger things to worry about.

Like when he comes back. When he comes in here, I can't let this place be as it is. It needs to be spotless, homey. Fresh and clean, just like Richard would expect it to be. The thought drives my battered hands forward. The bleach stings the cuts on my hands, but I barely feel it. There are more immense sorrows. I want to curl up on the rocking chair and scream. I want to crumple face down on the floor and sob until I can't sob any more. But that's a luxury I can't afford.

I have to keep us safe now. It's becoming more and more important, because it's just a matter of time until he comes back. It's just a matter of time now. My freedom from the chains is running out, and the shackles he'll impose on me are going to be much heavier. I brush the thought aside, but it's getting harder and harder to ignore. As the days go on, I know it's inevitable. It's all going to come crashing down—and then what? What will happen to him? To me? To us? I squeeze my eyes shut, shaking my head. Gideon. Sweet Gideon. Why did it have to happen like this?

I think back to that night, when my sweet baby called to me from the forest. Why didn't I get there faster? I should have been there for him. Why wasn't I there? Why didn't I do the right thing then?

I finish scrubbing until the floor is immaculate, just as it should be. I carefully tuck the rug back into place, smoothing out each tassel until all is well again as I've done so many times now. I rinse my bucket out and store it back in the closet where it goes.

I take a deep breath, steadying my resolve. If the Blessed Mother were still here, I'd kneel before her, pray for a sense of calm for what I'm about to do. Then again, I don't know if I could face her. I don't think she would approve. But maybe she would. She was a mother, after all. She knows what lengths you sometimes have to go to in order to protect your child. How did she feel when her son was up on that cross? Did she fantasize about crying out, about stepping in and saving him? I grab my head, my brains banging into my skull as a headache pangs through me. I can't get lost now. I must stay the course and figure out the best move.

I open my eyes, a new, steadfast resolve resting inside. It's time once more. The game isn't over yet—and I need to hurry it along. I have to finish what I've started and then make my getaway. But it has to be just right. Too soon, and the ends won't be wrapped up neatly, the escape pointless. Too late, and the prison I've called a house will consume me—and he'll win. He always wins.

But maybe not this time.

A new emotion takes the place of the fear, the twinges of guilt, the regret inside.

Anger. Sheer, unrestrained anger. *Hell hath no fury like a mother's wrath,* I think, as I head to do the good work I must do.

Night Five

I try to wiggle my wrists free, but I can't. Why can't I move a muscle? Why won't my wrists move? My toes? Nothing will move. My body is a frozen block of ice, stuck here, wherever that is. I will my body to move, but it doesn't cooperate.

Where am I? I look around, my bottom freezing cold on the metal chair. There is no light, no noise. The silence is what's the eeriest. I want to scream, but I'm gagged. I feel like I need to be sick. I'm trapped in here, and my blood runs cold at the thought of how I am at the mercy of the universe. I'm helpless in every sense of the word. I can't save myself from whatever horrors may appear.

I am naked, and the nakedness makes me feel vulnerable. My exposed body begs to be covered. If someone sees me like this . . .

I can't let them see me like this. I don't want to be exposed. I can't be. I will my hands, my fingers, my toes to move. I need to get out of here. I need to be free. It's no use, though. They're not budging. And then, sheer terror sets in.

I'm being watched. I feel eyes on me, can see them glowing red in the distance. Something's coming. Closer and closer the footsteps fall. I am frozen, screaming, shrieking, clawing my way out inside. Yet my body doesn't cooperate. No one knows I'm here.

'Crystal. Crystal, you've been a terrible girl, haven't you? You've done some unforgivable things. You better repent.' The voice is soft and condescending. I want to close my eyes, but even my eyelids refuse to cooperate. I know the voice. I don't want to see her. I can't see her.

A light shines down, as if we're in some demented play, on stage for all to see. It illuminates my mother in a way that is otherworldly. She is beautiful, more stunning than she ever was in real life. There is a glowing quality to her, and her hair is much longer. Is she an angel? I think she might be an angel. She ambles toward me, smiling, silent. I am afraid of what she might do. I don't want her to see me like this. I can't let her see me.

As she gets closer, I realize she's holding a perfect bundle, a black blanket around whatever it is. She walks closer, not saying a word. When she is right in front of my naked body, she shakes her head, grinning. She stoops down and puts the bundle eye level with me.

No. No. God no. What is this? My chest heaves, and my stomach lurches, but I can't react. I am a frozen doll, sitting placidly in the midst of this horror. For in her arms, right in front of me, is my baby. Sweet Gideon, cocooned in smothering black.

But there's one problem. This isn't my baby. This isn't the sweet angel who died before I ever got to kiss him. Sure, it's his face, his tiny fingers. But there's one important difference. This time, his eyes are open. And they're glowing red. Bright, demonic red, the kind that would send me running from my own child if I could.

'Your mommy's here,' my mother says, and I'm not sure if she's talking to me or Gideon. I want to kick her. I want to grab my baby from her. But I don't want to, either. Because I know this isn't my baby. The being in her arms looks up at me, and a paralyzing chill runs through my veins, freezing even my thoughts. I can't take this. I can't. This can't be.

Because as my sweet Gideon's hideous eyes bore a hole into my soul, his face turns into an impressive grin. He opens his mouth, wider, wider, until he's smiling bigger than the Cheshire Cat.

And then, all at once, from his mouth spews pointy, jagged, bloody teeth. They slap into my face, the raw roots on them slapping against me, splattering blood. This can't be real. I want to die. Please God, let me die right here.

Finally, mercifully, my eyes squeeze shut. I feel myself whirling, teeth hitting me left and right, a horrific cackle in the background whirling me around and around.

When things grow quiet again and I stop spinning, I will my eyes to open. I look down. I'm still naked, but this time, I'm walking. This time, I'm not frozen. In fact, I'm the opposite. I can't stop. I want to stop, but my muscles don't listen. My feet are working under their own volition, carrying me forward, forward, forward. Where am I going now? I wonder as my feet plod through mud and grass. Every now and again, I step on something sharp. It is when I look back as my feet move forward that I realize the sharp objects are teeth. Always teeth. So many teeth. Where's Gideon? My feet finally stop, and I'm in front of the familiar yet unfamiliar sight.

The decrepit house with the haunting red aura about it. I want to stop, to hesitate like I have before but I can't. My feet *lead me right up the porch, right through the door, right into the kitchen. And finally, my feet stop. I glance around for a moment, wondering what's next. Is Gideon here? Where is he? What can I do? What should I do? That's when I hear it. That's when my whole body rocks with grief and fear.*

Because from somewhere in the house, there's a guttural scream that's terrifying enough to rattle both the living and the dead. Suddenly, though, the scream becomes my own, and I'm whirling about the house, slamming into walls and trying to make sense of this place that isn't a place at all.

Chapter Twenty-Two

Sleep has become a rarity, but not for the right reasons. I should be having sleepless nights because of Gideon's cries—not the cries of terror and guilt. I should be up rocking his sweet body back to sleep, not swaying myself in protection against the harsh reality of my fears. I should be awakened by the cries of my child, not by my own screams from the nightmares that plague me every night. I sit and stare into the room, tears welling. Who have I become? What have I become? And what will become of me now?

These are the questions that have no answers, not today at least. I'm growing weary of this. I'm tired, so tired. But I know it's not over. It won't be over until I know Gideon's safe for good. It won't be over until I've protected Gideon and his memory. And, a shakiness erupts within as I realize it won't ever be over, not really. Hair dye and a new town can't cover all that's transpired here, no matter how much I wish I could just let it all go.

Dread seeps into my pores, my chest, as I nod at this truth. I can't put it off forever. This power, this freedom, is short-lived and not far-reaching. Because behind the semi-quietude of the house with Richard's disappearance, there is always the underscored fact that he will come back. He will come blasting through that door any moment to rip down this façade of freedom. He will shred any hope I had of building a safe, peaceful life of choice and autonomy. He will shatter the remaining pieces of who I am. And even if I get away, escape, how long will the freedom last until he hunts me down, a wounded piece of prey who was, for one shining moment, at the top of the food chain?

This time, when he comes for me, it will be worse than before. This time, there will be no mercy. It will make all of those other moments look like child's play. He will devour me once he finds out what unforgivable things I've done.

At least there will be comfort in knowing that for these few days, I've done my duty. I've protected Gideon. And I've made the world a little bit safer now. I stand from the kitchen chair, yawning. I march into the bathroom and peer into the mirror.

'You can't quit now,' I command myself. I look past the bags under my eyes and the gray pallor of my skin. I look into the irises looking back at me. I see the truth in there, and it shocks me. A grin spreads on my face as I shake my head. I think back on the past few days, consider all that's been accomplished. I think about how I underestimated myself, just as Richard always does. But things have changed, and I'm not the same Crystal. Looking through the hazy glass, I recognize something I've been burying deep within.

This isn't just about doing what's right. It's about seeking what's mine. It's about grabbing onto power I haven't had. Sometimes you can't just turn the other cheek. And whether that's something to be afraid of or to be guilty about, I don't know. But it is what it is at this point, and I can't surrender yet.

'HERE, BOY,' I SAY, putting down the bowl in front of Henry as the ravenous dog devours the meat. 'I'm sorry I've not been doing a great job at taking care of you.'

I do feel bad. I've been too distracted. I need to do a better job at caring for Henry. Not that Richard would care. But I'm not like Richard, I reassure myself.

I'm not him. I'm not.

I stroke the dog's fur with shaky hands, and, once he's done eating, blood dripping from his jowls, he rubs his face on me. I ignore the smears of blood as I rub his ears, settling into the dirt with him. Richard would never let Henry in the house. He said the dog was lucky enough to get this patch of dirt and some food and water. The thought bubbles within, a fury rising. Richard's not in control anymore. He's not here to tell me now. I smirk at the thought, untying the rope from Henry and clutching his collar.

'Come on, boy,' I say. It might be nice to have him inside, the guard dog within the house. Just in case. You never know who could show up. I lead the dog to the house, and he trudges inside, sniffing wildly. He's not used to being in here. I watch him explore. I smile, thinking about how nice it will be to have a companion now, to snuggle in with him. I picture myself sitting in the rocking chair, cradling Gideon, Henry at my feet as we look out into the clear evening. But then the unthinkable happens.

No. Damn dog, no. No. No. I rush toward him in horror as he scratches at the rug, sniffing and moaning. Scratching,

scratching. All of the tassels are skewed, and everything is messed up. Dammit, he's messed it all up. Tears start to fall.

'No. Henry, no. You'll ruin it,' I argue, yanking the dog back. He has laser beam focus on the area, and I shake my head. He's ruining it. I'll have to clean again. I'll have to clean. *I'm sorry. No. Don't think about it. Just breathe. Breathe. Breathe.* I'm sobbing now, my head racing. This was a terrible idea. What will I do? The dog jolts away from the scene after a loud noise crashes through the house. Something must have fallen. What was that? Henry lets out a massive bark, backing away from the spot, momentarily forgetting about it.

I rush to the kitchen and find some leftover meat. I entice the dog with it, and his barks go silent as he follows me. I make a beeline for the tree, throw the meat in his bowl, and tie him securely to his place in the world once more.

When Henry is back where he must be, I sink into the dirt, staring ahead. Tears fall as I think about the loneliness and about the harsh fact that in some ways, I guess I'm not any better.

I'm not any better than Richard. Maybe I'm worse.

Father, forgive me. Forgive me. Forgive me.

Chapter Twenty-Three

The familiar, tissue-thin pages beneath my fingertips, I rock slowly, methodically as I stare out the window into the darkness. My head lightly presses against the headrest, and I close my eyes shut after a long moment, tracing the ink on the pages as a blind woman reading braille would do. But I don't need to feel out the words with my fingertips. So many verses are etched into my skin, into my mind. I just haven't listened to them lately. Why haven't I listened? What's happened to me?

My fingers glide over the words—words of sin, of guilt, of resurrection. Tears leak from my eyes as I think of all that's transpired and how there are no verses to soothe my tortured soul now. I should be reading, should be repenting. I'm a sinner now. I'm such a sinner. But I'm also weary, and I just can't bring myself to read the words. Maybe it's just the exhaustion of all that's happened, or maybe it's just the debilitating fear of what's to come. Perhaps, though, it's something darker.

Perhaps it's that as I gain strength and independence, I realize a harsh truth—God has forsaken me, long before I had forsaken him. What kind of God lets a man like Richard walk this Earth? What kind of creator would let a God-fearing woman like me suffer at the hands of a monster? Or become one in her own way?

My fingers trace over the page, left to right, my mind's eye seeing the words.

James 1:12 Blessed is the one who perseveres under trial because, having stood the test, that person will receive the crown of life that the Lord has promised to those who love him.

But this crown of life is a gory one, a demented one. It's a crown I wouldn't mind cracking, I comprehend, as my mind flashes back to the harsh truths of the life I live in this house.

'RICHARD, I'M SORRY. I'm sorry.' The whimpered words sliced into the stagnant, damp air between us as my choking sobs racked my pale body. I could barely see through my tear-filled eyes—but I discerned that all-too-familiar, complacent grin on Richard's face. My stomach sank once more.

My naked thighs clung to each other. My wrists were tied too tight behind my back, and my shoulder blades were aching. The tearing and straining of my body accompanied the debilitating throbbing of my head. I ached to reach up and rub the growing bump on my head from where Richard cracked me in the skull with the wrench. Sticky blood dribbled down, crusting over, but I was too woozy and too restricted to do anything about it.

How long had I been there, naked and wet, tied to the dilapidated metal chair? How long would he leave me there, the chill in the air nipping at my skin and causing goosebumps to emerge? He walked closer at the sound of my pleas, and the stench of bourbon lingered between us. The smell caused me to involuntary shiver even more. Bourbon. Of course it was a bourbon kind of night. He straddled me, his dirty jeans brushing against my cold skin. I trembled, dropping my face down and to the left to avoid his eyes. I saw the pocketknife glinting in his left hand.

'I bet you're sorry, you slut,' he replied, his words a burning bellow that sank into my ears, down my throat, into my core. My body tensed, waiting for the blow. But it didn't come, Richard's plans demented by an alcoholic rage.

Instead, his left hand raised in an agonizingly slow fashion, methodically poking into his target—my cheekbone. The knife burned into my flesh with its metallic bite, and I whimpered. He leaned in, his hot breath smacking into my face and drowning out any hope I had that it was almost over. I cried and implored him to stop, which I knew was a mistake. Richard loved to hear me plead with him. He lavished in my tear of desperation and terror. I was only feeding the demon within him.

'Tell me. Do I provide for you, Crys?' His words had a lilt to them, a sarcastic, chilling tone that told me his true intent.

'Y-yes,' I stammered, the knife point stabbing into my cheek. I squeezed my eyes shut now and tried to steady my shaking.

'Do I give you everything a woman could want? Do I take care of you?' His words were tenser, angrier. They slapped into me.

'Y-yes,' I repeated, not moving a muscle for fear of the knife carving deeper into my flesh, stabbing my eye, or worse.

'You're fucking right I do. I do everything for you. Because I'm a good man. I provide for you. And how do you thank me?'

I moaned. The knife stabbed a little harder. I felt a trickle of blood.

'I said how do you thank me? Huh? Do you provide me with wifely duties? Do you make me dinner or take care of your chores? Do you provide for me like a wife should a husband? No. No, Crys. No. You fucking slut around this town when my back is turned. You go whoring around wearing sinful outfits like I'm some moron.'

'Richard, please,' I cried. I didn't dare move, terrified the knife was going to end me right there. 'I didn't mean to—'

'You didn't mean to what? Be a slut? Cheat on me?'

'It was just in the house. Honest. I didn't wear it out of the house. And I'd never cheat on you. I love you.'

I pictured the red shirt with the lacey neckline. I knew when I picked it up at the consignment shop that Richard wouldn't like it. Why had I been so stupid? Why had I thought I could get away with such a sinful shirt? He was right. I should've been more modest. I wished I could go back.

'Well, you're going to learn your lesson. Aren't you?' he panted, and I could feel the knife trembling in his hand. He wasn't just pissed. He was excited. He was empowered by my fear and by the opportunity to punish me. And I was pathetically at his mercy. Always at his mercy.

A long moment passed where I feared the worst. Maybe this would really be it, I thought. Maybe he would slit my throat. Who would know? Who would miss me? His words from earlier fights, from past threats, echoed in my brain.

No one. There was no one. Richard was it. I was pathetically at his mercy.

Just as I was preparing to say goodbye to the life I'd lived, the knife clinked to the floor.

'Look at me,' he demanded. I jumped at his word.

'Fucking look at me,' he repeated, grabbing my chin and whipping my head toward him. I looked into the frenzied eyes of the man who was more fiend that human.

'Don't ever disobey me again. Don't ever disgrace me by wearing those sinful outfits. You hear me? You're mine, Crys. You're mine. I decide what you do, what you wear. It's me.'

I nodded. 'Yes, I'm sorry. I'm sorry.'

Richard released my head, and for a moment, I thought he might untie me. I thought my punishment might be over. Instead, he backed to the corner of the garage, pulling out something red. I shuddered, realizing what it was. The red shirt. He caressed it between his fingers, shaking his head.

And then, he grabbed the gasoline can from the corner of the garage and a lighter. I trembled, my body aching.

'Please,' I wanted to whisper, but the word didn't leave my lips. It was pointless, I knew. He would do what he wanted. I watched in uncontrollable terror as he tossed the shirt on the gravel in front of the garage, dumping gasoline on it.

'Wives,' he said as he held up the lighter, 'obey their husbands. Plain and simple. You'd think you'd understand that by now.' He shouted the words as if he was a pastor giving a sermon. And then, with a flick of the wrist, the shirt was on fire. For a moment, I thought he would catch, too. But he didn't. It wasn't his sin to bear.

It was mine.

I watched as the shirt turned into black smoke. I stared, naked and tied, as Richard stalked away, leaving me in the garage to stare my sin in the face.

'Father, forgive me,' I whispered into the cold emptiness of the garage, the smell of gasoline and smoke around me as

I wondered if the burning shirt was the hellfire that would finally consume me. And deep down, perhaps I'd even hoped it would be.

'GIDEON, FORGIVE ME,' I say, rocking back and forth, my hands cradling the baby that isn't there. Tears fall as I remember the warmth of the fire that day years ago, of the freezing cold of my bare skin as I waited for Richard to return. As I awaited a savior who was vile and nefarious.

He always came back, though. No matter what, he always came back. He was, whether I liked it or not, the savior who claimed my life, who led me through the world. Freedom from him is still tainted by the scars from the past, from the hold he has on me. I can dye my hair, leave the state—but he'll always be there, like the smell of smoke that clung to every fiber of my being, every hair on my head, interminably. I rock back and forth, staring out the window, thinking about how much torture I endured at his hands because—why? Why did I let it happen?

It was a question I never allowed to sneak in. I'd always done what was right, what God would want. And Mama had always told me that God wanted pious women who stood by their men. But what kind of God would approve of that? What kind of God would let such a heinous being into my life? The past week had given me the space and the strength to see it all so differently.

I shake my head at the hypocrisy of it all. How could I not see it? How did I not see what a horrid, wretched being Richard was? Why did I bow to him?

All of the scars on my body. All of the permanent marks. I was not allowed to have tattoos because they were the devil's mark—but Richard was covered in them. And, in his own way, he marked me with the mark of the devil—all the scars, the burns, the bruises. But not now. Because now, it's just me. Just me and Gideon making the rules.

We are the ones making the marks now. I chuckle at the thought, thinking about the possibilities as I reach for my glass of bourbon and thirstily drink it down.

Night Six

My arms won't move. I struggle and struggle, but the clinking of metal as my arms remain splayed sends terror through me. I slide my wrists up and down, but they won't move left to right. The cool metal cuts into them. I'm handcuffed. But it's not my bed, I realize with a start, my eyes adjusting to the blackness. The room is sterile, white, and unfamiliar. Where am I? Tears rise as a scream fills my throat.

And then I look down at my arms, bare now except for the cuffs. Up and down the arms are marks, pox marks dotting my flesh. Am I sick? I must be sick, I decide. I bite my lip to stifle the tears, but it's no use. They flood down as a burning sensation spreads through the veins in my arms. It hurts. They're on fire. They must be on fire.

But when I look back down, I see the pox flaking off. My skin is peeling off, flaking, puddles of blood oozing down my arms. It hurts. It hurts so bad. I feel stab after stab after stab, and my head feels woozy. Darkness. It's dark.

When I blink, I'm relieved that my arms are free. They don't hurt anymore, but where the skin once was, muscle and tendon and bones are the only things left. I shudder at the horror of it, taking in my surroundings.

I'm in the forest again, and the drum is beating. But this time, I stand in a patch of dirt, a circle of leaves around me. On each leave is a leathery, dried up strip of something. Prunes?

Leather? What is it? I crouch down and take a look, reach out and touch one with a wary finger.

Skin. They're pieces of skin, shredded, marked, and stained flesh.

I yank my hand back as words appear on the skin. Letters and numbers. Leviticus 19:28. I shake my head. It doesn't make sense, I think. I didn't do that. I didn't. Why me?

The forest clears, and the house is in front of me. The red haze oozes and bubbles around the house, as if cocooning it. I think I can hear the drum beating, beating, beating from inside. I shudder, but I know what I have to do. The pull of the house is too much.

I walk up the creaky steps with a confidence I don't feel. My arms are wrapped in bandages now. I reach for the doorknob. Inside, the house feels alive. It seems to be in motion, but as I look around, I don't understand why. I turn toward the door, but as if a presence notes my thoughts, it slams. I rush to it and yank on it. It doesn't open. Panicking, feeling claustrophobic, I stumble toward the windows. I try to open them, but they scald my hands, the sills and glass burning hot. So hot. Everything is hot.

That's when I notice it. My feet. They're sticking in something, almost like glue. I look down. A beet red, oozing substance swirls around my feet. It's flooding in. Where's it coming from? It looks like it's coming from the door in the kitchen. That makes no sense. But the blood rises like floodwaters, to my ankles, to my knees, to my chest. The whole house is a swirling pool of blood, and I cry out, aching with the thought it will soon suffocate me. It's hot and sticky. I want out of here. I need out of here. I pound on the window, screaming, yelling. I'm going to drown. I'm drowning.

But as I look out the window into the distance, a figure appears. A savior. A helper. My heart swells as the blood flows up to my chin.

The figure moves closer. My heart sinks. It isn't a savior or a helper.

It's something else entirely.

Chapter Twenty-Four

Heart racing, I jolt upright. I reach for the lamp beside the bed, needing light in the ever-growing darkness. My eyes land on the nightstand, the glass from a few days ago still in its spot cradling its gory treasure. The Bible sits right beside it. I grab the holy book from the side of the bed. I find the page that Richard quoted to me so often, about wives obeying their husbands.

I yank the page out, shredding it with my teeth. I spit it onto the ground.

I flip in the good book to Proverbs 31:25 where my new bookmark sits. It's a quote I read but didn't understand—until now.

She is clothed with strength and dignity and she laughs without fear of the future.

Strength and dignity. I've reclaimed them both, I realize, my fingers savoring the feel of the bookmark that I've placed in the Bible. It's a bit limp but effective. I stick it back in the page, my new favorite page. I close the book, and it sticks shut.

Strength and dignity—but am I truly fearless? I close my eyes, trying to imagine that beach, the wind in my hair, the scent of the salty air. I could be there now. I could have left when I had the chance, taken the cash and left, believing that God would make it work.

As badly as I want to be standing on the sand, a new future ahead of me, I don't regret my choices. There's a peace in me from what I've done. Freedom can't always equate to the feelings that retribution, that setting things right, can bring.

I've made my mark now. Richard's marks are almost gone. All is well. All is right. I think I hear screams in the distance, but I shake my head. Gideon's not screaming. No. He can't be. He can't. It's in my imagination. He's okay now. Gideon's where he should be. I roll onto my side after tugging on the lamp cord. I wipe my hand on his pillowcase, and then I drift back into a peaceful sleep.

No more nightmares come. Instead, I dream of Gideon's face smiling at me as he builds the sandcastle. Sweet, sweet Gideon.

You're welcome.

Chapter Twenty-Five

My hand freezes in the sudsy water, clinging to the dish as the warmth slaps over my arm. Heart constricting, I steady myself with the other hand on the edge of the sink.

Gravel crunching. A motor running. The car cruising up the driveway.

Is it just my imagination, or is he driving faster than last time? Is this it, is this when it all comes crashing?

Just breathe, I tell myself, but it's no use because I suddenly don't remember how.

Legs trembling, I let the dish sink underneath the water and grab a hand towel, hurriedly drying my hands as Sheriff Barkley parks the car in Richard's typical spot. My eyes fall on the rug in the living room. The tassels are straightened, the bleachy smell of cleanness assaulting my nose. Still, even I can detect the subtle hint of the off-putting odor. This is no good. No good at all. I rush to the door, painting on my best poker face. I screech open the door, stepping onto the porch hastily. I know I look anxious. But any wife whose husband was missing would be, right? *Just breathe. Don't think about it.*

'Sheriff Barkley, did you find something?' I call into the gentle breeze as he adjusts the brim of his hat and ambles toward me. His face his drawn, and there is no warm smile, no kind eyes. Just a serious man about to deliver some news. My heart constricts again. The moment is here.

'Mrs. Connor, we need to have a discussion. I thought it would be easier for me to come to you rather than making you come to the station.'

I keep my face complacent. 'What is it?'

'He stares at the door, as if asking for me to invite him in. I don't budge, acting like it would be an imposition.

'What can you tell me about Richard's garage and his business dealings?' he asks, point blank. I want to breathe a sigh of relief, but instead, I stare at him quizzically.

'The garage does all right, I suppose. Richard doesn't really talk much about it. Seems busy enough. It keeps food on the table with the support from the state, of course. Why?'

Sheriff Barkley pulls a photograph out of his pocket.

'Did you happen to see this car here a few weeks ago, by any chance, Mrs. Connor? I need you to be honest.'

I glance at the silver car, squinting. I do remember the car being here, sometime before Gideon was born. I remember seeing it in the driveway. I nod slowly.

'And did Richard say anything else about it? About the work to be done on it?'

'Sheriff, I don't understand. Richard's missing. What does this car have to do with it?'

Sheriff Barkley doesn't change his emotion. He's an expert at his poker face. 'Well, as you know, I've been doing some investigating, which means I've been digging into some of Richard's customers, some clientele. Some sources have been willing to share with me some theories about your husband's garage and what's happening there. Do you know what a chop shop is, Mrs. Connor?'

I shrug noncommittally. 'A bit. I've heard of it. But as I said, Richard doesn't involve me in the business.'

Sheriff Barkley nods, turning his attention to the garage. 'Well, it appears that Cody and Richard have allegedly been running an operation for quite some time. But apparently, Richard has been doing some side deals of his own, handling some bigger acquisitions and not being so forthcoming with clients. I think it may have something to do with his disappearance.'

I tap my foot, staring off into the distance as if considering the possibility. I think about the wad of cash under the floorboard, next to my hair dye. My sanctuary money. I feel heat rising in my cheeks, as if Sheriff Barkley is a walking lie detector test or a telepathic who can read my mind. I remind myself to calm down, to not give it away. He doesn't know about the money. Right?

After a long moment of silence, I shake my head. 'I feel like such an idiot,' I murmur, tears welling. 'How could I be so stupid to think Richard was really supporting us fixing brakes and engines?' The sentiment is true. I do feel idiotic to not have realized that Richard's business was less than savory, and that even without him disappearing, it was probably on the verge of crumbling.

I look back to Sheriff Barkley. His poker face cracks. The kindness is back. The pitying look for the weak, stupid, mindless Crystal is back. He softens his expression.

'I'm sure Richard is very private about his work. For good reason. He's involved in some serious stuff. There are some major accusations being thrown at him that could lead to serious charges.'

'Do you think this has something to do with why he disappeared? Do you think someone could have taken him? Or do you think maybe he knew he was about to get caught?' I ask, carefully placed terror cracking in my voice, thinking about how perfect either scenario could be. I can feel the sunshine on my face, can almost taste the salty air.

'I think it's a distinct possibility. Look, Mrs. Connor, if I'm going to crack this case and find your husband, I need to get more proof.'

'Okay,' I murmur, fear now creeping into my voice for real. Richard, Richard, what mess have you entrapped me in now? How will I solve this? Standing at the sink, I thought it was all over. Now, though, I realize I'm not ready. I'm not prepared to throw in the towel.

'I need to do a search, look for clues.'

'You can't. Not without a search warrant,' I reply. As soon as the words are out, I regret them. I see suspicion building in his eyes. I look guilty as hell. But I can't have him searching, snooping. I'm not ready. Not yet. I have to keep Gideon safe. That's my priority.

'You're right. I can't. But we know each other. Don't we? You trust me, don't you?'

I stare back at him, and we study each other. Neither one of us wants to show our hand.

'We have the same goals, Crystal. To keep you safe. To figure out what's going on with Richard. Isn't that what we both want?'

'Of course,' I reply robotically.

'I need to solve this to keep you safe. So I can leave here and get a search warrant, turn the house and the garage upside down all night. Or you can let me do a more thorough search of the garage, where I suspect I'll find what I need. It's up to you.'

I stare at the man who has now played his hand. What to do? What to do? Richard would be furious at me for letting him into the garage, especially if what Sheriff Barkley is saying is true. It could condemn him. Not that he doesn't deserve it. And if I don't let him search the garage—what's next? If I let him into the house, I'm done. It's all finished. I can't risk it. I have to keep Gideon safe.

'Follow me,' I murmur, leading Sheriff Barkley away from the porch and toward the garage, praying it'll be enough to pacify him, to buy me more time.

I still have work to do, after all. I'm not quite finished, and Gideon still needs me.

THE LEDGERS AND PAPERWORK in an evidence bag, Sheriff Barkley stands in the threshold. After tearing the garage apart, Sheriff Barkley found the proof he apparently needed tucked away in a bottom desk drawer in the makeshift office. I stand nearby. My arms are crossed as I study the spot where the hammer and the specks of blood once were. My hands tremble. Did I miss something? Did I clean well enough?

'Crystal, listen to me. I know you're a good woman. I do,' Sheriff Barkley says.

I avert my eyes to the ground. This may be debatable, even if he doesn't realize it. I scratch my arm absentmindedly, listening to Henry's barks.

'I don't want you getting wrapped up in something, going down for something with Richard's fingerprints all over it. I need you to cooperate with us, okay, Crystal? Can you do that?'

I look up into the kind eyes of the sheriff, a man I hardly know who has been kinder to me than any man. I don't deserve his kindness. I hate that at some point, probably in the near future, those kind eyes will look at me with a new realization that I'm tainted, that I'm not who he thinks I am. For now, I relish in that look. For now, I'm still Crystal Connor the innocent in his eyes. A naïve part of me wishes I could stay that way forever.

'Of course,' I reply, my voice wavering.

'Crystal, this is all crashing down. It's going to fall onto Richard. Keep your hands clean. I would hate to see a sweet woman like you suffer for his behavior. And I would also hate to see you get hurt. Desperate men do desperate things. You need to be careful.'

I nod.

'I have some paperwork to do. Some leads to look into. We're going to find Richard, and when we do, he's going to be in a lot of trouble. I want to find him before he comes back here. I think he's going to feel the walls closing in around him, which makes him dangerous. Please be careful, and please call me if you find anything that might be of help.'

I blink, staring at him. In his eyes, I see a man trying to protect me. A good man. Nothing like Richard. However, as Sheriff Barkley pulls away with the paperwork and a suspicion that the chop shop theory will lead him to Richard, I stare in disbelief.

Sometimes even the good men get it so, so wrong. And sometimes the weak aren't the ones who need protected the most.

Chapter Twenty-Six

I stroke the dog's grimy fur, stiff and dull, as he devours the food in his bowl. He could be so good, I think. A different family, a different piece of dirt to call his home. A different life.

Things could be so different.

My fingers absentmindedly grab his fur as my mind wanders, thinking about all that should be different. Thinking about all that *is* different. Nevertheless, there's little solace in this. The nightmares don't just haunt my sleep, after all.

The crunching of gravel under tires startles me out of my demented memories and turmoil. Fear settles with the dust, but it's dulled somehow. Terror is exhausting. My weary soul struggles to break free.

Beneath my sore fingers, Henry's hair spikes to attention between his shoulder blades. A low growl resonates as the car comes to a halt nearby. It takes a moment for recognition to dawn on me, the car unfamiliar—but when the lanky man gets out of the car, his face partially blocked by stubble and a ball cap, my stomach sinks. I could identify that walk, that gait anywhere. I know the way he swings the crowbar, the way his chin juts out.

But one thing I don't know, one fear that startles my soul awake is this: does he know the truth about what I've done?

FROZEN AND STOIC, I stand up straighter, clasping my fingers to steady the trembling that's rocking my body. The black crowbar swings cockily as he nears me.

Despite his poised gait, he looks haggard somehow. It's more than the stubble on his chin. It's the torn shirt, the discernible bruising on both eyes. Cuts and scrapes mar his face in spots, and the exposed flesh on his arms is raw.

Henry snarls, jumping wildly on the end of the rope. His enormous paws stomp into the ground, all of his hair on his back now outstretched in a display of aggression. I step aside to avoid being ensnared by the whipping rope and the dog.

'Where the fuck is it?' Cody yells, his voice edgy and inconsistent.

'W-what?' I stammer. There's an untamable surge that gleams in his gaze at my word. He is a man undone, a man seeking something. I don't think he cares what it costs him at this point—which is even more dangerous than the usual Connor behavior.

'Don't play with me. After all that's happened, don't play with me, bitch. Where is it? Where's the goddamn money? I know it's here.'

'I don't know,' I lie, thinking of the money tucked safely away, waiting for me when I'm ready to use it—which will be soon. Very soon. It has to be soon.

I step backward, hands still up, as Cody inches forward. Henry snaps at him. Cody huffs and sneers at the dog, then at me.

'I've just spent days and days answering for Richard and the missing money. Death threats, torture, you name it because that bastard didn't follow the plan. He didn't deliver what he was supposed to, trying to skim money off the top. And now he's missing, and I'm the one dealing with his mess. I'm not playing anymore. Give me the damn money. I know you know where it is.'

'Cody, please. I don't know what Richard's done, but I'm not a part of it. I don't know anything about money. I don't. But Sheriff Barkley was here, and he searched the garage.'

'You think I'm going to believe you, you lying slut? You're covering for him, aren't you? This whole innocent act is the perfect cover. He's too much of a pussy to face to the truth, to deal with the mess he's made of this whole thing. Stealing a few cars here and there isn't a big deal. But he's messed with the wrong people now, and he's taken it to the big leagues. He fucked over our supplier, big time. Kept a bigger cut than he should've, and now they're after me. Where is he? Where are you fucking hiding him?'

Cody lunges closer, but Henry goes insane on his rope, causing Cody to second-guess his moves.

'He's not here. I've told you. I haven't seen him. I'm actually very worried.' I sob now, praying he'll buy into my words and leave. I can't deal with this complication, not when I'm so close to being finished, to getting away with it all.

Cody snarls, his face looking similar to the growling dog beside me. 'Where is he, Crystal? Huh? Is he in the house fucking hiding? Has he been there this whole time? Is this asshole stowed away letting me clean up his mess, just like when we were young?'

Cody turns, heading toward the house. I rush after him, my legs moving faster. My need to stop him is stronger than my desire for self-preservation, than my ability to reason.

'No,' I shriek, but he turns on me. The rage within him explodes, and he tackles me to the ground. He is on me, my back slamming against the damp earth in a familiarly painful way. The crowbar against my throat in a familial show of strength, he presses the air out of my chest, the scream out of my mouth.

He is the complementary branch of Richard's family tree, for sure. I choke and struggle and gasp, the well-known flirt with death once more a part of me. This time, though, there are no stars or fireflies to welcome me. And Gideon is far away now. This time, my soul is also unclean. So unclean.

But I'm getting ready to say goodbye, nonetheless.

Will he get what he deserves, in its entirety?

Will he be found?

Will he return?

What will become of Richard when I'm gone?

The questions rattle in my dying brain when suddenly, the snapping sound echoes through the forest and the train comes barreling at me.

Chapter Twenty-Seven

The screams aren't my own.

They are of a guttural, raspy variety that do not come from my lips. When the shock disintegrates and my breathing comes in waves, this is the concept that rattles me the most: the screams aren't mine. My lungs ache, burning with the need for oxygen.

I'm breathing.

I'm not screaming.

I'm okay.

Tears fall as I heave in air over and over, choking on dust and oxygen as the shrieks and cries reverberate. They sound out over the vicious growls, over the scuffling and the pleading whimpers.

I scurry backward now, watching in horror as a new power is asserted. The broken rope still loosely attached to his collar, Henry surrounds his target, lunging at his prey. It's an easy catch for him, the scrawny man no competition for the muscular, powerful machine of a dog. Blood pools and spills as the ripping of flesh sounds. Specks of the red liquid fly and scatter haphazardly, some landing in Henry's grimy fur. I watch in awe as my mastiff makes quick work of Cody. I watch until the screams subside. I watch as Henry devours flesh and meat, a hunger I've helped create for him. I don't know how long I sit there, stunned, watching nonetheless. I can't stop watching.

But eventually, after a long while, I rise up. *There is cleaning to be done,* I think with a start, stretching my legs and wiping my hands on my apron. There is so much cleaning to be done, and I'm an expert at it.

I AM STILL WEAKENED from the scuffle and trauma. Cody is small, scrawny compared to Richard. Nonetheless, dragging his mangled corpse is no small task. Nor will cleaning the blood be easy. If he comes now, I'm finished.

Breathe. Don't think about it, I command myself. *Just keep focused on the task at hand.*

Henry is gone now, the bloodied dog having taken off for the forest at the sight of freedom. I don't know if he'll come back. I hope he doesn't. I'm happy for him. I wish him a new life where he is his own master—because that, I've come to realize, is what makes a life truly filled with luck: freedom. Freedom is the true master. Not money or power or domination. Not fancy cars or big houses or beauty. It's the freedom to go as you wish, to choose your own life.

Freedom is the real god to be worshipped, praised, and kept holy in this world. How has it taken me so long to see it? It could be too late now for me, but perhaps Henry can flourish on his own.

The sight of Cody doesn't sicken me, another sign that so much has changed. I'm stronger now. In fact, I'm intrigued. I see the marks and mauled flesh, and I take it in. I imprint it in my mind, wanting to remember just how his skin flaps and the look on Cody's deadened face. I smile as his limp feet clink up the porch steps, dragging behind him as I grab him under the armpits and yank him to the screen door. It's hard work, and sweat pours from my forehead, but it feels good to be strong. The blood trail on the porch and on the kitchen floor angers me as I drag his body. So messy. This will take a lot of meticulous scrubbing, and I'm so tired. Do I have enough bleach left? I'll really have to put my muscle into it, and I don't want to, not for Cody. I need to keep Gideon safe and clean. I don't have time to tend to this nuisance. Still, adrenaline pumping through my veins, I'm energized. I ignore my throbbing arms and pull him onward.

When I reach the door in the kitchen's corner, my fingers reverently touch the brass knob. It's cold to the touch unlike in my nightmare. I yank it open, reveling in how it screeches on its unoiled hinge. Richard really should've oiled that. I take one more look at Cody, smirking at the fear-inducing grimace and the bloodied wounds. He is a messy sight, indeed.

Then, dragging him closer, I give him a swift kick down the basement stairs, rolling him and shoving him. His body flails in a bewildered heap until finally he is at the bottom of the basement stairs. I follow behind him. Sliding him and yanking him, I pull him to the back corner. Sweat pours down from the effort. I'm soaked through with blood and sweat. But there are no tears. I don't have tears to cry, not for him. It's worth the effort, though, I realize once I've succeeded.

After all, I want his body to make an impact. I want his death to be appreciated. Most of all, I want him to know that when the mighty fall, it's in a big, ugly way.

And oh, how they've fallen. Smirking, I turn from the gory sight to wipe my hands of it. I creep back upstairs to face the next burdensome task. But I'm good at cleaning. So good. Richard, Mama, Daddy—they taught me well. So well.

Chapter Twenty-Eight

It isn't until much later that the reality of what's happened sinks in. The blood cleaned, the red trails scoured away, I sit in the bed where this swirling spiral of decay began. Only then does my mind traipse backward, to other bloody sights, to other horrifying images.

I think back to that day when everything changed, that day not so long ago. It was supposed to be a hopeful day, a day to rectify what remained of my life. Instead, it had been the day that incited the beginning of the maniacal end.

All good things come to an end—but what about the bad? The depraved? Do things of malice also come to a finale, or do they just continue on their merry way, torturing the downtrodden, the damned? I don't know anymore. I don't know anything at all. Maybe I never did.

I rock myself in the dusky room, the sunlight filtering through the blinds as dusk settles on the horizon. It's too early for bed, but I'm exhausted. The day's been a grueling one, and I need rest. The splatters of blood on my T-shirt beg for me to change, but I'm too tired. How do you even get blood out of fabric? How will I clean up this mess?

My eyes are heavy with exhaustion, the turmoil of the past week plaguing me. Has it only been a week? Only seven days since the Crystal Connor I once knew transformed into a being I hardly recognize? Has it only been a week since the sins of my soul burned in anguish, filling me with a regret I can never reconcile for?

The Bible sits on the nightstand in its familiar spot, opened to the last page I read. The bookmark rests against the splayed pages, a visual reminder of all I've messed up. It may as well be a sign from God—I'm doomed.

I hit my head against the wall, terrified to fall asleep. I *can't* fall asleep. I know what's coming if I give in, and I'm not strong enough tonight to let that happen.

Tears fall. I rock back and forth like I have so many times. If I close my eyes, I can feel the weight of him in my arms, see those chubby cheeks, and remember what it was like to clutch him to my chest. I wish I could hold him once more.

And then, I hear it. My eyes bolt open, my heart surging with disbelief. It can't be. There's no way. But yes, as I silence my breathing and will my pounding heart to be quiet, I'm sure I hear it. Faintly, in the distance, I hear the sounds of muffled cries, of screams, of him needing me.

I take a deep breath, maybe the first one in ages. The cries I've craved resonate through the house like a welcome melody. It isn't too late. He *is* crying. My heart leaps to hear the sound I'd so desperately wanted to hear all this time. I rest my head against the wall, feeling like maybe all will be okay. I sit, listening to the cries, the sound calming my soul instead of grating on my nerves. I'm so happy to hear his shrieks.

After a few moments, I'm not tired anymore. I stand from the bed, clutching at the locket around my neck, the familiar piece of soft hair inside. I don't have to open it to know it's there. I can feel him close to me. It soothes me to know he's close, even after all that's transpired. I cross the floor and peer out the window, studying the tree line I've seen so many times. At first, I couldn't look out there. The memories were too real, the scene too fresh. But things are different now. I'm different. In many ways, I feel at peace.

Everything is just as it should be. Everyone is right where they should be. And he is safe. I've ensured that. I've done all I can for him. We're all fulfilling our purpose. There was a time not long ago when I wasn't sure I'd get the chance to live out mine, to see mine through. But now, I feel like maybe I just didn't understand what he had in store for me. Maybe I was just blinding myself to the truth I couldn't bear to accept. I had a different purpose, a different role to live all along. I hate that it took this tragedy to understand that, but I guess the Lord really does work in mysterious ways.

I glance out into the fading light, perusing the tree line. The darkness of the forest is macabre in a way that's familiar but eerily unsettling. I'm okay with it, though. I've come to learn that life is sometimes meant to be uncomfortable.

But just as the cries are quieting and the silence of the house pervades again, I catch a glimpse of something that sends icy, sheer terror through my heart. The peace that reverberated within is now shattered, an icy chill spreading like a virus in my veins.

'No. No. No,' I plead, shaking my head. My fingers clench into fists, trembling.

I put a hand on the window, unfurling my fingers with great effort. My trembling digits feel the grimy window. I should really be embarrassed about the thick layer of dirt.

How long it's been since I've washed the window. Despite my fear, I can't help but wince at the grime, the scratchy filth irritating my fingertips. It's like I believe touching the chilled, defiled glass will snap me back to reality. It will save me from what I saw. Certainly it wasn't. It couldn't be.

Suddenly, like a sign, it appears again, right in the tree line, an angry, vicious sight that sends terror pulsing through every single one of my limbs.

I bite my lip so hard I'm pretty sure it's bleeding. I devote my energy to steadying my breathing as I try to look away, but I can't. My gaze is glued on the spectacularly petrifying sight before me. I know what that means. I know that he's almost here.

And I know that I am, in fact, doomed in every way imaginable.

For out in the distance, it stands, confident and cocky in its glare. I know for sure the glowing eyes are staring at me.

The goat. It's back, standing watch, right in the spot where dear Gideon was. How is it back? It feels like a lifetime ago when I saw it. Where did it go, and why is it back now? I must be imagining it. Tears fall, and I shake my head. Squeezing my eyes shut, I try to make it disappear. Please, God, make it disappear.

'No,' I exclaim. 'No, please no.'

But it's too late. It's too late for me. And maybe it's too late for Gideon. Maybe I've doomed us both. Maybe I'm not mother material after all—and maybe I'm not the good daughter I once thought I was. Maybe, just maybe, it's all gone too far.

I cry myself to sleep, knowing peaceful dreams won't come.

Knowing what dreams will plague me—but not strong enough to fight against them, even if I want to.

Night Seven

'Hello?' I mutter, clutching my arms against my chest as I wander about the dusty lane. My feet are so cold, and I have goosebumps all over me. I'm naked and alone, staring up at a moonless sky. The stars are tiny specks, but they don't illuminate my path. I'm lost, but there are no trees this time. There is only the dusty path and blackness.

'Hello?' I murmur again, not sure who I'm talking to. I look down and notice long black hair cascading down my shoulders. My stomach churns. This isn't my hair. Whose hair is this? It's not mine. I shake my head. Something's wrong. Who am I?

I pick up my pace now, running, running toward my destination. I feel a pull, even in the darkness, toward something. I run on and on, my breath barely coming, my body still chilled. My bones ache, throbbing from the effort. I feel like I've been hit by a bus, but I run forward.

I make it through the red haze, but it's thicker now. It's like a thick fog settled over the scene. I'm scared to breathe, afraid the redness will seep into my lungs, will choke me from the inside out. I can barely see in front of me, the air so thick, I can feel it weighing on me.

A drum beats in the distance, a ricocheting, steady beat. It seems to get closer and closer and closer. I cover my chest with *my arms, still aware of my nakedness. And then the fog lifts, whirling up in a cacophony of sound. When it's gone, I blink.*

In front of me, a body lies in a pool of blood. Who is it? I wonder, shaking my head. Who is here? I wander toward the body, startled and confused. Did I do this? Is this my fault? Who is it? Questions whirl, muddling my brain. I lean toward the body, needing to see the face. But before I can reach the person in a dire state of death, I am pummeled to the ground, something furry slamming into me.

I lay on the ground, naked and terrified, but screams won't come. They never come, my voice silenced by this murky world.

It stands on my chest, biting at me, a low growl that is unnatural. The black goat takes chunks out of my skin. Fear surges through my body as blood seeps. But then a louder growl resonates, and the goat runs off. Henry comes dashing from the forest, standing on the body to my left. I turn and see the dog, covered in blood. The goat is gone, the goliath dog in its place. Will he claim me next?

For a moment, we lock eyes, and I know I am safe. Run free, boy, *I think, willing him to safety. I desperately want him to be safe and free, more than I've ever wanted anything. He does, and for a moment, I look up at the now starless sky, a hint of red floating above me like a cloud.*

I blink, and I am now standing in the middle of the house, the one that is familiar yet so different. The bloody, mangled body from outside stands upright now, propped against the wall.

Cody's eyes are missing, and his throat is chewed out. A greenish slime drips from his face, and I shake my head as I vomit. He's dead. I killed him. I did this, I realize. I'm at fault.

The basement door creeks open, as if in invitation. I know what I must do. I walk across the room, my skin warm now. I'm no longer freezing, and the goosebumps are gone. The long, black hair is gone too. I recognize myself. I feel more like me, like Crystal. I take his arm and drag him toward the door, but my skin begins to burn as I touch him. Tears fall, my flesh singeing and melting and disintegrating. I struggle and strain, getting Cody to the basement door. But just as I'm about to push him down, his face morphs.

It isn't Cody.

It's Richard.

I jump back, startled, as his mouth twitches. I kick him down the steps, his body tumbling and tumbling and tumbling for what feels like an eternity. I shut the door, leaning my back against it as I crumple to the wall, feeling a sense of relief. It's okay. He's gone now. He's away. I can forget about it. But something sticky touches my backside, my legs, my hands that are on the floor. It feels like warm paint that's congealed in the sun. I pick up my hands.

Red. Red everywhere, all around. It puddles and pools, oozing from under the door. I scuttle away and scurry toward the center of the kitchen. But it's no use.

Red fills the kitchen, dripping, dripping from under the doorway, flowing in like a river. I cry out and hurry to the door to the outside. It's locked. I pull on the doorknob. I can't get out. The blood works its way up, to my knees, to my hip, to my chest. I'm going to drown. I'm going to drown. *I make my way to the window in the kitchen, pounding on it. I try to yell for help, but no words come out. And just as the blood gets to my chin, a figure appears in the window.*

It's him. He's come.

But he's too late, I realize, as blood gurgles in my throat and I sputter and cough.

It's all my fault. He's too late. Just breathe. Just...

Chapter Twenty-Nine

Blackness promises to drown me as I shove my way through the trees. A branch scratches my bare legs as my dress hikes up. Blood stains the delicate fabric, but I don't have time to care. I needed out of that room, away from that dream. I needed away from the blood that threatened to choke me. I needed away from that vision of him in the window, standing there. I need to take care of this before I can't.

Twigs continue to assault me as I make my way to the spot. I shudder at the possibility the goat or Henry will be here, just like in my nightmare. I worry that maybe they haunt this sacred spot. I shake my head, though. This is no nightmare. None of them have been nightmares, in honesty.

This is real life. It's all my life.

I'm here. Mama's here, Gideon. I'm here, just like I should've been on that very first night when Richard tossed you into the forest like a meaningless sack of rubbish. I'm finally here.

I should have held him that night he was born, rocked him in my arms. I should have cradled his lifeless body and shown him he was loved, that he mattered. I should've never let him out of my arms. I should have rocked him and rocked him and rocked him.

I feel the need to pray, to be absolved, but it's been years since I've set foot in the little church in town. Richard never liked me going there. He always said I could pray at home, that the women in the church would put ideas in my head. Besides, I don't feel I could show my face now. This is the closest to a sacred spot I could get. This is as close to a confessional as I feel comfortable. I find the spot etched in my mind, the specific spot that cradled Gideon's head. It's a simplistic patch of dirt. I sink to my knees, the night air swirling around me and chilling me as I lay in the grime, right where Gideon was. I think about his bluish body discarded here, laying here for days, waiting for me to come. I should've come right away. I hate that it took me so long to rise up.

Trash.

Richard's biting word rings in my head. I shove the beast's word aside, rubbing my face on the ground. He wasn't trash. He wasn't. He isn't.

Tears flow as I think about the nightmares that are more than just fantastical relics of a processing mind. They are the dark realities of who I've become. Deserved or not, these reminders of my motherly love are also symbols of a soul gone black.

If Richard hadn't thrown Gideon here, right here, would things have been different?

I don't know. But in some ways, I do. In some ways I know that it was the final moment that shoved me to become who I should've been long ago, who I perhaps always wanted to be deep down. The thought sends a chill through me. I shudder. It's not easy baring your soul, but it's even harder to face up to the fact that maybe it was never as pure as you thought. I heave in the dirty air as I think about all that's happened. My mind flashes through the images, through the torturous moments. It's like I'm watching someone else's life, but I gasp as realizations settle in.

It was me. It was me. It was all me.

I gasp and choke, my hands shaking. These hands that once trembled with fear and fragility now quake with an insidious power they don't know how to handle.

I'm sorry. God, I'm sorry. I'm sorry.

I rock back and forth, shaking, trying to shut out the bloody scenes. Trying to mitigate my blood-stained hands and assuage myself of the rising guilt and damnation.

It was for him, I remind myself. I did it for Gideon, to get retribution for him. I did what needed to be done. Gideon. Sweet Gideon. I'm sorry. I failed you. I didn't come soon enough. But you're safe now. I did the right thing. It was all for you. You're forever safe now.

Safe. Safe and sound.

I lean up on my elbows and then sink back onto the heels of my feet as I peruse the spot. He's not here. Gideon's not here, I remember with a sober grin. It eases the guilt and nullifies the bloody images. I remember once more why it had to come to this. I remember those choking hands, those threats, that clinking body banging off the bed. I remember his cutting words about our angel. I remember him tossing Gideon here, right here. It was good that I came out here. It gave me a faith and memory stronger than any church pews could. I grip the dirt with my fingers, digging in, remembering. Reliving.

No matter what happens to me now, I've done the right thing. The dirt's reminded me. This spot has helped me strengthen my resolve. It was messy. It was hard. But it was the right thing. I nod, wiping at the tears.

My work is done. It's done now. The blood is almost wiped clean.

It's time to make my escape, to make a clean break. But the thought of leaving my baby forever, it's terrifying. Daunting. Am I strong enough to do it?

Or should I take another way out? What's right? What's wrong? Who's really to say?

I swipe at my tears, deciding that I need to make my own path. I've got my retribution. I've set things right.

It's time for Gideon and me to leave this place, to never look back. I decide to head inside, to pack my suitcase and dye my hair—and then to head for the new life Gideon and I deserve.

Mama's coming, Gideon. Mama's coming at last.

Chapter Thirty

D aisies.
    A bundle of daisies, freshly plucked, sat in a crude excuse for a vase on the table. I leaned down after coming in from hanging the laundry, sniffing the vase of daisies. They were my favorite. I'd told him that on the night we'd first met.

He remembered.

I snatched one of the daisies from the vase, feeling the silky, fresh petals between my thumb and forefinger. I breathed in, just breathed in, smelling the scent of the flower. Of life. Of my life.

Wandering to the window in the kitchen, I peered out. Richard came walking toward the porch, up the stairs. His shirt was grease-stained, his jeans torn. He ruffled his hair with his dirty hand, leaving a mark on his stubbled cheek. He stopped and peered in the window, smiling.

'Hey,' he said once he was inside the door.

'Hey,' I murmured back, the morning sunshine casting a backdrop to the scene that was memorable, serene. He walked across the kitchen, kissing my cheek.

'I'm sorry,' he murmured, kissing my neck, pressing his forehead against mine when he was finished.

I squeezed mine shut, nodding. I willed my hands not to automatically touch the cigarette burns on my chest, the scars of what he'd done last night.

'I just . . . the bourbon . . .' he offered.

I peered into his eyes, seeing a softness behind them. Last night there had only been ugliness. Pain. Anger. Now, there was a sweetness, a concern. Somehow, his harsh words, the bruises last night, the searing flesh under his sadistic sneer—they melted away. They made this softness stronger.

'I love you. I just lost my temper. I'm scared, Crystal. I know I have to take care of you,' he murmured, his hand finding my belly. 'But when the baby comes, it'll be different. We'll be a family, and I'll be better. I will,' he assured.

The bruise on my arm, on my chest, faded. It was going to be okay. He was different. He wasn't Daddy after all. He just needed time to learn how to be a good husband. And he needed this baby to help him figure out his purpose. This baby would help us both find our place, find happiness. We could still salvage some kind of joy.

Sure, he had his moments. Even in the years since we'd been married, I'd realized life with Richard would be volatile, not unlike my upbringing. But there was hope. My hand found my belly now, too. There would be hope in this baby. Our lives would be different. My baby would have a chance to make something of himself or herself. He or she would grow up loved. I would make sure of it.

And maybe with time, this softness in Richard's eyes would take over. Maybe this small life growing inside of me would be the answer. Maybe I could make him be good. I could stand by him and help him. Richard tucked the daisy behind my ear, kissing the tip of my nose.

And in that moment, I remembered. It really was my job to help him be better, to be good. I had to help him. God wanted me to help him. I could do that. I could live out that purpose.

'I love you,' *I whispered to him as he turned and walked out.*

It'll be okay, *I promised myself once he was gone. I put the daisy back in the vase, submerged the bottom of the stem in the water. We'll be okay. He's a good man deep down. I can make him be a good man. If I just work hard enough at it.*

God, let us be good.

Chapter Thirty-One

Scarlet. Scarlet Gideon.

That's who I'll be now. That's how I'll take a piece of him with me. That, and the hair in the locket, I realize as I touch the necklace resting on my chest.

I return my fingers to their task, playing with the rug that's beneath my cheek. I roll the threads of the single tassel forward and backward between my sore thumb and forefinger. Back and forth, back and forth, as my cheek rests on the gritty texture. My eyes are close to the tassel, and I spend time watching it roll back and forth, thinking about all of the moments and memories and things that will never be.

My suitcase sits at the door, the money from Richard's illegal dealings tucked carefully in the front. I have a map and an address to get me to the women's shelter in South Carolina. I've finished everything I needed to. Now it's time. While I still have a chance to make a run for it.

But I've realized I can't take Gideon with me, not completely. And that's a hard thing to come to terms with.

It wasn't supposed to be like this. *I wasn't supposed to be like this,* I think, tears falling as I stroke the floor. I see the rocking chair out of my peripheral vision, the one where I would have spent hours rocking my baby. Now it will sit empty forever, guarding a baby who never really could be.

I love you, Gideon. I love you.

It's the phrase that plays over and over in my mind, whirling about like a carousel that's been left to its own whims. I think about all that's been lost. I think about how sweet my angel was. Is. Will always be.

I stroke the rug as if I'm stroking his warm cheek. I breath in, closing my eyes as I think about baby powder and sweet, milky cheeks and the scent of his lavender hair. I don't know how long I stay on the floor, but darkness falls outside and soon, I sense the solitude of the darkness. I need to go. I need to say goodbye. It's just so hard to rip myself away. I feel like my heart is glued underneath the floorboard, like a piece of my soul is there.

I should go check on him. I should go dry his tears. That would be the merciful thing to do. He must be scared. But I don't. I shake my head. I need to be with Gideon, here, right here. I can't leave him. I won't make that mistake again.

Never again.

My back aching, I carefully lift myself from my spot.

'I'm never going to stop loving you,' I assure the sweet child, my legs creaking as I carry my deadened legs to the rocking chair. I plop down, resting my weary feet. I clasp my arms around the child, the memory of him. I rock him, back and forth, singing the lullaby I never got to sing.

Over and over I sing the words, never quite ready for it to be the last time. I'm pretty sure I hear screams, but they are weakened whimpers and easy to ignore. It'll all be over soon, I realize. I need to spend a few moments here. I need to savor these moments, these last moments.

I did what I could. I tried to protect you, Gideon. I tried to make this place safe for you. I did my best. I really did. Mama would do anything for you. And I did. Oh, I did.

Just breathe. Don't think about it. This is not the time to feel guilty. This is a time to savor, to enjoy, to relish in the feel of him so close. Otherwise, it was all for naught. I can't let everything be for naught.

I rock and rock, my mind going blank. I'm thankful. My mind hasn't been empty for days. I rock and rock and rock and rock in the darkness. I feel his warmth against my chest. I feel his cheek against mine. I love you.

And then, a knock. A yelling at the door. A command.

I clasp my arms to my chest.

'He's here, Gideon. He's come back.'

I stare at the suitcase. Could I make a run for it? My heart beats wildly. I could grab my suitcase and run for it.

But I can't put Gideon down. I can't. My arms continue cradling him.

And I know that the time has truly come. I can't say goodbye. The sea water evaporates, the sunshine turning to gray clouds. The warmth becomes icy, and the only grittiness underneath my toes comes from the dirty floor.

It's time to pay. He's shown up at last. He's here, just as I always knew he would be eventually. I surrender to the inescapable truth, resting my head back as I succumb to the darkness within, as he kicks in the door, and as he steps in front of me, weapon drawn.

I look up at Sheriff Barkley, a formidable force frightened and shaken. I've known since the beginning it was only a matter of time until he came, until he showed up. I knew he would come. I feared it, I anticipated it. I looked over my shoulder, wondering when he'd come back. And now he's here. It's time. What does he know?

He knows enough. He knows enough.

'Crystal, get on the ground.'

'I'm sorry,' I plead, tears falling as I look at him. He's come at last. I knew he would come. All this time, and now he's here. He came. He did. He showed up. It's done now.

'I'm sorry. I tried to clean,' I plead as Sheriff Barkley coughs, walking toward me to grab my arm. I hear vomit roiling in his throat, and anger rises in me. He should show respect. He shouldn't be standing here, I think as he leans down to me.

'No, please. Gideon. He needs me. Please,' I argue, clawing toward the floor, my fingernails scraping the wooden plank now that the rug has lifted up in the struggle. I can't leave him. He needs me. Who will keep him safe? I need to keep him safe.

'Crystal, come on. Come on now,' Sheriff Barkley says, choking and sputtering as he pins me down. My eyes burn as he lifts me up.

'No. My baby. What will happen to him? Please,' I argue as Sheriff Barkley slaps cold metal on my wrists. I hear him reading me my rights, but I don't hear him all the same. My teary face is pressed against the splintered wood, sobs racking my body.

I feel close to him here. He's so close. *Mama loves you, Gideon. Mama will always love you.*

At least Richard can't hurt him now.

'Please take care of my baby. He needs you to take care of him,' I argue as Sheriff Barkley lifts me up and leads me out. I turn around to look at the floor, at the gravesite of my sweet, miracle baby. I blink through the tears. And I don't think it was protocol or sheriff-like. I think it was just a sign that out of all of them, Sheriff Barkley was the only man who was the real deal. Because as he led me out of the house, down the steps, Sheriff Barkley said the words I'd been needing to hear all along. The words that could have changed everything.

'I'll take care of him, Crystal. I'll give him the burial he deserves,' he promises as he lowers my head and helps me into the back of the car. Looking out the window, I hear him call for backup. I hear him utter radio codes and watch his graying face as he leans on the car, his sweaty palm leaving a print. But when I turn to the right, my blurry vision from crying focuses on something else.

Off in the distance, in the middle of the woods, he is there, proud and tall.

I squeeze my eyes shut, shaking my head. Just breathe, I tell myself.

When I open them again, he is gone. The goat is gone, and I am still here.

It's over now, I realize, shaking my head.

God forgive me.

Chapter Thirty-Two
Richard
Last Wednesday

It's strange how the familiar can become unfamiliar in the darkness, how what you thought you knew can be tinged scarlet with a new perspective.

Beams of light radiate through the two windows across the damp, stale basement air. What I wouldn't give to touch that beam of light, to feel the glow on my ragged, scarred body—or what's left of it. I wiggle the fingers I have left, trying not to think about all the blood I've lost. Trying not to think about how much my life has changed, how much I'm missing. How life will never be the same. Mercifully, I passed out after she sawed through the first one. The bitch didn't even know how to saw it off properly, the rusty blade gnawing at it over and over and over in ragged strokes.

I look back to the window. I'm starving for the sunlight like I once thirsted for the bottle. But perspectives change. I'm different now because I have to be. Who would I be if I escape from here, away from the clutches of that maniacal bitch? I always knew she was a psychotic bitch. But my biggest mistake was that I underestimated her.

She was the weak one.

I was the strong one.

But dammit, in a moment of weakness, I let her win.

It's hard to tell how long I've been down here. The moments blur together, the setting of the sun basically irrelevant. The only thing that tells me it's been too long is the fact that the throbbing pain has stopped. My body is weak. I can't hold on much longer.

I've lost so much blood. I'm in and out of consciousness so frequently, I often wake up thinking I'm dead. Will I survive this? Is it worth surviving?

I hear banging upstairs. What is the bitch doing now? What torture does she have in store for me? She can't keep me here forever.

It's going to be over. It's all over.

Who will I be if I survive? A surge of something familiar radiates through my veins. I'll be who I always was—but stronger. More powerful. And more vengeful. She won't get away with this. I'll make her pay like she never had before. So much pain. So much torture. She'd become a madwoman I can't understand.

My head lolls again, drooping onto my chest as my eyes fall back to the dirty floor and sleepiness starts to take over. My own vomit and blood pools beneath me. I am a wreck, a fading disaster. I am a victim. My face contorts at the stark realization. Dammit, I'm no one's fucking victim.

I rattle the metal chair against the floor in a futile display of the small amount of strength I have left. It's pointless. I know she'll be back any moment, through the door that I walked through so many times. I can picture all those nights I'd threatened to toss her down the stairs that now taunt me.

She better kill me. She better kill me because if I get out of here, there will be no stopping me next time. Things will be different, fingers or not. I can still make a fist. I can still make her suffer.

As the door clinks open, I raise my eyes in defiance to stare at the captor who once wore my ring. Now, in her left hand is a knife . . . my knife. I steady myself for the pain that's to come as the psychotic woman comes closer, pointing the knife at my eye.

'This is for all the times you fucking looked at me with your judgmental eyes, all the times you made me look into your eyes before you beat me,' she announces.

I shudder, powerless in her sick, twisted game. I give her credit. She's darker than I ever was. More twisted, eviler. The knife pokes toward my eye, and I try not to piss myself. I vow to never show her the weakness she once showed me.

I'll be strong, stronger than her. I'll fucking survive her endless torture. She'll screw up. She's not that smart. And then, I'll make her pay. Flop her body right beside that dead baby she was so obsessed with.

She'll pay alright, I think, even as I scream in pain, my cries muffled by the carefully placed duct tape.

The woman always has to pay.

Chapter Thirty-Three
Sheriff Barkley

Sometimes the most defiant, the most fiendish ones are right under your nose the whole time.

From the second that woman walked into the station, I knew something was wrong. Maybe it was the overly sweet smile coming from a woman who had suffered so much. Or maybe it was the fact she was looking for a man no sane woman would ever miss. Regardless, I knew Crystal Connor was up to something from the second I found out Richard was missing. Maybe it was intuition. Maybe it was just obvious. Regardless, it broke my heart.

That woman's been through enough. I can't blame her for what she did, even if I should. She's broken, more than we could've ever known. And in truth, maybe it's my fault.

She tried her best. For a woman with little experience in the criminal world, she did okay. Hiding Richard's trucks back in the woods. Hiding Cody's car beside it. Buying the supplies at the hardware store the day after she hid Richard. Asking questions around town and making it seem like she was worried about where he could be. It could've worked. She may have gotten away with it.

Except for the hikers who found the vehicles.

Except for the fact she didn't take the suitcase she had packed and get out before it was too late.

I was going into the house to tell her about the discovery, to weigh in on the good news about the vehicles and how I was closer to answers. I had a search warrant in my pocket as well, ready to do what I should've done earlier in the week. I suspected I might find the answers to Richard's and Cody's disappearance with Crystal. She knew something, even if she wasn't letting on about it. And then we came in the door and found her—weeping in the living room.

That by itself wasn't damning.

It was the smell. The wicked, unmistakable smell of the decaying corpse. It made sense now why she'd always met me on the porch. It made sense why there were so many bleach containers in the garbage. She had tried to clean it up.

What wasn't as obvious was that the smell was coming from the floorboards. Like some sick, twisted Edgar Allan Poe story, the decaying body was in the house, tucked away under a few splintered boards. And what was more surprising?

It wasn't Richard's body or Cody's there.

It was the baby's.

I had been shaken by the sight. I had been shaken for Crystal, for the agony she'd gone through. I had so many questions. Was there foul play at work in the baby's death? Was Richard responsible? And then I'd gotten the call from my deputy who had wandered into the basement.

'Get down here quick, Sheriff. You're going to want to see this,' he bellowed after yelling for 911 to be called.

The sight I saw was something for the books, something I hadn't conjured up in my worst nightmares.

In the back corner of the basement, hanging onto life by a thread, was the town's infamous badass, Richard Connor, now looking only bad and not badass. Not looking so strong. Not looking so alive.

Tied to a metal chair in the back corner, way out of sight, his legs and hands were bound. The first thing I noticed as the deputies untied him and removed the duct tape was the blood. Pools and pools of blood, coating the floor. And it clearly wasn't coming from what appeared to be Cody Connor's body, which was sitting next to his dilapidated brother. Not a spot of his body was whole, not a piece of him preserved. My eyes took in the sick, twisted painting that was Richard.

The blood was oozing from Richard's arms, skin apparently missing. His arms were mangled, meaty messes. Most of his fingers were missing, the stubs crudely wrapped in bandages. She'd done just enough medical care, it seemed, to keep him breathing—but not much more.

The removed duct tape revealed missing teeth, and a sliced and branded tongue. I didn't know how he'd ever speak again, or if he would.

His left eye was gouged and cut, pieces of the eyeball removed.

His toenails were all gone, placed in a nice and neat pile in the middle of the floor.

The man who was once a legendary strong one in the town was now nothing but a heap of bleeding flesh and broken body parts. He looked pitiful, and sorrow actually leaped from my chest for the man I had once wished would disappear.

Looking at what was left of his mangled face, I felt like maybe he wished he could disappear too. He murmured and mumbled, but we couldn't make out a word. He would have a long road to recovery physically—but his shivering, his moaning told me that he would have emotional trauma too. Who could blame him after all?

I ran a hand through my hair after taking off my hat. To imagine that Crystal Connor, the frail, sweet woman we all knew, could do this. Did she really do this? Was it her? I shook my head.

To think how dark her soul must have been to pull this off. To think about the torture she must have endured to feel that this was warranted.

I couldn't begin to fathom.

As we continued our nightmarish search of the house, we found other relics from Crystal's week of retribution.

Pieces of Richard's eye in the glass upstairs.

The leathery bookmark she'd made of his tattoos perched in the pages of her Bible.

The lock of her dead baby's hair in the locket around her neck.

A few pieces of finger in a bowl in the fridge. The missing ones were unaccounted for.

I sat down in a chair, thinking about all that had transpired. Thinking about how the most horrific man of the town had been degraded to a pile of deteriorating flesh. Thinking about how the most heinous, disturbed criminal in the town was a woman we'd all overlooked.

Thinking about how it's all my fault. How it's all of our faults, really. We let her get to this point. We knew what Richard was like, but we closed our eyes. We closed the windows. We turned our heads. We let her suffer at his hands for years, ignoring the warning signs, the look in her eyes. We let her endure it all on her own.

What did we expect? What did he expect? Everyone has a breaking point, and everyone has a darkness lurking within.

I visited Richard in the hospital the next day. He's not well. It will be a long road to recovery, and he'll never, ever be the same. The doctors say he's suffering from emotional issues as well as physical issues. He cries out often. He cries often. He whimpers and shudders away from everyone's touch. He may have set out to be a strong man, but even the strongest can be broken.

A tortured man. A tortured soul. How will he ever be the same?

It's over now, I told him as I stood beside his hospital bed, looking out into the sleepy town of Forkhill.

But I know it's not. Because for him, it's all really just begun.

Chapter Thirty-Four
Crystal

I stare at the plain, cement wall, thinking about how it all transpired. Thinking about where it all went wrong—or where it all went right, depending on how you look at it.

My mind floats back, reviewing every detail of the night I stood up to him, of the night I seized the power.

I'll have plenty of time to think about it, I realize. I'll have plenty of time to replay every single detail over and over and over.

'DON'T EVEN FUCKING try that again,' he shrieked in my face, his nose against my cheek, his eyes lasering into me as I panted, everything aching.

He stood up, staring at Henry. 'You shut the fuck up, too. You're next,' he warned, kicking dirt at the dog before stumbling back to his garage, leaving me on my back.

Tears fell down my cheek as I stared up at the sky, the stars above a wonderous sight in the midst of the chaotic hell that was my life. How much pain can one woman endure? I didn't know if I was strong enough anymore. I didn't know if I could carry this burden. I asked God for strength, but he was silent.

Henry quieted, and after a long moment, I sat up, my head aching. I drug my worn-out body toward the dog, who greeted me with a tail wag. I leaned against him and clutched his fur. I cried into him as I thought about what was going to happen to me and wondered where it all went wrong. Then again, I considered as I rocked my body gently in the dirt by the doghouse, I knew exactly where the road to hardship started.

After letting my mind wander to that first night that Richard came into my life, I glanced up once more at the sky. I steadied my gaze, focusing on a single star, wondering if it was fate or chance or choice that brought me to the crossroads I stood before.

I could endure a lot, as I'd proven over and over again. I could handle Richard's aggressive sexual deviancies or his cutting words. I could stand the cigarette burns on my chest and the bruises and constant fear. I could stand by my man. I could follow my covenant. I could tolerate Richard's abuse and attitudes—if it were just me.

But I had someone else to think about, to protect. Gideon needed me. I pictured his tiny, frail body, withered and decaying in a heap in the forest. I pictured him, alone and terrified, wondering where I was. It was a sin to disobey your husband—but wasn't it also a sin to abandon your child? Wasn't my true purpose in life to protect Gideon, to care for him? And he needed me so much. He deserved the reverence and care I could give him. I needed to do my duty, to live out my purpose.

Richard wouldn't let me give that to our son. Sometimes, sacrifices are required in order to do what's right.

Father, forgive me, *I silently pleaded as I stared at that star for a final moment, taking a deep breath to strengthen my resolve. And then, I waited for the right moment to strike.*

I'm coming Gideon, *I said inside.* Mama's coming.

Night 51
Prisoner #312
Smithfield Correctional Facility

The sunshine is beaming down as I sit cross-legged in the center of the dusty road. There's a raven in the tree nearby, but it's quietly perched. It seems to look down at me. I smile at it, it's beautiful black feathers a stark contrast to the purple flowers budding in the tree. I lean back and sun myself, stretching out my pale legs. It feels good to be in the sun. I always love the sun.

I hear a whimper, and my heart beats fast. But when I shield my eyes and glance down the street, I see a small child walking toward me. He's wearing overalls and a purple shirt. He's not wearing shoes. His blond hair billows slightly in the light breeze. I stand and head to him.

When I get to him, he reaches up toward me, his chubby arms outstretched. I look into the blue eyes, see the familiar jawline. I know this boy. My heart swells with recognition.

I languidly pull him into me, closer and closer. Gideon. Sweet Gideon. I kiss his cheek, my lips savoring the moment. I hug him close, the feelings of warmth from the sun now flooding my veins and marinating my heart. I turn to the left when a rustling startles me.

Another familiar face. Henry. The dog looks thicker, happier. His tail wags as he approaches, and I beam at him. I reach down to pat his head, and he nuzzles into me.

They're okay. They're both okay.

I set Gideon down. The boy walks off into the forest, following Henry. I try to follow them, but I'm stuck. My feet won't move, cemented to the road.

'No,' I say, shaking my head. This can't be. 'Gideon, wait. Gideon!' But the boy and the dog continue on. They don't pause. They don't look back. They walk straight on into the forest, as if swallowed by the tree line. Tears fall, and I panic. I need to get to them. I need to get to them. I tug at my legs, lunging forward. It's no use. I'm trapped. I'm stuck. I can't get to them. I can barely breathe.

Another rustling to the right. I turn, looking at a much darker tree line. A murder of crows perches in the trees, thousands of them cawing and flapping in a wonderous yet horrifying sight. And that's when I see him emerging from the tree line, bleating and charging.

The black goat. He's come for me. There's no fooling him. There's no pleading innocent when he knows the absolute true color of my soul.

I'm still glued to the spot, unable to move an inch. Tears fall as I surrender to the reality. I raise my arms out and look to the sky, waiting for the fatal blow.

But it does not come.

Night 354
Prisoner #312
Smithfield Correctional Facility

B *lack Emptiness.*

MY EYES BLINK OPEN with a start, and I gasp until I take in the surroundings. Once I realize where I am, I inhale slowly, closing my eyes again in relief. I'm where I always am. I'm okay with that. And most of all, I'm thankful. Thankful that yet again, no dreams came to me. I suppose this shouldn't be a surprise, not really. After all, there aren't many dreams to be had when you're alone, all alone, day in and day out. Eventually, the dreams dried up with my hope of seeing the light of day. The dreams of Gideon and Henry, of what had happened, of the goat, all disappeared. In many ways, it comforts me. It was too painful to live those dreams over and over.

I take in the lonely surroundings, the emptiness. I am also comforted by the solitude. Being around the other women didn't suit me. They learned that really quick. I've heard it didn't suit them either. Who can blame me though?

I know what I did was wrong in those first days after I tied Richard up. I just couldn't help myself. Just like Henry, I'd tasted blood . . . and I wanted more. Oh, did I want more. That doesn't always stop when you put someone behind bars. In fact, I found that the hunger grew.

I don't remember much about the first night in jail. After Sheriff Barkley had hauled me out, shrieking and crying because I didn't want to leave Gideon, everything became a blur. I remember being terrified—not for myself, but for Gideon. What would happen to him? I hated not being there to watch him, to care for him. I knew no one else could take care of him like I had.

When I'd finally fallen asleep on the dank mattress that night, I'd dreamt of Henry. I was standing in the middle of the yard, naked and alone. I was shivering, blood running down my legs. And that was when I saw him. Henry, foaming at the mouth, blood seeping from his teeth. He snarled, walking closer and closer. I realized he had something in his mouth, something so large. And then the mastiff who had saved my life that night dropped the bundle at my feet.

I shrieked and shrieked in my dream, the decaying corpse of Gideon rolling in the grass, flopping in ghastly contortions beneath me.

I screamed and cried so hard in my dream that I must have been shrieking and crying in real life. The next think I knew, I was opening my eyes to the sight of guards banging on the bars, warning me to quiet down. I couldn't go back to sleep that night. I was so convinced that just like the other dreams, it was real.

I know now that that dream was just that . . . a dream. Unlike the seven before it, the nightmare was just a figment of my overactive imagination. Henry was out, roaming, free and clear. And Gideon was safe now. He had to be. Sheriff Barkley had promised me that much. He'd promised Gideon would get the respectful burial he deserved. I always knew he was a good man. And he is. He truly is. He came back to visit me a few times, to assure me that Gideon's grave is taken care of. He's even shown me a picture. Sheriff Barkley puts flowers on it and keeps it clean. He pulls the weeds and makes sure it looks nice. I know I could've done a better job, kept it cleaner. But Sheriff Barkley's doing his best, and I'm thankful for that.

He's also come to say he was sorry. He says he's sorry he failed me, that he didn't help me. I've assured him over and over it's not his fault. He's a good man. I made my choices. We all make our choices. We all choose to listen or to ignore the dark callings of our soul. He is not at fault for mine.

I've learned, too, that dreams aren't real, not typically. But the seven, the ones I had during that week that changed everything, well, they were different. I think maybe those nightmares were my mind's way of processing what I was doing, and what I had to do. Maybe they were a type of purgatory inflicted by God, to show me what was happening to my soul. Maybe they were supposed to scare me into stopping. But the opposite happened. Those dreams gave me power, made me hungry. Somehow, those dreams made it all make more sense. They gave me the strength to continue on. They gave me a place to grieve, to feel guilty, and to repent while also knowing I needed to finish. I needed to strip Richard of his power, to make him understand what weakness truly was.

In a way, being in here has brought me a sense of peace I never understood before. True, I'm a prisoner of this dark and musty cell, alone more often than I'm not. I have few choices, limited freedom, and very few things to fill my day.

Still, there's a freedom here that I didn't have at home. I'm alone with my thoughts, and the few choices I have, well, I get to make them. And I do find ways to occupy myself. There's a trustworthy Bible under my mattress. It isn't the same one as at home, of course. That one's in evidence now. Sometimes I wonder if they left in the lovely bookmark I made. I don't know. I'm sure Richard's tattooed skin is quite leathery now. What a fantastic bookmark it would be after all. I'm sad I didn't get to see it.

When I don't feel like reading the Bible, there's always cleaning to be done. These floors won't clean themselves. Richard always liked things clean, but I guess over time, I learned to like that too. I take pride in my cell. It's clean, so clean in here. It makes me happy.

I'm glad all the formalities are done now. All the questioning. All the court appearances. How I hated answering those questions over and over. I had nothing to hide. I told them everything they needed to know. I'd walked them through those seven days, the basement fiascos, the reasons behind it. I'd told them every detail they needed. I hid nothing. The truth sets you free—but I guess sometimes it just doesn't. It really doesn't.

The trial was hard. I had to hear strangers talk about Gideon like he was something to pity. I heard them talk about his death like it was a simple line on a piece of paper. I hated that. But there was one interesting thing about the trial. While my appointed defender was trying to strum up pity and sympathy, I was busy.

I was staring at Richard.

I hadn't really thought I'd see him again after that day they took me away. If I had realized it was our last day together in the basement, maybe I would've done things differently. Maybe I would have said something. I don't regret it. It's just interesting to think about.

When I got to trial, it had been a while since I'd seen him. He hadn't come to visit me. I was glad for that. I didn't really have anything I needed to say to him. All was well. Gideon was buried. He was at peace. I'd helped Richard repent, and I'd taken back my power. I'd served my purpose. I had nothing more to say to Richard.

So at the trial, when I saw him for the first time, I couldn't stop staring. I really don't know what I expected. I'd seen him in the basement, after all. Still, those days, I wasn't completely focused. I was too busy to look at him, to properly take it all in. In some ways, I guess I'd detached from him, almost forgetting that he was Richard.

But looking at him in that courtroom, I couldn't help but gasp. Was this really the man who had ruled me with fear for so many years? Was this the same monster who had thrown my baby into the woods like a heap of trash? Was this the man who I had let overpower me for our entire marriage? It couldn't be him. It couldn't be.

Because the specimen before me, well, he was hardly a man let alone a powerful one. He wore the scars of those days, but he didn't wear them well. Richard was broken, his face sunken in and gray. Even from across the room, I could see that his dark eye was tearful, remorseful, powerless. He walked with a limp, his hands in his pockets. He never took his hands from his pockets now. He would never be hitting someone again I betted. Those stumps for hands would be pretty useless in a fight.

There was no swagger to him anymore, no defiance. In fact, when I watched him from my seat, I realized something. His head was no longer held high. His eye rarely lifted from the ground when he talked. The strong had fallen. The weak had risen. Our places had shifted, and I doubted Richard Connor would ever be in control of anyone again.

It was a little bit sad, I guess. He did have spirit, that one. But I suppose I was also a bit proud to know I had finally broken him after all.

Crys had proven to be Crystal, and even though I had been damned in the process, I had risen up in a feat of strength no one had expected. I had won in so many ways, and Richard wouldn't be winning against anyone again. He would understand his sins of the flesh, and maybe he could find a way to forgiveness—something I still had to work on myself.

We were all safe. I had done that for us.

I pluck at the hole in the mattress like I do so often. If only I could have some thread and a needle, I could fix this right up. I was never the best seamstress, but I was good enough. I could make it work. I turn to my side now, stretching out my left hip. I let my mind wander today, a luxury I don't always afford myself. I let it drift back to the

basement, to those days I don't often peruse in my mind.
It doesn't do to look at the past. What's done is done. But
something about today is different. Something makes me
want to look back.

I hadn't really had a plan when Richard had thrown me
to the ground that evening, drunk as usual. Tears and rage
swirled in a dangerous concoction. It wasn't about what he'd
done to me. I could handle some bruises, some scars. No, it
was much deeper than that. It had been about Gideon, about
what he was denying his son. I wouldn't have that. I couldn't.

So when I wandered to Richard's garage and found him
stumbling over himself with bourbon breath, I knew I had
to act fast. Without thinking, I'd stomped toward him with
the fury of a grizzly in mating season and swung at Richard's
head with the passion I'd been holding in for a long time. It
was a passion I didn't realize was in me until it emerged in
full force.

The sickening crack against Richard's face stunned me,
and as he crumpled to the floor, I'd wondered if I'd swung
too hard. I gasped, thinking I'd killed him. The hammer
clanged to the floor as I'd covered my mouth. I'd killed him.
I'd really killed him.

I fell to the floor, Richard resting on his back. I crawled
to his body, gasping and shaking. I felt for a pulse, relieved
when I felt the thudding. He was still alive. I stared into the
blank face of the man who had forsaken our child, and the
rage bubbled again. I wouldn't let him get away with this.
He'd gone too far. I would take care of Gideon. I would keep
him safe. I would make sure he was close by, treated with
respect and care. I could still look out for him. And I could

still make sure Richard knew that what he had done to our son, well, it was wrong. It was time Richard paid for his sins. It was time for him to repent.

Dragging his dead weight through the garage, into the house, and through the basement hadn't been easy, especially in my condition. But I found a will deep within, and with each step down into the damp, dark abyss, I gained strength and courage. The excitement over the fact that I would be able to prove my love for Gideon drove me forward.

Once his body was in the basement, I'd fiddled about, pulling on the single string to illuminate the room with the bare lightbulb. I'd found the corner of the unfinished, dirty room to be a perfect spot for storing my new prisoner. I managed to prop his limp body onto a dirty metal chair in the corner by a beam. The same metal chair he'd once tied me to when he set my red shirt on fire. I was a quick learner, even if Richard didn't realize it. Some zip strips, rope, and a gag later, and my improvised plan was seemingly coming together. I brushed my hands off, proud of my handiwork. I wasn't the stupid, weak Crystal everyone thought. I'd managed to pull off the unthinkable.

Now, I was free to make him pay. Still, there was something else to be done.

I had planned on burying Gideon in the backyard, a simple stone to mark the grave. Still, the thought of leaving him outside in the cold, dark night, the threat of animals in the forest nearby, well, it didn't seem right. I wanted Gideon in my arms, in that rocking chair. I wanted so badly to nurse him, to love him, to protect him. Tears welled as I retrieved his sickly body from the forest edge, cradling him as I carried him into the house. I carried him inside and found myself heading straight to the rocking chair. I'd held him for an hour or so, the smell of his body sickly, but the craving to be his mother stronger.

It hadn't been easy prying up the floorboards in the living room, not at all. I'd had to return to the garage—I hated leaving Gideon alone—to find some tools. The hammer in a pool of blood made my own blood curdle. I'd have to clean that up later, but first thing was first. Gideon was always first.

I'd retrieved the tools and struggled for quite some time. After what felt like forever, sweat pouring down my face, I'd managed to find a safe spot for Gideon, a place he could be close to me. That's what we both needed. I would keep his gravesite clean and well-kept. I would watch over him. I would have him nearby, and Richard couldn't stop me. Richard would never stop me.

As I tearfully put the board back and cleaned the gravesite, I meticulously put every thread back in place of the rug. I laid down, resting on top of Gideon, my labor of love done for the moment. I knew, though, it would never be done. I would show Gideon my love for him by keeping him safe and clean and nearby. I sang him a lullaby as I rested on the rug.

That was where I'd fallen asleep.

It was the next day that the plans with Richard really began. I knew that it would be impossible to keep Richard from disturbing Gideon, and I knew after what I'd done, he'd kill me if he got the chance. I couldn't have that. If I was dead, who would keep Gideon's grave clean and neat?

Richard wouldn't. I had to make sure to protect Gideon, to keep him safe from Richard.

And that's when I began.

I started with his fingers. The fists that had hit me over and over, had bruised me and marred me. The fingers were the first to go. God, the blood. At first, it was difficult. I didn't have the stomach for it. I didn't have the heart for it. It hurt me just as much as Richard. I didn't realize how tough of a job it would be with that dull saw. Even through the gag, I could hear his screams. I was glad when he passed out. It was easier to wrap his fingers then, to tend to him. I always was good with nursing skills. Maybe I should have went to school for it. I spent the evening hurling that night, and after giving Henry the snack I knew he craved—the fresh meat—I went to bed.

That was when the dreams began. That was when my living nightmare haunted me even in sleep. That was when I knew I was truly damned.

Day after day, I lived that waking nightmare. Tending to Richard, stripping him of his power, and tending to sweet Gideon, keeping his living room gravesite clean and neat. Richard always liked things clean and neat, after all. I needed to show him that our son mattered because he did. I needed to keep him close, to be near my baby.

The whole time, nevertheless, I knew my purpose would be short-lived. I knew he would show up. I knew it was only a matter of time until Sheriff Barkley figured out what I was doing. Even when I fantasized about my plan of escaping, I think I knew, deep down, I'd never be able to leave Gideon. The thought of leaving him alone, untended, was horrifying.

I'd bought the hair dye. I'd made the phone calls. I'd even planned my destination and packed the suitcase. But I think I knew my bravery, my courage had limits. And even after I was done with Richard, after the final sacrifice of him, I knew I wouldn't be able to leave Gideon's final resting place. What kind of a mother abandons her child? I'm no monster, after all. I'm a good mother, I am.

I'm surprised it took him as long as it did for Sheriff Barkley to show up. In a way, I was glad when he found out. I was so tired then. I was exhausted from covering my tracks, from protecting the hidden treasures I had lurking in that house. I was tired of living out my role. Still, I knew I had to finish what I'd started. Thy will be done.

I don't know when it happened, the true madness of this journey. But somewhere along the line, there was a shift in me. I'd like to pinpoint it to one moment, but I don't know if I can. It was too complicated, and my feelings ran so deep. But at some point, the pain I felt hurting Richard turned to something else.

Pleasure. Thrill. Enjoyment.

I started to enjoy the torture. His pale face, the grayness spreading—I liked it. No, I started to crave it. What started out as a noble cause perhaps turned into something else. I loved flirting with the line of life and death—and then using my power to bring him back over. I liked being in control. I liked having physical domination over him.

For the first time, I started to understand Richard and maybe even appreciate him. I got the addiction, the thrill of hurting another. Suddenly, all of those moments he was so abusive to me—well, I understood them. I got him a little bit more. Being the one in control is addicting, like the most heinous drug or the most elusive addiction. There is a high that goes with it that you can't explain. It's just too bad it took so long for me and Richard to bridge the gap between us.

I think about Richard often now. Some days, I think about the past and what drove us to this point. Most days, I just wonder what he's doing. Has he found a new version of himself as I did? Has he found a way to make peace? Or is he still the broken man I last saw? What color does his eye glow now? I wish there was some way to know. But he hasn't come to visit me. I guess I can't really blame him. I've tried writing to him a few times, but I never know what to say. I don't know if I want to say anything to him, in truth.

Sometimes I wonder if he visits Gideon's grave, but I'm too afraid to ask. I don't know if I want him there. I just don't know. Parts of me are still tainted by selfish urges and dark thoughts. I'm not perfect, after all.

Some people I've come across have expressed their pity for me. My public defender, Sheriff Barkley, random visitors. Some nice women from a local church group come in once in a while to lead prayer services. They look at me with sorrowful eyes. Apparently, my story made the news everywhere and stirred a lot of questions about domestic abuse. Sheriff Barkley said that's the good that's come out of this whole thing.

Other than losing Gideon, I think this is what I hate the most. The pity. I don't want people feeling sorry for me. I don't want any of you to feel sorry for me. That's what I want people to realize. I've lived my life. I've done my deeds. I don't know what will happen to me when I leave here, but for now, I am safe. I am where I'm meant to me. I've done what I was supposed to do. I was a good mother in the only way I could be. I protected my child. I made sure he knew he was loved. I did my best, and sometimes, that's all we can do.

I look up at the ceiling, stretching, and thinking about how I used to start mornings on my knees. Ever since I could walk, Mama had me on my knees, praying, begging for forgiveness.

Forgive me, Father. Forgive me.

My, how things have changed. I know there's no point. My God is a merciful God, it's true, but I knew when I started this whole road there would be no turning back. I knew there would be no forgiveness. I didn't care, though. And maybe, in truth, I no longer want forgiveness. Maybe I've found enough strength in myself that I don't need someone else's approval for the first time in life. Not Richard, not my father's, and not a higher being.

I don't care about myself, my own soul's status. All I've ever cared about is Gideon. And I think I've accomplished my goal. I've shown that child what he meant to me. I've protected him. I've made sure no one can hurt him. I've made sure his father understands what my father didn't. Children are a gift from God. All children. No matter what.

And so, no matter what, I've done something meaningful in this life. I've loved my children, both children, with the ferocity of a true mother. That's enough for me now. I'm okay with what happens and with what reckoning comes down on me.

Even if I spend the rest of eternity as a tortured soul, all is well.

All is well, indeed, I think, standing to greet the day. I stretch for a moment before I get to work. There's plenty to clean. I smirk thinking about how proud Richard would be to see me in my old, familiar role. If only he had known that behind that sweet, dutiful housewife, someone else was lurking.

Forgive him, Father. Forgive him.

Acknowledgements

First and foremost, I want to thank my amazing husband for always believing in my stories and for encouraging me to chase my dreams. I love you so much. You are my best friend.

Thank you to my parents, Ken and Lori, for instilling a love of writing and reading in me and teaching me to work hard. I love you both.

A special thanks to all of my friends and family members who have supported me on this journey, especially: Grandma Bonnie, Jenny, Lynette, Ronice, Kay, Alicia, and everyone else who has been there along the way.

Thank you to all of the book bloggers and bookstores who have supported my authorship. Thank you to the ATA and especially Audrey Hughey for believing in my dreams, picking me up when I felt like quitting, and encouraging me to dream big.

I also want to thank every single reader who has picked up the words of a small-town girl with big, lofty, bookish dreams. I couldn't do any of this without you.

And finally, thank you to my best friend, Henry, for always being there to greet me with those soulful eyes and big heart, no matter what book sales look like or how many pages still need edited. I hope we have many more years together.

Did you love *A Tortured Soul*? Then you should read *The Christmas Bell: A Horror Novel*[1] by L.A. Detwiler!

From USA Today Bestseller L.A. Detwiler comes a disturbing paranormal horror novel that will bring hell to the holidays and chilling fear to the festivities.

Some Christmas ornaments should be left in the attic.

When Candace Mills, 26, heads home for the holidays to visit her mother and ailing grandmother, she's expecting a peaceful, dull Christmas. She has no idea, though, that a single Christmas ornament is about to send her into a whirling chasm of evil.

---

1. https://books2read.com/u/bW1NRM

2. https://books2read.com/u/bW1NRM

It starts with the Christmas bell, scratched and worn in one of Grandma Anne's boxes in the attic. Once they put it on the tree, Grandma Anne starts to say terrifying things and act strangely. Candace and her mother assume it's her dementia talking—until they start to have dangerous encounters with a fiendish being.

As the secrets of Anne's past involving her twin sister rise to the surface, the women face sinister horrors from a dark force looking for revenge.

Will any of them be able to survive, or will they fall prey to the malevolent secret Grandma Anne is harboring from her past?

Read more at www.ladetwiler.com.

Also by L.A. Detwiler

A Tortured Soul
The Christmas Bell: A Horror Novel
The Christmas Bell: Rachel's Story

Watch for more at www.ladetwiler.com.

About the Author

L.A. Detwiler is USA TODAY Bestselling author and high school English teacher. Her debut thriller, The Widow Next Door, is a USA Today and International Bestseller with HarperCollins UK/Avon Books. Her second thriller, The One Who Got Away, released in 2020 with HarperCollins UK/One More Chapter. The Diary of a Serial Killer's Daughter released in 2020.

L.A. lives in Pennsylvania with her husband, Chad, their five cats, and their mastiff named Henry. Her writing has appeared in several women's publications and online magazines. She also writes romance under Lindsay Detwiler, including her popular Lines in the Sand Series.

Join her Readers' Club with this link: http://eepurl.com/gkZ2Sf

Read more at www.ladetwiler.com.

Printed in Great Britain
by Amazon